FROM THE ANNALS OF THE TRUST

FROM THE ANNALS
OF THE TRUST

Myron Curtis

iUniverse, Inc.
Bloomington

FROM THE ANNALS OF THE TRUST

iUniverse books may be ordered through booksellers or by contacting:

iUniverse
1663 Liberty Drive
Bloomington, IN 47403
www.iuniverse.com
1-800-Authors (1-800-288-4677)

ISBN: 978-1-4759-7031-9 (sc)
ISBN: 978-1-4759-7032-6 (e)

Library of Congress Control Number: 2013900221

Printed in the United States of America

iUniverse rev. date: 1/8/2013

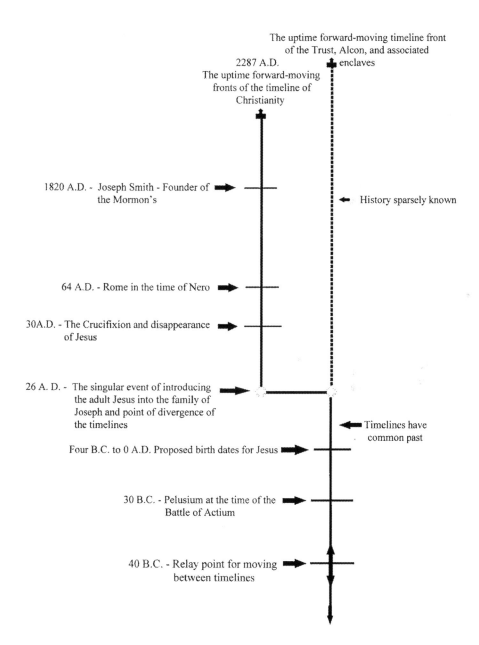

The uptime forward-moving timeline front
of the Trust, Alcon, and associated
enclaves

2287 A.D.
The uptime forward-moving
fronts of the timeline of
Christianity

1820 A.D. - Joseph Smith - Founder of
the Mormon's

History sparsely known

64 A.D. - Rome in the time of Nero

30A.D. - The Crucifixion and disappearance
of Jesus

26 A. D. - The singular event of introducing
the adult Jesus into the family of
Joseph and point of divergence of
the timelines

Timelines have
common past

Four B.C. to 0 A.D. Proposed birth dates for Jesus

30 B.C. - Pelusium at the time of the
Battle of Actium

40 B.C. - Relay point for moving
between timelines

Prologue

The ability to travel in time took those who probed its potential it into a series of bizarre and conflicting events.

Compelled by rival factions of the Church, the New Essenes and the True Church—the assumed name of the traditional Catholic Church—our time travelers made the first jaunt back to Biblical Judea to probe the beginnings of the Christian movement. It was revealed that there were significant variations in the Gospel accounts and that the various players in the Biblical story, especially those of Jesus, Barabbas, and St. Paul, had different roles from that recorded. But more fundamentally, they found that the Jesus figure so central to Christian dogma was not a homegrown prophet with divine attributes. He was an agent from another timeline sent by his organization, The Trust for the Fusion of Science and the Spirit. With the altruistic mission to establish an enduring culture of moral and ethical behavior, they sought to link with the prevailing faith, Judaism. To this end, the Trust agent and Jesus figure, Adrian Beike, and his cohort, Francois LeBrust, recruited followers, devised miraculous events, and orchestrated Jesus's martyrdom.

However, the action of introducing Jesus into the family of Joseph had created a pivotal event, one of such import that it initiated an alternate reality with its own timeline. From the future of this timeline the travelers: Brant Conjular, his companion and confidant Lila McEntire, scholar and prime field operative Parzan Rajulk Petrov, tech Lovencroft Smithe, Daily World reporter Millicent Hopper, and historian Erik Korbach, all embarked on the first mission to investigate the veracity of events described in the Gospels. At the close of this first venture into past eras, a chronicle of the events was written and placed in the restricted archives of the Government Science Institute (GSI). [1]

The potential for conflict within the Religious community; however, led those of the first mission to make only a repressed and selective release of the true historical events and to suppress the discovery a new timeline. This was to avoid siding with one or the other contenders to the truths of Christianity in order to prevent undue tumult and stress in the world of faith, and to seek a cautious approach to revealing the existence of an alternate timeline.

The second venture to the past had no such antagonists contending for the true facts of Christianity at its nascent stage.[2] Setting aside the revelations of the first mission, the travelers were persuaded to a more constructive course: to sort out details of the growth of the Faith after it took root. This took them to Rome in the time of Nero and the period of St. Paul where to their surprise they again encountered Francois LeBrust, still working to promote the values of the Trust.

Brant Conjular as head of the Institute of Temporal Research (ITR) entourage decided that in order to determine the nature and possible dangers from the link to LeBrust's timeline, they must maintain contact with it. Their efforts took Brant into the alternate timeline itself, where he fell victim to its bizarre aspects and had to be rescued.

Growing weary of his epoch-by-epoch approach to shoring up the Christian Faith, LeBrust appeared at the uptime present of the Christian timeline, and positioned himself in the Vatican as Press Secretary. In this post, he could continue to monitor the Trust's inroads into the world of faith.

Alerted by various leaks, General Carlin Bromfsted, Intelligence Chief of the U.S., sought to uncover any successes of the ITR regarding time travel, but was thwarted by the actions of LeBrust. He shelved for the moment, his efforts to expose the ITR, but his suspicions would linger.

A surprise visit to the Christian timeline by Adrian Beike, revealed that the home compound of the Trust in its own timeline had been invaded by rogue forces and was no longer a viable location for transferring between timelines. Beike and the Trust leaders made plans to resettle and initiate a new contact point in order to continue pursuing its altruistic aims.

Barry

The bus pulled into the Obamapolis station. It was early morning, but the sun was up, and the streets were already bustling with citizens hurrying to work or some defined mission laid upon them. Barry alighted from the bus clutching a tattered bag containing his modest belongings. He surveyed his new surroundings.

So, this is Obamapolis, he mused. *I thought I would never get here, but after my dismal experience in Palestisraelia everything pointed to the United States as welcoming to strangers and the one place I might find opportunity … I must first find some place of lodging, then search for employment.*

Picking up a paper at the terminal's newsstand, he scanned the local offerings.

"Hmm" … *Most of them are too expensive for now. I must settle for the most modest of accommodations until I can find a job … Here's something.*

> **Small Room, furnished.**
> **Bath to share. Window**
> **looks out on alleyway,**
> **$100/week. 740 Colin**
> **Powell St.**

He purchased a map and unfolded it.

Here, here it is, some distance from this place. Glancing at the rising sun, he twisted the map so that its orientation roughly matched the surroundings. He looked up. *That way, more or less,* he thought, eying the maze of intersecting streets emerging from between buildings. *Maybe I can walk it—save money.*

He folded the paper and the map and stuffed them in his bag. An hour later, he pulled up in front of the house on Colin Powell.

This has to be it, more of a slog than I figured, but it looks decent enough.

A matronly woman answered the door and looked him up and down with only tentative approval.

"My name is Bass, Barry Bass. I wish to inquire about the room for rent. May I see it?"

The woman paused for a moment to decipher Barry's articulate but thickly accented English. "It's upstairs, but you'll have to use the stairway on the outside she said pointing to some steps just peeking out from the corner of the house."

She fumbled with a key chain. "Here, this is the key." Then, with a furtive glance at Barry she added, "I'll come with you."

Mounting the stair, which terminated on a landing, she again fumbled with the keys finally selecting one. The door creaked open to reveal the modest enclosure.

"I'll take it. Here is a week's rent," said Barry portioning out funds from his meager holdings.

The door closed, leaving him with his thoughts. *There is no sense wasting time.*

He again scanned the paper for possible jobs. After a period, he had only checked a few possibilities. He sat thinking. *Too many jobs in these listings require at least a minimum of training and familiarity with this culture. Even my modest mastery of the language does not give me advantage, but something here that may fit me.*

He put down the paper and took his weathered copy of the bible out of the bag, reading until the sleep overcame him.

"You start in the morning," said the dispatcher. "Be sure you are here at the airport by 4:00 A.M. The place gets busy by five, and we want it spick-and-span by that time. The job is seven days a week."

"Thank you, I am grateful to have the job," said Barry thinking,

Inconvenient to get here, but I don't have a choice. I should be able to find a church with a late service.

The next day, as his shift ended, he looked at his watch, which read 2:05 P.M. The bus from the airport wound its way back through the suburbs to the center of Obamapolis and the terminal.

There, thought Barry as he spied the church spire though the trees. *I didn't notice it before, The True Church, just what I was looking for.*

He entered the sanctuary just as Holy Communion was underway, and strolled forward with the stragglers as the last of the meager congregation received the Host. The service concluded and Barry hesitated before approaching the confessional. *I may as well get it over with … I must do it, but need to watch what I say and how I say it. My background is confusing, even to me. Such holding back bothers me, since that is against the purpose of confession in the first place.*

"Bless me, Father, for I have sinned," said Barry as he settled in the confessional. He voiced several minor transgressions again hesitating before saying, "I long to experience once again the impact of his presence."

The Priest paused before saying, "It is well that you are imbued with the impact of his spirit."

"That's not exactly what I meant," said Barry, suddenly trapped in the confines and strictures of his faith regarding truth, which was in fundamental conflict with his experience.

"Then, what do you mean?" asked the Priest.

"In the interest of acting in good faith and following the imperatives of truth, I confess that I was once had the privilege of being in his divine presence."

The priest was quiet for a minute before responding. "You perhaps are hearing voices or having delusions concerning the savior. It stands outside our function to advise you concerning this. I suggest you consult the secular medical experts for options in treatment. For now, you must give token penance for such thoughts, even if they are not under your control. Please voice a series of twelve Hail Marys, one for each of his holy followers, and endeavor to resist such erroneous musings in the future."

"Yes, Father."

Maybe I do need help, thought Barry. *I sometimes think I have imagined it all.*

He settled in the routine of the job at the airport, off at midafternoon, home to rise early the next day. A few weeks passed.

So, what is in the paper today? He thought as he rummaged through the pages of the Obamopolis Daily Herald. *Most of what is important is on the front page and then there's the gossip and sports: I can understand a little of it. Football looks big, but I will have to have someone explain it to ...*

He paused, stared at the picture, and read the caption.

Winners of Women's Competition
The bruising tussle between several contenders at the Sports Arena ended in a tie between two contestants. Pictured from left to right are Athena Flack and Lila McEntire, winners, and runner up Fran North. The small but packed arena responded enthusiastically to the ...

That woman, I have seen her before, sometime in the past, he thought. *It is the first hint of a connection between my sudden transformation from the primitive world of before, one I have thought I may have imagined, to this one. But this person, who is she?* He slowly mouthed the name in the caption, Lila McEntire.

The Dissolution of the Trust Enclave

All was quiet for the moment in the enclave, home of the Trust for the Fusion of Science and the Spirit as searchlights combed the rolling landscape. Binzing, chief of the Division of Science in the enclave, and the Trust officers gazed out from one of the landings that served as lookout posts spaced regularly along the wall encircling the city.

"Maybe they decided to call it off," said Binzing.

"Not likely," said Danbro, chief of security. "We are not facing docile Garuletzsky.[3] We did only play-war with them."

"Yes, but even they could get nasty if aroused. Fortunately they joined us to rid the area of that Xerjinko [4] rabble," said Binzing. "This time it is serious. Somehow the insurgents have bypassed the Garuletzsky land holdings to the north and west, to besiege us."

"The obvious answer is that they looped around them, maybe arriving by boats or by land hugging the shore of the great inland sea," said Danbro. "The Garuletzsky lands do not extend that far. If they used boats, it would have taken a lot of them judging by the numbers in that first surge."

"I would agree," said Binzing. "It appears that there is a new alliance of the rogue enclaves from Gallodeutchia. After the Flood of Deutchia[5] when everything fell apart, the hostile forces were fragmented. Now they have achieved a pack mentality and are joined in the common cause of conquest. I am sure exaggerated rumors have made their way north attesting to our riches, which is ironic, since our 'riches' are mostly intellectual—knowledge of how to make something out of little or nothing."

They watched in silence for some moments, before Binzing gave a nod and turned to leave. Just then, a volley of shots came from the folds in the landscape. Some scored on the array of searchlights, sending sections of the wall's expanse into shadows, illuminated only by the wash of those remaining.

"They are using their primitive firearms to extinguish the lights," said Danbro. "In the darkness, we will have less leverage against their superior numbers."

"Just in case we will not be able to hold, we should gather the women and children into the armored autobuses and send them south to Alcon," said Binzing. "Then the rest of us will have to fight our way out of here. If that happens, they will take casualties from our superior weapons and probably not pursue us far. Why should they? Once we are clear, they will have the spoils of the enclave and the Trust. That will irritate the Garuletzsky because, as we all know; they depend on us for the modest technical advances they have embraced for which they trade foodstuffs. In any case, we don't want to get in between when they tangle.

"I must leave now. I must attend to something. If you must fall back, assemble at the Trust Chapel with the rest of our forces who have already donned their body armor. I will join you there."

Binzing rushed to his headquarters in the Trust Science Center. Adrian Beike was there to meet him.

"I got your message. How is it going at the wall?" asked Adrian.

"Not good. I think the rats are going to overrun us. I am ordering evacuation of the women and children now and am putting the rest of the enclave on alert. I addition, for some time, I have had the gold assets of the Trust loaded onto the trucks so that they will be ready to go in case of an emergency. We may need them later to bargain for a place to settle and resources."

"How about our work on fostering the new ethical movement in the other timeline?" asked Adrian. "LeBrust and I already have much time and energy invested in it. Are we going to chance that it will continue on its own?"

"For now, yes, it's a pity we will have to put it on hold, being the one Trust success in the time travel venture. However, to preserve and push forward our efforts achieved so far is why I have summoned you here. I have a plan."

"I am glad to hear it," said Adrian with a tinge of disgust. "LeBrust and I went to considerable trouble, and if I may say so risk, to plant the seeds of that movement to grow around my Jesus character."

"I realize that, and the time when it is too late may be fast approaching," said Binzing. "While this transfer point is still available, I want you to transfer to the other timeline to secure our contact and continue the work we started. You will be marooned there until we can establish a new transfer point and reconnect. Ideally, we would stage from the vast double continent to the west beyond the great sea. That, of course, is impossible until both our timelines can establish downtime relay points there so that we can make contact below the node of intersection of our timelines. So for now, Alcon is our best choice. This may take a little doing, even though they are a branch of the Trust and in tune with its overall aims. The Alcon keepers are not aware; however, that we have extended the common Trust mandate by using time travel.

"As we constantly remind ourselves, both our technology and that of Christianity's timeline are location specific," said Binzing, pressing on. "We can only transfer through time to and from the specific geographic location where we have set up a facility, so you must go now before we are overrun, and this site is still active. You should travel downtime to the still-operable bounce point below the intersection of our timelines, to where they coincide, and we have a common history. Once there, you can transfer uptime within the Christian timeline from the common point here in the enclave and inform Brant Conjular of our predicament. With his cooperation, you can get a fix on the Alcon location, go there and set up, and transfer to a date we will agree upon now. We think eighty-six years downtime from the time we introduced you into Judea as Jesus will put us well within the period when our timelines coincide. With the cooperation of the Alcon authority, we will setup and transfer a delegation down to that point to meet you. Naturally, Brant will have to search for Alcon since a settlement with that name does not exist in their timeline, and they will have only limited knowledge of where the Alcon location actually is. After you again link with us, we can, with the aid of their own Temporal Reciprocators, [6] move freely in their timeline to and from the Alcon staging point."

"All right," said Adrian after a pause. "That is a mind-rattling plan with many uncertainties, but we will have to go with it. I will connect with Brant Conjular and inform him how to establish the new link, but

I will need some geographical markers for him to be able to identify the Alcon site."

"As you know, Alcon is to the south where the landmass curves to the west around the Great Inland Sea, but short of the River of Majesty,[7] which carries so much earth and silt that it has extended the land."

"That should narrow it down enough," said Adrian. "Other than that, given what may be the final opportunity to further the Trust's mission in the foreseeable future, I may take advantage of the path we still have to the other timeline at this location and go where my instincts tell me. Of course, any time spent advancing the interests of the Trust during this diversion would be irrelevant to my timely appearance at the uptime terminus of the other timeline."

"Yes, but should you undertake a side mission on behalf of the Trust, do it first before going to the uptime present of the other timeline, where you can find out the results of your efforts. In addition, guard your actions carefully in such a venture. Tinkering with the natural flow of history might create a pivotal event, creating yet another timeline which will take you with it."

"I am beginning to wonder if that is so bad," said Adrian half joking.

"Perhaps not, but you could be irretrievably lost within it," said Binzing as the lights went out.

Binzing glanced at the mirror of his armored autobus, which was taking the rear position in the motorcade as it moved south.

"They aren't following us now. Thankfully, we got everyone out. How far is it to the Alcon facility?"

"Around 275 kilometers," said Danbro. "With a caravan this size, it will take at least eight to nine hours to do the distance. It is fortunate that we had the foresight to plan for an emergency evacuation."

"This road is not too bad since it relates to before breakup of the nations to the north bounding the Great Inland Sea," said Binzing.

The sun rose and bore down on the procession as they moved south and then west, with the land as it curved around the edge of the sea.

"The Alcon enclave should be in sight anytime," said Binzing. "By necessity, it should look like some sort of bastion since, like us, they have to constantly repel incursions from outside. Our *wavant* [8] communications with them have always been friendly, and like all our sister enclaves, they have embraced our values and the principles of the Trust. Fortunately, they have retained their interest in science as a key to survival, but as far as we know, they have not explored its potential beyond the practical. I cannot imagine how they will respond when I reveal our efforts to extend the influence of the Trust by using time travel."

The Trust caravan traveled some thirty minutes more when suddenly a complex of buildings appeared in the distance: a system of low-lying structures standing in a ring around an array of multistoried ones.

"They have a different system of defense than we did," said Danbro.

"Yes, the flat terrain here with little forest or plant life gives limitless vision. Whatever the specifics of their defense scheme are will probably be revealed as we get closer."

As they approached the edge of the settlement, a lone vehicle stood parked in the middle of the road along with a group of men, silently waiting. The caravan stopped. Binzing maneuvered his car around the long line of his cortege and approached the front, joining those in the leading car already in discussion with the Alconians.

Alighting from his car, he faced a man adorned in a modified version of Arab dress: a shortened *thobe* topped by a conventional *ghuttra* and secured by a black *igal*.

"Welcome to Alcon," said the man. "My name is Marzin Jut, primary rector of the Alcon Trust Enclave, which automatically encompasses the title and responsibilities of chief executive of the enclave. We have been expecting you and have prepared temporary accommodations. You will have to endure this inconvenience until you can lend your efforts to finding a way forward."

"We humbly accept your offer and are grateful," said Binzing, matching Jut's formality. "As you know, we all are subject to conquest by forces known and unknown and must stick together for survival. We have much in common and the advantages of being the sole repositories of science knowhow in the known world. With these tools, along with our unity and cooperation, we can thwart any chaos that unfettered elements seek to inflict upon us. It is unfortunate that we succumbed to such banditry before we could enlist the aid of other enclaves."

"Yes," said Marzin Jut. "Perhaps more contact is essential for our survival, but we are spread out wide, and material help is always slow in coming. Events often overtake us before it can come into play. Now with regard to your settlement here, your followers must be exhausted from the stress of the evacuation and the weariness of travel. Please instruct your convoy to follow us to your temporary accommodations."

Binzing gave the signal and with his car in the lead, followed Marzin Jut through a checkerboard of uniform structures and into the confines of the Alcon enclave.

"They certainly have a different scheme for defense than we did," said Danbro.

"Look at those … those pill boxes, for want of a better word, with the holes in all sides. Any attackers must run the gauntlet of them to reach the center of the settlement. Overrunning or bypassing one only brings fire from the rear along with a frontal attack from the next ring of these demi-fortresses."

"Ingenious for this flat terrain," said Binzing. "There are probably tunnels connecting them with each other and the operational center of the enclave. In the convoluted topography of our ill-fated enclave, I'm not sure it would have worked."

The convoy arrived at an array of low profile buildings.

"These buildings were storage facilities hastily emptied of essential items, which have been scattered and placed elsewhere in the enclave," said Marzin. "You and your company will have to endure the discomforts of barracks style living for a period while we temporarily assimilate you into our community. There is certainly strength in numbers, but it reaches a point of diminishing returns at some point where the logistics of supporting it surpasses the available resources. We calculate that with the addition of you and your followers we will approach that limit. Hopefully, none of our other sister enclaves are in trouble. We would be unable to help them."

"Again our profound thanks to you," said Binzing. "We will sleep the night and my entire contingent will be ready to lend their skills to whatever your plans are in the morning."

The Trust followers finally settled in the Alcon enclave. Binzing conferred with Danbro. "It is a bad time to bring up the time travel issue because of the huge job of settling the enclave here, but I will just have to do it and see how he reacts."

"Better sooner than later, you have a deadline to meet," said Danbro.

"Yes. We have to tell him. Essentially, we must wait and see if Brant

Conjular finds us in the time window, we gave Adrian. Until then, we can concentrate on re-building the community while we look for a long-term solution."

Three weeks passed before Binzing had the confidence to broach the subject with Marzin. "I will take the evening meal with Marzin. The end of day setting should be the best time to talk to him.

"At least it is done," Marzin was saying. "We have in place our modified defense ring. Now we can concentrate more fully on your temporary settlement."

"Yes our men and yours seem to be working in harmony," said Binzing taking a breath. "Now, I feel it necessary to bring up an unrelated matter which we encountered because of the demise of our enclave. Our ventures in science on behalf of the Trust took us into a new realm of proselytizing."

"Oh? Where did it take you?" asked Marzin. "From what we know of the tribes and clans that lie between our two enclaves, it must have been a formidable task."

"It wasn't a question of where, but when."

"I don't follow you," said Marzin.

"We discovered a way to travel in time."

"That is quite remarkable," said Marzin slowly after a pause. "How does it promote the mandate of the Trust?"

"It worked this way: We planted one of our agents in the millenniums of the past to plant the seed of Trust values to see whether it would take hold. We expected it to grow within our history, flourish, and have a dominant presence somewhere even if we are now unaware of it, that is, at least strong enough as not to succumb to the vagaries of civilization. However, the unexpected happened. The insertion of our agent was a singular event of such cosmic import that it initiated a new timeline, a parallel reality with its own history. We don't know how such a seemingly nonscientific event influenced the flow of time. That question lies within that foggy interface between science and philosophy. The fact is, the alternate timeline exists and, from its future came its representatives to probe the origins of its own unique history. Our agents have met and interacted with them.

"It is pleasing to know that the Trust has spread its message in such a unique way," Marzin said after a long pause. "Is there any value to pursuing it further?"

"Well, yes," said Binzing. "We have agreed with the other timeline that unrestrained interaction could be counterproductive, even dangerous, but that discrete contact should be maintained. Reports from their agents and ours now established there indicate that their world has progressed much further than ours has. Peaceful nations exist side by side throughout the entire globe. You will recall for instance that we know little of the chaos in portions of the vast double continent beyond the broad sea to the west, not to mention the little known lands in the east. In the other timeline, those are peaceful and settled. We may have much to learn from them.

"But now to my purpose in bringing it up at this time," continued Binzing. "We would like to reestablish contact with this timeline since it was lost when the Trust enclave was overrun. We plan to solicit their help in relocating. We have brought with us the technology we need to resume contact, but we need an adequate power source to make it a reality. It should not add to the other disruptions caused by the settlement of our people here since only a few specialized personnel are involved. We need only your permission to go forward."

"I will have to consult the council," said Marzin after again taking refuge in silence. "The negatives of our current situation are evident, but we have a confidence in what we have established even if imperfect. We have a symbiotic relationship with the more primitive inhabitants nearby with whom we trade the fruits of our knowledge for food and other basics of existence. We assume your enclave had a similar arrangement."

"Yes we did," said Binzing. "And now that we are gone from there, the Garuletzsky, an agrarian cult dependent on us must look elsewhere. Even though the supply lines are stretched, you might try contacting them to your mutual benefit.

"But regarding the timeline contact, we would appreciate it if you could consult the council as soon as possible. We have arranged a rendezvous fifty seven-years downtime of the node representing the intersection of our time streams, where we have a common past. That would be 2462 years in the past from this, the uptime point of our timeline. They will be coming from some 2288 years in their future as they reckon time. In their time stream, they discovered the ability to travel in time almost two hundred years before we did. The contact we are seeking has its uncertainties since they have only an approximate location for this Alcon enclave at the rendezvous date."

Two days passed before Marzin summoned Binzing.

"The council has met and approved the contact and authorized the use of our power source for your venture under the condition that a full report is given concerning the events leading to the discovery of the other timeline, and what has occurred since. We were caught off guard by this development and have yet to fathom its full implications."

"I will have my staff assemble the report as soon as possible," said Binzing.

A week later, all was ready. Binzing addressed the Alcon council and prime field operators of the Trust. A handsome woman stood to the side.

As you know, our agents, Adrian Beike and Francois Lebrust were sent to consolidate contact with the other timeline and are now functioning within it to further the aims of the Trust. Since the demise of our enclave, we have been forced to establish a new contact location to maintain a link to this other timeline. We must now draw on our reserve of personnel prepped for such missions. After some thought we have agreed on Kara Satin since, she is the only agent in the pool who has not been compromised by the upheaval in our community. She has been thoroughly briefed on the results of previous contacts and is eager to move us forward. I have asked her to say a few words.

Kara stepped forward. A neat one-piece jumpsuit clashed with her overall appearance—a shapely silhouette topped with a coif of coal black hair pulled back and wound tightly into a bun. Strong but delicate hands shifted pages of notes as she turned toward Binzing.

"Thank you Daner," said Kara. "Our technician, Lors Roux, informs me that the transporter is in place and ready to power up to send us downtime to the selected rendezvous point where our timelines coincide. Once there, we will have to branch out and search to make contact with the other timeline since no common cross-reference for the geography could be determined. Before the dissolution of our enclave, Daner instructed Adrian Beike, our advance envoy to the other timeline, to direct the agents to this general area at their temporal equivalent of our 2288-year downtime point. I hope that this site will be free of both inhabitants and hostile forces since, in the near future since we will have to return to it to reconnect with Alcon. We know a little of the history of the era. It is at that time in transition from local control to that of the aegis of the Roman forces, which we know from our own history, dissolved during succeeding years although the details of its demise have been lost. Dolf Barret has had experience with those of the other timeline, so he will go to identify the envoys. For protection, we will carry stunners, and lasers. We also have some small and large items to trade for food and other things to sustain us, all of which we will each carry in nondescript bags. We are ready to go as soon as the council gives the word."

Kara and Dolf both stood wavering for a moment.

"Lors warned me about the immediate effects of time transfer, but I guess we had to experience it to get the real impact," said Kara

"You're right there," said the tottering Dolf. "It is like a mixture of vertigo and intoxication, but it passes quickly."

Kara panned the desolate landscape. A vast stretch of water appeared several hundred meters from their position. "At least we didn't land in the middle of some bustling market. Assuming we have our rendezvous times in sync, I would also assume that Adrian and the envoys of the other timeline would judge that we had headed for the nearest populated place."

"Yes," said Dolf. "If we stick close to the shore we should encounter some settlement dependent on the fruits of the inland sea. If the others have transferred to this general area, they will probably do the same thing."

"We need to put some markers here, so we can find this transfer point again. As reference, we can use some of the sparse landmarks to find them," said Kara. "That small inlet there will do, together with the mound just visible to the southeast. They should be enough to clue us in."

They planted stakes to delineate points on the circular area that defined the reach of the TRs, the transport reciprocators they carried.

"Okay, let's keep the sea in sight and go in that direction," said Kara gesturing to the west.

They had plodded over the sodden landscape for an hour before Dolf pointed to the southwest. "What is that?"

"It's a colony," said Kara. "I can just make out the walls. Whatever it is, between here and there are islets of habitation leading up to it, so it must be of a considerable size. We will have to cross that stream of water flowing into the great sea to get there. It is the only sign of a concentrated population we have seen, so let's give it the once-over. At least it narrows down the search area the others will have to cover in order to rendezvous with us."

Another half hour passed before they stood in front of the walls of the fortified town. Two soldiers lounged lazily at the gate, casually viewing the natives as they entered. The populace freely moved in and out with purpose, some unburdened and others loaded with various items for consumption or for some other use unknown.

"Should we enter?" asked Dolf.

"Yes—carefully," said Kara. "It is likely that neither of us will be able to communicate with anyone. We are separated by millennia time-wise. There is no telling what languages they speak. If we are challenged, you must attempt to communicate in whichever primitive form it might take. Doubtless women are subservient in this world. Also, we are in luck. Our choice of garb looks generic enough so as to not raise suspicion."

They moved through the gate past the soldiers and into the heart of the settlement, Dolf a few steps in the lead with Kara following behind. When they were clear of the soldier's scrutiny, they paused to look around. Some taller structures surrounded a square fronted by stalls full of foodstuffs and other items for survival in the simi-desert conditions.

"Those were Roman soldiers guarding the gate," said Dolf. "From what we know of history, they have taken over this area by now."

"Everything is built of mud brick, probably the only thing handy in this region," said Kara. "We need to learn the name of this place and find somewhere to settle, so Adrian and Francois can connect with us here."

"I am leery about inquiring about lodging here since we can't speak the language, and they are probably suspicious of all strangers. But the alternative is to exit the city and camp out in the open, so we will have to improvise."

Kara again scanned the scene.

"There are beggars all around. Maybe we should join the club. They go about unnoticed, and some are in that condition because they can't speak or hear, which would serve to cover our language deficiency."

"A good idea but our garments are too pristine," said Dolf.

"A few rips and a little mud should fix that."

Stopping to trade for a small jug of water, they retired into the shadows of one of the buildings.

"Here, let me distress your robe then you can do mine," said Kara. She ripped Dolf's robe in a few places.

After a few minutes she stood back. "Okay, now a little muck to finish beggarizing you," she said with a chuckle while smearing some soil mixed with dirt on Dolf's face.

"How do I look?" asked Dolf.

"Great, I feel like giving you something myself. Oh, we have to muss up our bags too," said Kara.

Dolf repeated the process on Kara. They returned to the edge of the square.

"I hope they get it together, so they can zero in on us," said Dolf. "I wouldn't want to remain in this state indefinitely. Keep your weapons handy. This beggar status doesn't lend us much protection from those of a superior class, which is just about everybody on the social scale."

"Assuming they used the same logic about where and when to connect in this sparsely settled area, we could expect the ones from the other timeline soon," said Kara. "If, after a few days there is still no sign of them, we will know there is either some delay in the other timeline, or we got our signals mixed up. Now, we can't look like the Beggars Society of … of whatever this place is, so let's separate but stay in sight of each other. We can meet later and assess the situation."

The day stretched on, and with the approach of dusk Kara signaled Dolf who had planted himself some hundred feet away.

Kara's attention was on Dolf's leisurely approach. She was unaware of the retinue of natives who had approached from the opposite direction. A short bark of the local language rang in the air. Kara turned to be confronted with a large bearded man and two servants. He fixed her with a patronizing stare, which she could tell signaled trouble. In spite of her efforts to disguise her appearance, the lure of her feminine gifts still showed through.

The man spoke in soothing but firm tones and gestured to one of the servants. Kara scrambled for her bag of supplies and weapons and gave a quick warning glance toward Dolf, but was too late. The servant reached down and hoisted Kara to her feet.

Dolf was quick to recover her abandoned bag after he prevailed in a short dispute with a fellow alms seeker. With both bags slung over his shoulders, he watched as Kara was hustled toward a cluster of low profile buildings.

This is something we did not consider, thought Dolf. *This beggar disguise works to a point, but we are fair game to anyone with perverse sexual proclivities.* He followed the group of men into the maze of dwellings and shops of the settlement. Several yards in front, they finally disappeared into one of the houses. *I must rescue her even if it means blowing our cover.*

Dolf cautiously tried the door of the closed door, which was locked. He took out his laser and melted the primitive lock, which secured the door. He was just about to push it open with his foot when he heard a muffled cry followed by a stream of exclamations whose tone signaled meaning even in an unknown language.

He must have grabbed the hot metal latch, thought Dolf.

He nudged the door open with his foot to face one of the servants he had seen at Kara's capture. The muted invective diminished to a whimper as the Dolf and his surprised adversary regarded one another. Dolf reduced him to a heap with his stunner before he could raise an alarm.

Better to eliminate this complication and at the same time give him some temporary relief from that singed hand, thought Dolf.

He carefully made his way through the house as muffled voices echoed through the hallways.

There, it's coming from behind that door.

He drew closer and heard signs of a struggle and unmistakable protests in Gallo, the official language of the Trust. He burst into the room and found Kara half-clothed and struggling with the bearded owner and a servant. The standoff lasted only an instant before Dolf sprayed the two *thobe*-clad locals into a tangled mass of recumbent flesh. On impulse, Dolf rushed to the traumatized Kara and embraced her, lingering there for a moment. As if suddenly aware of his impulse, he stood back and mumbled, "I ... I feared for your safety."

Kara's eyes remained fixed on Dolf for a moment as she gave him a faint smile. "You were just in time. I couldn't have held them off for long. We will have to be more careful as we go forward. Now, what do we do with these bodies? They will be unconscious only four to six hours."

"We'll truss them up along with the one I did in at the entrance and find some place to sequester them," said Dolf, returning to the moment. "Then we can use this place as headquarters, but there's a limit as to how long we can continue. The captives will have creature needs and must have some kind of interaction within the city which will mean intruders from outside."

"Yes, and because of our language inadequacies, we will have to sequester anyone who stumbles in here," said Kara. "We could soon have a room full of locals clamoring for food and release. On top of that, we are known now. Once we let them loose, we will be fugitives. Perhaps we should leave as soon as possible, take to the country side, and watch for anything atypical that enters the city."

"If we go that route, we will need something to protect us from the dangerous predators that haunt a simi-desert," said Dolf. "A couple of improvised hammocks should do it if we can find some place to suspend them. I saw some fish nets drying outside one of the shops just as we came in, no doubt the property of some local fisherman who profits from the fruits of the inland sea."

Dolf and Kara left their unconscious captives in the house and made for the gate.

"There," said Dolf, pointing.

As they neared the gate, they saw a fisherman who, having no way to preserve his recent catch in the steamy weather, was dealing with some citizens in an effort to dispose of the last of the days take.

"The nets are still there," said Dolf. "It's a little big for a hammock, but with some clever folding or cutting we can rig something usable. I will try to bargain it out of the owner without knowing a word of their language."

The fisherman took in the ragamuffin duo as they approached, both still in their beggar's disguise, and decided that they were unsavory, probably loony, and definitely unfit to frequent his place of business. With the wave of a hand, he spouted in the local language that which clearly meant, "Begone, and don't loaf around here."

Dolf took out some gold coins he had brought along, flashed them at the fisherman, and pointed to the net. After a few takes on the beggar pair along and an exchange of grunts, the man, now convinced that they were indeed daft, accepted the coins and gave over the net. The same Roman soldiers, still lounging about, paid them no attention as they passed back through the gate. The daylight waned, and the black of night closed in as they wandered back across the barren steppes, which embraced the city.

They walked until the city was a comfortable distance away. Dolf pointed to a dead tree. "We can string the net from those limbs and drape it to form two compartments. I think," he added tentatively.

After a half hour of frustrating manipulations, the two looked at each other. Kara swung over, dropped into the bowels of the net, and motioned Dolf after. The two lay converged in a shapeless mass and soon succumbed to slumber.

III

A.D. 2288
In The Christian Timeline

Brant Conjular of the Institute of Temporal Research and Gerald Frondner, head of its parent organization, the Government Science Institute, met in Frondner's office in Obamapolis.

"I have an old-fashioned hand written letter from General Bromfsted," said Frondner. "The military seems to be up to date in its weaponry, but still twentieth century in communications."

"I must admit to some nostalgia for old ways of keeping in touch. So, just what does the restive general have to say?" asked an amused Brant.

"Nothing direct, but he gave some vague hints that the little show we put on to throw him off the track of our time travel escapades may not have worked. Here, see for yourself."

Brant scanned the letter.

Dear Dr. Frondner,

I must thank you for the kind invitation to your costume party in celebration of the breakthrough by the GSI's subsidary, the Institute of Temporal Research.

As to the occasion itself, the minute breakthrough of sending an object back in time almost a full second is most astounding. Adding to the excitement and festive atmosphere, were those present who themselves almost seemed to have sprung from past eras. We anxiously await the next step, greater penetration into the past. May we sooner rather than later, actually visit some of the places suggested by the costumes and the curiously authentic behavior of the attendees.

With sincerest regards,
Carlin Bromfsted

"Apparently, the old curmudgeon doesn't miss a thing," said Brant. "I believe he still has suspicions about the unexpected results of Onsley's mission to shadow Francois LeBrust." [9] I think we should let him simmer in half-knowledge and vague innuendo until, god forbid, he has firm evidence of our activity. Then we can meet the problem head-on."

"We will just have to keep an eye on it and try to stay ahead of him," said Frondner. "Now, the reason for this get together is to talk about the overall results of our time travel ventures and decide where to take it from here."

"I'm with you on that," said Brant. "The wealth of historical data we have gathered, especially the clarification of the events defining the Christian tradition, is astounding, but the discovery of another timeline has complicated matters. Despite their claim that our timeline is an offshoot of their own, we, in our own bumbling way, have a stable world while theirs, by their own assessment, is in chaos with only islands of advanced culture."

"I'm feeling that we should help them to preserve their progressive enclaves in hopes that the whole shebang will morph into a more stable world," said Frondner. "Beyond that, perhaps we should resolve any outstanding issues between us and then let the link go dormant, since there's little more we can or should do. One thing is for sure. Given what we know of human nature, unfettered interaction between us could be a disaster for both timelines—another reason for keeping the whole thing secret."

"Sadly, I must agree," said Brant. "We have enough to do in probing our own history. Of course their bumbling surrogates, Adrian and Francois, are here on a crusade for the Trust, which seems harmless enough but still implies no mandate for continuous interaction between our timelines."

"While we are on the subject, what do you make of Adrian's

showing up the other night with all that depressing news of events in their timeline?" asked Frondner. "And what was he saying about some activity to promote the values of the Trust some three centuries ago in this hemisphere? Aren't we in enough trouble with Francois LeBrust worming his way into the Vatican?"

"Maybe we should all get together for dinner and ask Adrian just what he was talking about," said Brant with a chuckle. "I can't imagine what he would be doing this side of the Atlantic at that time that had anything to do with the altruistic aims of the Trust, or, given the staging restrictions of time travel, what he would have gone through to even get here. As far as the present contact between our timelines is concerned, the Trust's problems throw the whole issue into a state of uncertainty. As he tells it, Binzing wants us to figure out where this Alcon settlement is, go there, and link up with his emissaries. To find it, we have agreed on his suggested time, thirty-one years below the A.D. 26 date of the intersecting node of our timelines where our histories coincide. It is safely below the date where Adrian was introduced as the adult Jesus into the culture of Judea, which initiated the new timeline. We will go there and look around for them. It sounds easy, but there are some unknowns. We at least agree on what a year is: one lazy swing of the earth around the sun," added Brant sarcastically. "Other than that, we know only that this Alcon is somewhere on the north coast of Africa, and we have only a general idea of what's there at that time."

"This is bad timing. All this confusion and must-dos now when we are under Bromfsted's radar," said Frondner.

"I agree. As far as Bromfsted is concerned, I don't think our little charade of a celebration last month got him off our backs," said Brant. "But to the immediate, the issue of contact with the other timeline must be addressed before it trickles away. Once done, we are back to considering what I mentioned before, letting the link go dormant until there is some reason to revive it. I hope that we can keep it secret. To now, we have been able to conceal the whole time travel capability itself, not to mention the ensuing ramifications of it.

"As to the goal of contact, we will have to get together with Rajulk to decide upon a target for the rendezvous. He is well versed on the history of the area. He can help us to pin down the temporal and geographic location of this Alcon. What I understand from Adrian is that it is somewhere short of the Nile delta as you travel southward from Palestisraelia, then west as the Mediterranean coastline curves around. You will have to consult some historical maps to determine a likely site. In any case, we won't have to hit it on the nose; we need only to get close."

———————

Rajulk pored over the outspread out map.

"It would be around where Pelusium was," said Rajulk, pointing. "I don't think there's anything there now except some ruins. A branch of the Nile used to run through the area, but it is silted up now. Hmm ... The 31 B.C. target year is when the Battle of Actium took place, and just before when the Romans swarmed in. We would not want to be around when that gets under way and caught up in the chaos of war. The Romans under Octavian are defeating the forces of Antony and Cleopatra, and the Egyptians are in a period of transition from the Ptolemaic to the Roman era. Considering the Trust's vague knowledge of the ancient past, the choice of date may be unfortunate. In any case, we are stuck with that date and certainly need to tread carefully in an atmosphere of Roman domination."

"Okay," said Brant. "The Pelusium location is a go. Its desolate state in the present may give us some advantage when we request permission from the Egyptian government to set up our equipment there under the standard phony research ruse."

"Let us hope they don't come nosing around when we do," said Rajulk. "We were lucky when we used that deception without a hitch more than once on the missions to Palestisraelia."

After some wrangling, the GSI received permission from the labyrinthine Egyptian bureaucracy to establish a base in the isolated coastal area east of Cairo.

"We have to zero in on a specific site before Seth can set up, and we can't get too close to historic Pelusium," said Brant. "Even though it was the Roman's presence that put it on the map, it was there before under somebody's authority. We, as well as the Trust envoys, could end up transferring into the middle of some bustling market."

"Have you decided on the team?" asked Rajulk.

"My preference is that it be just us, you and me, although when Lila gets wind of it she will want to go for the unknowns and excitement of it," said Brant. "She is reckless and takes too many chances. It wearies me especially because of my involvement with her."

"Oh—and Frondner brought up what Adrian was saying about activity in this hemisphere three centuries ago."

"Yes, I remember him saying that. I wonder what he meant. I am amused at the trouble he would have gone to even get here in that time of primitive travel," said Rajulk.

"I have no idea what he was talking about," said Brant. "Like I told Frondner, we should ask him. I hate to get distracted from our main goal of establishing contact with the Trust's main contingent, but we need to clear the air. I have suggested we all get together for dinner to ferret out what mischief he and Francois may have engaged in, while blindly stumbling forward with the Trust's mission. Adrian is another loose cannon, like Francois, so we can expect anything."

The ambient noise was loud, but not so intrusive as to prevent easy conversation in the crowded restaurant where Brant, Rajulk, and Lila decided to meet with Francois LeBrust and Adrian Beike. The relaxed air gave Brant his first chance to appraise Adrian since his return to the Christian timeline.

My first impression sticks, thought Brant. *He is like the Indiana Jones from those old films, ruggedly handsome and physically fit, but he shares with Francois that zany mindset of the Trust actives.*

"So Francois, when do you have to return to your duties at the Vatican?" asked Brant. *I would surely like to know how he managed to establish himself there.*

"I fear I must get back to Rome soon to mollify my superiors," said Francois. "I have been gone too long and have no more excuses for being absent. I could appoint myself as Vatican attaché to America, but that would be like demoting me from the illustrious position of Vatican press secretary."

"I see what you mean. Oh, Adrian," said Brant easily as he changed his the subject. "It is a pleasure to see you again. I feel somewhat weird for saying it but welcome to our timeline. I have a vivid recollection of our conversation when I visited the biblical era, where in the interest of the Trust you had immersed yourself in the role of Jesus. Your ordeal as Jesus chills me when I think of it. It is unfortunate that it took the demise of the Trust's enclave to bring you here.

"Yes, the situation of the Trust enclave is uncertain. We hope it can be resolved satisfactorily by finding a new place to settle," said Adrian.

"Our hope is that we will be able to stay in contact with your timeline and the Trust by following the Binzing's suggestion that we do so," said Brant. "Other than that, you mentioned a previous visit to this hemisphere before arriving at the now, the uptime forward moving terminus of this time frame. Was it in support of the Christian movement?"

"Yes, in the immediate sense, but of course with the long range goal to promote the values of the Trust," responded Adrian amicably. "I decided to make use of my temporary exile to give a boost to Francois's efforts and at the same time get a feel of life in this part of the world that was somewhat inaccessible and undeveloped in our own timeline. I went to considerable trouble getting here by primitive sailing ship in the first place. Then of course, I had to make the same arduous trip back to the transfer point in Jerusalem in order finally to arrive here at your uptime present. Finding myself here, I had first to familiarize myself with your culture and devise a means to survive before traveling to this hemisphere. Fortunately, I won't have to do that again if we follow Binzing's suggestion and establish a new link on this side of the … the Atlantic I believe you call it. If we can do this, it will save me that trip dreary back again under the primitive conditions of your nineteenth century to link with my fellow citizens of the Trust."

"So, what exactly did you do on your little side trip?" asked Brant in measured tones, uncertain as to having established Christianity what additional activity this side of the Atlantic could be in line with the aims of the Trust.

"Well, after some consideration, I choose the location of Palmyra, New York based on media reports of the period. I looked for candidates who might embrace the values of the Trust. In particular, I sought out either those whose behavior signaled an ardent leaning to the spiritual for persuasion to the aims of our movement, or those who approached them persuaded by intellect."

"Did … did you find such?" asked Brant with a glance at Rajulk.

"Yes, at least of the first category, a perfect specimen," said Adrian, leaving his answer hanging in the air.

"Who … uh that is, what came of it?" asked Brant in the silence that ensued.

"I had hoped to find that out when I reached here."

"This man, how did you approach him? That is, did he think you a little daft as you broached, uh … whatever you broached?" asked Rajulk speaking for the first time.

"First of all, it was not a man but a lad, no older than fifteen or so years," said Adrian.

"How could one so young possibly give impetus to the Christian movement?" asked Brant.

"I wasn't sure he would, but, as it said, I hoped to find out by probing past history when I arrived here up time to see if anything had come of it," said Adrian.

"Can you tell us more of what happened?" asked Brant with another side-glance at Rajulk whose raised eyebrows signaled that something bizarre may be coming their way from the unpredictable Adrian.

"Well, it came to a head in Palmyra New York," said Adrian staring off into space. "As I said, I had spent weeks investigating him and had hopes that the little side trip with all its inconveniences was not a waste of time. On this occasion, I watched from a shaded glade some one hundred yards away as he strolled from the clustered houses and shops of the town into the countryside. I needed to get him alone to try any *mumurastation,* at the same time hoping that the weeks I had spent investigating him on my tedious side trip had not been a waste of time.[10]

"As I watched, my subject turned left to and around some clustered foliage. I thought he might be going to relieve himself, which I considered not the ideal moment to engage in ethereal dialogue. He finished what he was doing and emerged from the bushes.

He then looked around and sauntered over to a stand of stately oaks some fifty yards away. I sidled to the right to converge on him although he was temporarily out of view, at the same time delving into the bag I was carrying to pull out a robe of my devising. I slipped it on, fastened a choker length wooden cross around my neck, and draped the bag over one shoulder with the thought that the whole getup would be hard to explain should anyone else see me.

"When he again came into view, I continued to watch him as he entered the dome-like domain of the oak grove and looked around. Choosing a hardy specimen, he sat down, leaned against its massive trunk, and dozed off. I took in the scene. The foliage soared high over the moss-covered space below. Light filtered through the gently moving limbs above, casting sprinkles of luminance on the shadowy landscape.

It could not have happened better. It was the perfect setting for what I was trying to do. I activated the LED lights emanating from the top of the robe behind the neck, which framed my head in a ghostly aura, then quietly moved into his purview. An inadvertent crackle of some brush signaled my presence. His eyes flickered and opened. Still in the never-land of half-sleep, he stared at the apparition hovering before him.

"It was a moment before he spoke. He said, 'I have been expecting you.'"

"It was even better than I had planned. It fit with the impression of him I got from the locals. He's a dreamer, completely open to the paranormal.

"I affected the most statuesque pose in my repertoire and intoned, 'As divine messenger of Jesus who dwells in the heavenly realm of god, I have come to admonish you to follow and promote the teaching of him, our savior the Lord Jesus Christ, who died for our sins. You must find within yourself the inspiration of Jesus as applicable to this land, so distant from his original presence. Having done this, you must go out into the world and bring others to embrace his teachings in their new form. I submit that this is your mission in life.'

"Now completely under my spell, he said 'But how can I do that? I am too young. Nobody will listen to me.'

"I said to him, 'You must persist and find the way. As you achieve age, maturity, and stature, you will have an audience and a following.'

"Judging that I had pushed his weakness for the paranormal to its limits, I decided it was time to wind things up, so I said 'I must leave you now and return to sphere of transcendence from whence I came.' I backed away into the cluster of oak trunks, dimming my halo as I went until I was out of sight. I quickly removed the robe and accoutrements and stowed them away in my bag thinking that after considerable trouble and planning, I had done what I set out to do. Time would tell if it had been worth it.

"I thought over what I should do next. Should I poke around a little more to find other candidates to further the aims of the Trust, or go uptime, find Francois, and tell him about the trouble back at the enclave? Whatever I did, it should be before visiting the uptime terminus of this timeline since doing it afterwards was out. It could alter the time stream jiggering me into a timeline from which I could not be retrieved. Giving in to reason, I concluded that I had spent too much time furthering the Trust's mandate when the fate of the enclave itself was so uncertain. The thought of returning all the way to Judea on one of those primitive sailing ships just to transfer uptime within this time line was depressing, but until we can establish a transfer point here in the Americas it was the only way."

Brant and the others sat in open-mouthed silence as Adrian rambled on, somewhat unsure that at the pause indicating he may have finished, he had indeed finished.

"Uh … well, what was the young man's name?" asked Brant, groping for the right question to throw further light on the encounter and discover if it had any possible relevance to subsequent events.

"His name was Joseph Smith, apparently a common one in this culture. I had studied him for some time, first talking to the citizens in his community and compiling the various rumors floating around."

The name, Joseph Smith, rang silently and held suspended in the air as Brant and Lila turned to Rajulk since of the three he was the one more attuned to the humanities. If someone of that name surfaced, he would not be in the field of science.

"That was early 19th century," voiced Rajulk eyes unfocused in recall mode.

Jo-se-ph Smith, thought Rajulk as he slowly mouthed the name. *Surely, he is not talking about the Joseph Smith, of early Mormon history.* A moment's silence passed before Rajulk spoke cautiously.

"There was a Joseph Smith who was one of the founders of the Mormon Church, a somewhat eccentric manifestation of institutionalized Christianity. It now has millions of followers. It is even more captive of the mythological extrapolations of the Christian story than the True Church or the New Essenes who sent us on the first mission. Are you saying you had a hand in its inception?"

"I am not saying anything," said Adrian. "As I said, I hoped to find out when I got here, but your comments seem to suggest a mixed success."

"To say the least," said Rajulk. "The Mormons advocate your goal of an ethical society, but are burdened by a questionable history and a bizarre theology based on the appearance of Jesus in the western hemisphere. They have revised the timeline of the first part of the Bible we call the Old Testament, and have placed the Garden of Eden in Missouri, not far from here. They have retroactively invented a scenario to support their beliefs. They have even tried to equate the timeline of the Hopewell culture with that of the Book of Mormon.

"Let's see," continued Rajulk as he paused in effort to sort out what he remembered of Mormon history.

"In Antiquity, there were conflicting tribes. From one of the tribes came a prophet named Mormon who transcribed what would become the Book of Mormon onto some gold plates and gave them to his son Moroni. This is where Smith comes in. In the latter part of the nineteenth century, when he was seventeen, he received a visit from Moroni in the guise of an angel in some setting or other … uh yes, the Smith farm itself. Moroni told him where a set of gold plates was buried. Theee … the Hill Cumorah, that's it. Through a series of convoluted events, Smith obtained the plates, translated what was on them, and published it. In its current form, the Book of Mormon is comparable in their faith to the Christian Bible. Don't tell me you had a hand in all that?"

"I expected none of those details to spring from my encounter with Smith. To further the Trust's mandate, I promoted only generalities," said Adrian.

"Well, what you set out to do has the tail wagging the dog," said Rajulk, now in a state of incredulity. "The mythology has far exceeded the moral construct you promoted."

"That is unfortunate. I will consult with Francois to see what can be done."

"It is too late," said Brant. "Unless … surely, you wouldn't go back and try to intervene? You could initiate another timeline with a new reality."

"From all appearances, Joseph Smith didn't initiate a new timeline when he with my encouragement embarked on the quest for a new faith, so how would tinkering with it do so?"

"That's different," said Brant. "In the case of Jesus where this timeline was established by the singular event of his presence, we didn't go back to change anything, only to clarify exactly what happened. As a result, you are now able to move up and down within this the Christian timeline by virtue of the TRs we provided you, which were made available by a series of coincidences: the invention of time travel technology and events driven by the politics of the Church. In this case, you are trying to change the course of history itself. You could become marooned, and be forced to live out your life in a newly formed reality with its own timeline. Quite likely, there would be no one in its time stream to establish a thread leading to its past or future to rescue you."

"You lost me a little bit. Perhaps Binzing can explain it more clearly," said Adrian. "But maybe we can manipulate some of the items in the history of the movement you have described. We can't alter what someone said about being visited by an angel, but … what about those gold plates you mentioned that are so important to the Mormons. Where are they?"

"As far as I am concerned, there never were any, and the bulk of the Mormon community is probably little concerned with them," said Rajulk.

"That's the point," persisted Adrian. "Maybe we could conjure up some gold plates with nothing on them or something frivolous, to debunk the fictional basis of the faith. Then the congregants can concentrate on the positive elements of spirituality consistent with the values of the Trust."

"Even if you could do that, experience has shown that unless ethics and morals are tied to something mystical like religion, they won't take," said Rajulk.

"That's nonsense. Men of reason can rise above the trivial and embrace true values."

"Think so? You are new here, not like Francois who has come to a more pragmatic approach," said Rajulk. "Besides, the Mormons are a peaceful community and do good works. The spurious facts of their founding are secondary. And I hesitate to mention it, but it is only one of several bizarre manifestations of Christianity which have cropped up in this hemisphere since its discovery and settlement."

"We can only concentrate on one at a time for corrective action. Now, back to the gold plates, where can you get some gold here?" persisted Adrian.

"The amount of gold you would need to reproduce plates of adequate size to inscribe the Book of Mormon on would strain any budget," said Rajulk, hoping to quash any further talk of the matter. "Gold itself has not been used as money nor has currency been based on it for several hundred years."

"Well, where is it?"

"Besides what's scattered about used in jewelry and for occasional scientific purposes, the reserve of it is in a place called Fort Knox," said Brant, aware that the conversation had taken a bizarre and humorous turn. He glanced at Rajulk who just had turned away red-faced, on the edge of losing it. "Of course," Brant added, "there is a pile of it in sunken ships on the bottom of the sea."

"Why don't they just bring it up?" asked Adrian.

"They don't know where most of it is," said Brant patiently, with the feeling that he never should have mentioned it.

"What is time travel for? Can't you go back and find out where it is by accompanying it from its source?"

"We never considered using time travel for such a purpose," said Brant after a pause. "We don't think anyone should do such a thing. It would bring up yet another ethical quandary—saving the gold while letting the ship's crew perish."

"Well ... where else was gold lying about?" persisted Adrian.

Somewhat recovered, Rajulk waded in to rescue Brant from Adrian's frivolity. "After what we call the Gold Rush in the mid nineteenth century, there were considerable shipments of it were transported by horse-drawn coaches in the west of this country. They were a favorite target of bandits."

"With what I presume is our superior weaponry, we could just take it from the bandits," said Adrian. "After all, the loot of such thievery would be lost to its owners anyway. As a bonus to the community, we could remand the culprits to custody."

Brant sighed and did a long take at Rajulk who stood on the edge of losing it again and waiting for what came next. "Just as you had the say as to what we did in your timeline, we reserve the right to manage what goes on in ours."

With a nod toward Rajulk, Adrian said, "As I recall, your colleague here and Ms. McEntire, stepped outside our guidelines when you visited us, ignoring our request to let us manage your rescue from the Xerjinko."

"Okay, perhaps we owe you one," said Brant. *I must resist venting my opinion of the Trust's wimpy security forces and their ability to rescue anything.* "We still reserve the right to monitor your activities as you dabble in our history. For one thing, you may well meet your end messing with the nasty banditry of nineteenth century America. We wouldn't want your demise on our conscience, and on a more practical level, we need your help now as we try to reconnect with your timeline."

"The bandits you speak of couldn't be any worse than the Romans before and after the crucifixion," persisted Adrian.

"Certainly not worse in intent, but they had fire arms by that time," said Brant. "In any case, even with superior weapons we couldn't let you go alone. Being here in an atmosphere of mutual respect, we feel some responsibility for your safety, just as the Trust did when we experienced the down side of your timeline."

"Should we indulge them?" asked Brant after Adrian and Francois had left. "I don't think it would shake the Mormon faith, no matter what they found written on the plates.

"We can go along if only to get them off our backs and keep them from even greater mischief," said Rajulk after a pause. "It's rather clear-cut: help them get just enough gold to fabricate some plates with enough surface to inscribe whatever idiocy they have in mind and stay in the background as a backup in case of trouble. They don't realize how fast things can happen in the era of gunfighters."

"Okay, I'll get together with Seth and settle on a time window and a lucrative site from which to transfer the three of you," said Brant. "Fortunately, Obamapolis is not only at the geographic center of the original forty-eight states, but also near the epicenter of the old west. That should make things easier."

They crammed the transfer equipment into a van and traveled south from Obamapolis.

"Looks like an okay place for the setup," said Brant, spying an old barn some hundred yards from the highway. "That rotting old barn still has enough structure to hide any transfer boundaries we set up. According to records, the main nineteenth-century stage route ran through here. Dodge City is to the west about ten miles."

IV

Kansas 1860
Adrian and Francois's Effort to Obtain Gold

The sun blazed, bathing the mostly barren landscape in a shadow-less blanket of light. A primitive road wound through the low-lying hills below as Rajulk, Adrian Beike, and Francois LeBrust stood vigil.

"This hasn't worked out, in spite of the local lore," said Rajulk wiping his forehead, disgusted that he had agreed to the plan. "Several coaches have passed unmolested in the past few days. Maybe we should find another site. Besides, these horses, which we were lucky enough to get in the first place, need water"

"Patience," said Francois. "The visit to the city informed us that there have been two robberies on this route in the last month, and the local bank is smarting over the losses."

"So, it happened," said Rajulk. "What makes you think it will happen again and here? We chose Dodge because it is on the main route. Now, after what we went through to set up this ambush, it turns out that the famous Dodge City is no more than a bunch of grungy buildings, a hotel, and two saloons set amidst a broad area of ranch lands."

"It may not happen again," said Francois ignoring Rajulk's complaints. "But any bandits who might have such ideas should pass by here."

"The last bunch we followed ended up at a local ranch after a night in the local saloon," mumbled Rajulk.

They settled down. Adrian and Francois exchanged some occasional words in Gallogermanian, the official language of the Trust, which they used side by side with Anglo. [11]

"What's that?" asked Adrian, pointing to a cloud of dust.

"It may be a lone rider," said Rajulk. "No, there are three, maybe four of them."

The riders stopped. One of them pointed to a cluster of large boulders bordering the road. They moved slowly around it out of sight.

"They may be taking a break, but they could be looking for a place to ambush," said Rajulk, emerging from his languid state.

"The coach is due soon from Pueblo, and if that bunch is planning anything it should happen soon," said Francois.

They waited until dusk. No coach appeared, and the suspicious horsemen were still concealed behind the outcropping.

"Should we give it up?" asked Rajulk in mock disappointment.

"Just a little longer," said Francois, himself beginning to consider it a day wasted.

On cue, a whiff of dust appeared at the top of a rise to the west.

"It's late, but that may be it," said Adrian.

"We'd better move closer if we hope to intervene," said Francois.

The cloud of nebulosity coalesced into the dim outline of a coach as it approached.

"It is one horse shy of the usual complement," said Rajulk puzzled. "That's the reason it is late. They need an even number for stability when moving since the coach pulls to one side. One probably threw a shoe or something."

"I suggest we ride down, park the horses, and wait near there," said Rajulk pointing. "If they plan anything, that's the place they will try to intercept the coach."

They arrived at the base of their hill lookout, dismounted, and tied up the horses where they could not be seen from the road. Moving quietly through the boulders and scrub brush, they stopped short of the bandits' position and waited. Several minutes passed before they heard the faint sound of hoof beats and the rustle of the coach.

"Get ready," said Rajulk.

The sound of the coach grew louder until it appeared, turning around a large occluding rock some fifty yards away. It approached and passed by their position.

"Damn," said Rajulk. "Where the hell are they? Did we make the wrong call?"

Just then the four horsemen raced by in front of their watch and started firing at the coach that was now receding at a faster pace as it drew out of sight around yet another bend. Rajulk and the others mounted and galloped in pursuit. Rounding the curve in the road, they saw the coach pulled up. The driver was tending the guard, who was slumped over to the side. As the bandits converged on the coach, the driver took a bullet in the leg when he was slow in holding up his hands. He spun and fell off his perch onto the coach's tongue, the rigid interface between the horses and the coach. He struggled to right himself as the bandits approached. Rajulk raced to the center of action ahead of Adrian and Francois, but as he neared the scene, he was unable to single out the culprits against the background of the horses, the coach, the driver, and his companion. With his stunner set for wide-angle, he sprayed the entire scene. Cut short but not out, the bandits staggered and turned toward the source of their oppression, one or more trying to lift their guns to fire. Rajulk laid another stream from his stunner on the bandits, now in closer proximity. They reeled and fell along with two of horses in the background, leaving only the remaining horse along with the wounded coachman upright and conscious. Rajulk and the others approached the coach. The driver was slowly untangling himself from the confusion of recumbent horses and the functional accessories of the coach.

"Where is the gold you were carrying?" asked Adrian.

The driver, still dazed, focused for a moment trying to decipher Adrian's somewhat strange rendition of English, then gestured to the top of the coach.

Adrian nodded to Francois and said, "Help me muscle it down."

"Hold it. It wasn't supposed to happen this way," Rajulk force-whispered and added under his voice, "We were to wait till the culprits got the gold then confiscate it. I had to intervene because the driver and his sidekick, the guard, have been wounded. We can't just leave them. It is against our principles and certainly those of the Trust to harm anybody in the target areas we visit. We must abort this effort and try again perhaps somewhere else."

"You are right, but we didn't bring along anything for medical emergencies," said Francois with regret. "What do you suggest?"

The door of the coach slowly opened and the tip of a dainty shoe-clad foot appeared from the dimness of the coach's interior.

Now another complication, thought Rajulk as all stopped to focus on what came next.

The young woman stepped from the coach and coolly appraised the bizarre scene. The three original bandits were unconscious and scattered about. Two downed horses, still partially conscious, pawed randomly at something in the air, while the surviving horse stood quietly. The wounded guard was still slumped over atop the driver's perch, mercifully anesthetized by the spray of the stunner. The driver, along with Rajulk and the others, stood with eyes riveted on the anomalous apparition, so incongruous in the stark setting.

With bonnet thrown back, a cascade of coal black hair bathed her shawl-covered shoulders and framed a porcelain face of striking beauty. White gloves guesting delicate fingers extended upward beneath the shawl. A bodice of lace backed with satin of similar hue tapered to a dainty waist and adjoined to a splayed skirt extending to the ankles.

Adrian was the first to speak. "Uh ... madam, you will pardon our intrusion and the inconvenience we may have caused you. Though we happened on this occasion by chance, our presence is spurred by a greater purpose than may be suggested by the crude scene you now witness."

"And what would that be?" asked the woman.

Let's see how he answers that, thought Rajulk.

"It is too complex to explain in brief," said Adrian without missing a beat. "For now, we must provide assistance to the wounded and see you to your destination ... which is—?"

"Most immediately it is Dodge City, where I will pause for a rest from the arduous discomforts of travel by coach. After a satisfying rest, I will continue eastward to St. Louis where I can catch a train to my home in New York."

"It would be our pleasure to accompany you to Dodge," cooed Adrian in melodious tones.

"I would be most grateful for your protection after this scene of violence," said the woman, who then retired to the coach.

Now that is settled, thought Rajulk. *What do we do with the bandits?*

"What should we do with the Bandits?" asked Adrian, as if reading Rajulk's thoughts.

"Let's pile them on top of the coach, and hand them over to the

Sheriff when we reach Dodge," said Rajulk. "They won't come to for a few hours and they'll be groggy after that."

"You are wasting good bandits, and reducing our chances for a favorable outcome," objected Francois. "There may not be another opportunity in the foreseeable future. We should leave them and let them survive to continue their thievish activity."

"We can't do that," said Rajulk, amused by Francois's twisted logic. "They may kill someone in the meantime. Now, we are wasting time. The guard up there may survive if we can get to Dodge quickly."

They tied the three bandits on top of the coach and decoupled the two fallen horses from the coach, leaving them to their twitches. The wounded guard was muscled down from his perch and, along with the driver, placed in the coach.

"Madam, you will please excuse the temporary presence of your two brave defenders until we reach Dodge and have them tended to," said Adrian.

"It is the least I can do," said the woman pleasantly. "With whom do I have the pleasure of speaking?"

"My name is Adrian Beike, and yours might be?"

"Eugenia, Eugenia Winthrop."

The cozy exchange between the two did not escape Rajulk, but the immediate concerns of getting the wounded men to Dodge took priority. He harnessed his horse to the coach to match the surviving one, and the coach proceeded to Dodge. Rajulk, having taken charge by default, was perched in the driver's seat. The strange procession was greeted by a gathering of the townspeople as word spread.

"Can someone get help for these men?" said Rajulk.

The driver and the guard were taken away as the sheriff and the agent of Butterfield Stagecoach Company converged on the coach.

Rajulk thought fast. *We'd better offer some explanation before we are bombarded with questions like who are we, and what are we doing here in the first place?*

"We happened on the robbery as it was taking place," said Rajulk. "The culprits are those uh … at rest atop the coach. The driver and guard can attest to our account. The contents of your shipment should be intact."

"That is good to know," said the Butterfield agent. "We are grateful for your services."

Adrian was assisting Eugenia from the coach.

Rajulk listened, open-mouthed, as Adrian said, "It would be my pleasure to accompany you to dinner this evening, if we should find a suitable place here."

"I'm sure the hotel has some sort of dining facility, if modest," said Eugenia favoring Adrian with a generous smile.

"If eight o'clock is convenient, I will meet you in the lobby."

"That would be fine."

Francois, occupied with untangling the still-unconscious bandits from their perches, missed the exchange.

"Francois!" whispered Rajulk, now concerned with the escalating diversions from what he thought would be a simple quest. "Can you get Adrian back on track? He seems to be infatuated with that woman."

"What? Oh—I didn't notice," said Francois with a glance toward Adrian. "Well, it will run its course. It always does— or did, back at the Trust enclave. Even back in Judea, there was that girl Mary. His closest followers were always jealous of his deference to her. Adrian just likes women but never lets it interfere with his obligations to the Trust."[12]

Rajulk blinked, his face taking on a look of disbelief. *Mary … Is he talking about Mary Magdalene? Perhaps the rumors were true. Maybe she did play a larger role than has been passed down. I will file that away and ask Adrian about it sometime. The True Church has disputed her so-called gospel for centuries.*

"I suggest we arrange for rooms at the hotel for the night," said Francois intruding on Rajulk's thoughts. "Tomorrow we can proceed afresh, as planned."

"How is that?" asked Rajulk who had assumed that the original plans had to be scuttled.

"Nothing has changed. The gold would have been lost to the bandits anyway had we not intervened. The only difference is that it is temporarily in the custody of the bank."

"And how do you hope to surmount that little detail?" asked Rajulk.

"Such plans are in the process of development," said Francois.

The dining room was crowded and possessed a modicum of crude opulence belying the sense of desolation presented by a view of the town from outside. Francois signaled Rajulk to join him. Adrian and Eugenia sat in animated conversation to one side. From the corner of his eye, Rajulk saw her take something from her hair and give it to Adrian.

The evening waned, and all retired to their quarters.

"So, how do you propose to get your gold now?" posed Rajulk as the three assembled.

"We have talked it over and think a straightforward approach is best."

"What does that mean?" asked Rajulk, fearing the worst.

"The gold resides in the Butterfield office now which presents the best opportunity to get it before it is disbursed," said Adrian. "We can intrude on the office, stun the guards, take it, and make for the transfer point."

"I want nothing to do with this folly," said Rajulk. "Things can go wrong. They deal quite harshly with bank robbers in this era. They could hang you for it and me, too, because of my associations with you. Besides, it is at least five miles to that farmer's barn where we set up the transfer point. Unless we got a big head start, they could pick us off one by one with rifles while they are way out of range of our stunners."

"We don't want to draw this thing out forever," said Francois. "It is in the greater interest to execute the plan as formulated."

"When do you intend to do this?" asked a resigned Rajulk.

"Tonight after hours," said LeBrust.

"Tell you what," said Rajulk after a moment of indecision. "I will wait for you on the road about three miles out. If it goes okay, we can reach the transfer point, release the horses, and be out of here. Bear in mind, take only the gold you may need for the plates. It is in the form of coin and heavy. A couple hundred pounds should do it. That's a hundred each, and even that will slow you down. Any extra will reduce your chance of escape."

Rajulk was dosing off in the saddle as early morning approached. Moonlight bathed the hilly landscape, highlighting the rocks and dust-covered roadway leading eastward. He glanced at his watch—*four a.m. They are late*, thought Rajulk in a moment of indecision. *I will have to sneak back into town to find out, but if they are caught up in something, I may be implicated too because of the incident with the coach.*

The sound of distant hoof beats broke the silence of the night interrupting Rajulk's reverie. *That must be them.*

As they grew louder, the patter took on a contrapuntal character as the closer sound merged with that more distant.

Two riders were rushing toward his position followed by a quartet of masked horsemen appearing over a dimly lit rise a few hundred yards away, traveling at full gallop. As the duo approached Rajulk's position, Francois shouted, "Follow quick. They are after us."

They passed Rajulk without slowing down, each with two bulging saddlebags draped over his laboring horse. Rajulk rallied his own mount and went in pursuit of the two. Looking back, he spied four horsemen in hot pursuit. He topped a rise and again looked back. The four horsemen were, in turn, being followed by yet another group of riders.

Catching up with his frantic cohorts, Rajulk barked over the sound of the horses. "What's happening here? Who's chasing who?"

Francois gave voice amid the bounces and lurches of his horse. "It's the bandits we captured earlier chasing us and a posse chasing them. Keep going. How far is it to the transfer point?"

"At least a mile and a half," said Rajulk.

"The horses are beginning to tire. Each of us has around the hundred pounds of gold you suggested," said Adrian.

"I'm sure those following us are tiring too. Just keep going, and we should maintain our lead," said Rajulk astounded that the hapless pair had managed to pull off such a tenuous plot. "So at least you got the gold."

"Yes, but with difficulty," said Francois.

There were hints of dawn in the east as the charcoal sky gave way to a glimmer of red.

They continued for another quarter hour. "I think it's just over this hill," said Rajulk. "I recognize that abandoned wagon there. We passed it going out."

"Hurry, I hear them not far behind us," said Francois.

"There," said Rajulk as they topped the rise. "That's the deserted barn over there."

They closed on the barn as fast as the now waning horses could manage under the weight of the gold. A shot rang out, and then more. Bullets whizzed past their heads sending up dust as they slammed into the loose, dry soil to the front and side. They arrived at the barn, quickly dismounted, and dragged the heavy saddlebags off the horses, which now unrestrained, slowly scattered.

"Quick, over here inside the transfer perimeter," said Rajulk as he rushed to the spot they had cordoned off.

LeBrust and Adrian struggled with the saddlebags and pulled them inside the perimeter just as other riders drew up outside.

It happened all at once.

"All inside?" asked Rajulk, his attention momentarily on his TR.

"Yes—no, wait!" said Francois.

That was all that Rajulk heard as he activated his TR. The sound of gunfire pelting the barn abruptly stopped. He and Francois stood breathless. Only the stakes delineating the transfer area amid the remains of an ancient barn remained in their view.

Seth Richards, chief tech of the time transfer home base strolled over to meet them.

"There were three of you?"

"Yes, where is he?" asked a thoroughly nettled Rajulk.

"He slipped outside the perimeter just as you activated," said Francois echoing Rajulk's frustration but coloring it with a whiff of concern. "I think he dropped something, and went back for it."

"I can't go back now," said Rajulk after a pause. "The place is probably swarming with the sheriff and his men or the setting of a standoff between them and the bandits with Adrian in the middle of it all. Hmm … it's just a deserted barn, and seeing no special significance to it other than the chance convergence of them all, they will soon leave. As for Adrian, if he doesn't get shot in the meantime, he may be able to justify his presence in some way. I'll wait a bit, then go back and see if I can find him."

"All right," said LeBrust, deciding to make the best of the situation. "In the meantime, I will take this gold back to Obamapolis and start fabricating the gold plates. Brant can help me with the process. When Adrian gets back, we can decide what to put on them."

"Okay," said Rajulk. "Hopefully he didn't get caught in some crossfire. They may have him in custody. It depends on what take the sheriff has on the situation. Seth can send me back tomorrow, and I will find out what happened."

With relief, Adrian had settled into the transfer perimeter with the others and stared at the opening in the barn, which was once secured by the heavy door now lying in tatters to the side. A sparkle from the rutted floor punctuated the dimness.

What is ... that? I must have dropped it.

He charged out of the perimeter to retrieve the object, then turned and stared into the stark emptiness of the barn. Realizing what had happened, he fumbled around in his pockets for his TR. A noise in the doorway made him turn again to face the four gunmen silhouetted in the barn opening.

For a moment, all was still as the intruders faced only a lone Adrian, clearly perplexed by the absence of the others they had pursued.

"Wher are they? Wher's thu gold at?" said one.

"Go aheaden shootem Leroy, you cun see he ain't got it," said another.

"If we shootem, we'll never find it," said Leroy. "Thuthers musta slipped out th back.

The sound of hoof beats again pierced the stillness of dawn.

"It sat that damn posse!" shouted one of the gunmen from behind as a shot entered the black opening of the barn.

"Th'r shooten blind," said Leroy. "We ain't got no cover in here an thr'es no way out. How many ubum are ther?"

"Bout uh dozen or so."

"Well, we ain't got the gold," said Leroy after a pause. "The only thang they cun do withe us is put us back in jail fer breakin out. They cān't hang us fer that. And that thang with the stage, it's ther word agin ourn. This here hombre was one of the ones what brought us in after we was out, but it was him an thuthers what took the gold. It's damn confusin. I cān't figure it out, and maybe the posse cān't neither."

Leroy held up his hands and walked out of the barn followed by the others.

"All right, where is the gold?" barked the Butterfield agent, standing by the sheriff.

"We ain't got no gold. Them what we was chasin had it, and we was going to git it back fer ya, but we only caught up with thisun here," said Leroy pointing to Adrian. "Go in and see fer yer sef. Ther ain't nun."

"If you think we are stupid enough to believe that, you are quite mistaken," said the Butterfield agent who gestured to one of his men. "Go search the barn."

After a moment, the deputy came back.

"There's no sign of anybody else or the gold."

"If there was anybody else, they can't have gotten far. Check the other side. See if you can spot them hightailing it," said the agent.

"Nothing," said the deputy when he returned.

"Tie up these men and … maybe that other one too," said the sheriff pointing to Adrian. "He is one of the three who originally brought this gang into Dodge. We need to take them all in and sort this thing out."

The gang of four was manacled and hoisted onto their horses, now tethered together. Adrian double mounted behind one of the deputies on another horse, and the strange procession made its way back to Dodge.

Settling in the sheriff's office, the four fugitives plied him and the Butterfield agent with a confusion of disparate accounts of the events leading up to present.

"It was this here hombre what robbed the stage in the first place," said Leroy. "We happened to be ridin along and seen what was goin on and stepped in, but we got bushwhacked by this critter and a couple of others. They somehow put a hex on us, and we was hogtied to the top of the stage wher you found us at."

"On the contrary," interrupted Adrian who summoned his best slightly accented version of Anglo/English and proclaimed with a flourish, "Events didn't unfold that way at all. These three rapscallions intercepted the stagecoach and attempted to rob it. We overcame them and placed them atop the coach where, true to character, they took refuge in slumber. It was only through the intercession of myself and my colleagues that confiscation of the gold and, god forbid, the possible violation of the delicate flower of name Eugenia Winthrop who traveled within was thwarted."

Both the agent and the sheriff stared at Adrian as he droned on, mesmerized by his florid rendition of English in stark contrast with that of the ruffians. A moment's silence ensued after Adrian stopped talking.

"All that happened before," said the sheriff finally. "What I want to know is what just happened at that old barn. Who was chasing who? Immediately in front of us were these four and you were in front of them. It would seem that they were after you, and …

What you were doing out there in the first place?"

"Jes like I said," Leroy broke in. "He and them other hombres was makin off with the gold, and we was chasin em."

"The explanation is quite simple," said Adrian. "Unable to sleep, I happened to peer out of my window at the hotel. I saw that these gentlemen, whom I had assumed were confined, were once more on the loose. With haste, I dressed and followed them as they left the town and traveled toward some unknown destination hoping to report back their whereabouts to the authorities. I approached the mission with such zeal that I overcame and passed them as they took a brief respite during their flight. Only too late, did I discover that my role as lone pursuer had inadvertently changed to that of the pursued. I had become the victim of opportunity."

"He's fulla cow dung," said Leroy, his voice trailing off with a feeling that Adrian's ornate rendition of events would carry the day, and they were once again at the mercy of the Sheriff.

"You four are going back to the jail," said the Sheriff after a pause. "It's pretty clear you attempted to rob the stage. We have the testimony of Mr. Beike and Miss Winthrop to vouch for that."

The sun was rising as Adrian settled into his room at the hotel and looked around. *Didn't think I would use it again. Convenient I didn't check out. Now ... better stick around for most of the day and return to the barn later when things die down ... Sleepy, up overnight. Right now, I could use a nap.*

Adrian woke refreshed in early afternoon. *I'm famished. I wonder if that dining room is open.*

A voice intruded on his musings as he strolled through the hotel.

"Why, Mr. Beike, fancy meeting you here."

"Miss Winthrop, the pleasure once again is mine."

"I am delayed here since the next coach to the east only arrives the day after tomorrow," said Eugenia. "To pass the day, I have arranged for a carriage to venture into the countryside. Would you care to go along? When we return, it will be time for tea, that is, if they even serve it in this primitive place."

"Uh, well ... how could I refuse?" said Adrian as he weighed the rewards of the distraction with the task at hand. "As for tea, I'm sure they could conjure up some or a close enough equivalent to complement the pleasantries we associate with it."

Adrian watched as the coach pulled up in front of the hotel. To his surprise, Eugenia herself was at the reins. "Hmm" ... *Not exactly, what I thought she had in mind. My instinct tells me this is not a place to be wandering around in. I thought we would have some sort of an escort. I have garnered enough history of this timeline to know it is much like ours. Danger springs from where you least expect it.* He instinctively touched the left side of his rawhide jacket for assurance that his stunner was still there.

"Hop in," said Eugenia cheerfully, who in contrast to the excessive feminine accoutrements of their first encounter, had now donned a spartan but graceful rider's outfit of the period: an ankle-length dress, flared at the bottom to permit movement, and a short matching jacket covering a white ruffled shirt. An abbreviated cap of similar hue topped off the ensemble.

Adrian mounted the carriage and sat quietly as Eugenia skillfully maneuvered it over the way forward, which became increasingly rugged as they proceeded from Dodge to the flat outlands.

"You apparently have skills at managing horses," said Adrian, surprised that the jewel of a woman beside him was not the fragile being of his original assessment.

"My family has many horses at our home on the outskirts of New York. I learned to ride at a very early age. Indeed, my father Edgar Winthrop is known for his skills in breeding as a side interest. His success, of course, has been in real estate."

They continued for a quarter hour or so. "Oh, over there is an inviting spot of green in this eternal brownness," said Eugenia. "Should we stop for a rest?"

"Yes, if you wish," said Adrian. "That tree does indeed look lonely amid this austere plain."

Eugenia deftly secured the horse and carriage before joining Adrian in the shade of the tree.

"So, what brought you to such a primitive setting as the town of Dodge?" asked Adrian.

"It was my idea. I was in search of adventure to break the monotony of New York life, so when my father received notice that his wayward brother Alger had passed away, I offered to go the west and claim ownership of the assets he had amassed from some gold operations. Having now secured the documents attesting to the inheritance, I can make the return trip to New York. I have had my fill of less-than-civilized conditions and am anxious to return home."

They sat together for a while in silence before she leaned her head to his shoulder. Adrian slipped his arm around her. Eugenia slowly looked up, and suddenly the two were locked in a passionate embrace.

Adrian was the first to speak. "I am not sure what is to become of this. I am on a mission, which must take precedent over momentary passion, but I have not met anyone like you in all my journeys or at my place of origin. Whatever the future holds, I hope you will reserve a place for me. I will try to reach New York in some way to join with you after I resolve some pressing matters."

"Please do, I will wait for you," said Eugenia wistfully, with regret that their moment of togetherness was so brief.

This will be difficult, thought Adrian. *I don't know when the work of the Trust will be finished in this timeline. Even so, my choices are limited. I doubt I could persuade Brant Conjular that it was important enough to move a transfer facility to the New York area just for a romantic venture … It may be within his discretion to transfer me from the facility in Obamapolis, or some hub with a more convenient access to this era. From there I could travel by way of their primitive transport eastward to New York. Of course, an alternative would be …*

V

Rajulk Returns to 1860 to Retrieve Adrian

Rajulk, with his stunner ready, gave the signal to Seth. *Here goes nothing. I hope Adrian got himself out of it somehow.*

After the familiar disorientation of time transfer, he gazed at the stark emptiness of the barn.

As I expected, all gone, he thought as he put away the stunner. *Guess I will have to hoof it back to Dodge.*

He began the long walk back. Topping a rise, he once again gazed upon the modest settlement, which in time became the legendary Dodge City. *There it is. Now to find out what happened to Adrian?*

He entered the hotel and glanced in the dining room. In a corner, Adrian and Eugenia sat immersed in deep conversation. *He seems to have talked his way out of it, and ... there he is with that woman again.* He approached the couple.

"Oh, Rajulk, please join us for tea," said Adrian, as if nothing of note had happened since they were last together. "I was pleasantly surprised that they even knew what it was in this sad place. Of course you know Miss Winthrop from our encounter on the road."

"Why certainly, it is a pleasure to see you again," said Rajulk, who though responding to the moment, was itching to hear what happened after the botched transfer.

"Eugenia and I have decided to stay in touch and reconnect, that is, after we have concluded the work we have set out to do," said Adrian with a knowing glance at Rajulk.

I wonder how he plans to do that, thought Rajulk. *Surely, she won't stay here in Dodge after this brief respite.*

"She has given me this miniature portrait of herself as a remembrance," continued Adrian, producing the image.

"Just what is the work you do?" asked Eugenia advancing the conversation.

"Well," said Adrian with a glance at an amused Rajulk. "It is of a … a philanthropic nature."

"I hope it will bring you to New York," said Eugenia.

"If it doesn't, I will come anyway," said Adrian. "For the present I must go with Rajulk and concentrate on … on the task at hand."

"Adrian is right," said Rajulk, suppressing a surge of pent-up sarcasm to vent his displeasure with the distraction-prone Adrian. "I am sorry to intrude on your intimacy, but we have important things to do. I will retire to the lobby so that you can conclude your farewells in private."

After half an hour, Rajulk looked in the dining room. Adrian had just left the table and was coming in his direction. A distraught Eugenia was dabbing her eyes with a handkerchief.

Sullen and without speaking, Adrian joined Rajulk, and they stepped outside the hotel.

"We can double up on one horse from the livery stable and set it loose just before we transfer," said Rajulk.

Eugenia, her eyes still moist, returned to her room at the hotel. The next day, with all the complications surrounding the attempt on the stagecoach sorted out, she and two others boarded the next coach passing through and left Dodge.

"It will take around three days to reach Kansas City," said the driver. "Since no accommodations are available between here and there, we will travel continuously until we arrive. Of course, there will be comfort stops along the way."

After two days travel, the coach slowly pulled into a small town.

"Where are we now?" asked Eugenia as the coach stopped unexpectedly.

"The town of Lawrence," said the driver. "It is only about twenty-five miles to Kansas City, but one of the horses is laboring and holding back the others. When we find out what the problem is, we will continue."

The driver and guard went to examine to the laboring horse and, after some consultation, returned to the cab and addressed the passengers.

"The lead horse on the left has a problem with a shoe and has been limping, throwing off the balance of the team," said the driver. "We will have to stop here overnight and seek a replacement. There are some hotel accommodations available. You may wish to take advantage of them."

Eugenia alighted from the cab with the other passengers and sought out the hotel. Fatigued by the arduous travel, she retired early, only to be awakened by shouts, gunshots, and the smell of fire against the background of an upsurge of hoof beats.

She roused herself and went to the window. *This place has gone mad. I had better get dressed. If this is some kind of emergency, and that awful war going on down south has spilled over into this area, I must be mobile.*

Hearing the rumble of hurried footsteps outside her door, she stood indecisively. Rummaging through her bag, she pulled out and donned the trim riding outfit she had worn on her outing with Adrian. A peek out the door showed the occupants of the hotel rushing downstairs toward the exits. Joining the exodus, she and the others hurriedly ran out onto the dusty streets. Fires raged up and down the modest center-way of the town against a cacophony of continuous gunfire and the moans of the wounded and their grieving associates.

"What is happening?" she asked a man running past.

"Quantrill's Raiders, [13] Confederate sympathizers!" he shouted as he ran past but slowed and again yelled, "Hide or seek cover; they are shooting everybody!"

Maybe the hotel itself is the safest place, she thought as several more men ran past. *No, they may burn it too.*

She stepped out on the boarded walkway fronting the buildings and cautiously made her way out through the darkness accented by the gleam of fires reflected from windows. She paused in front of an opening between the buildings. *I must escape this place ... Anywhere away from the chaos of whatever is happening here.*

Slipping through into the enclosure completely devoid of light, she emerged into the dimness of night and an open countryside filled with silhouettes of trees, houses, and unidentifiable figures scattering to escape the violence.

A fixture of the landscape moved—a figure loomed out of the grey tableau. "This way," said a voice, obviously that of a woman.

Better than indecision, thought Eugenia as she followed the figure.

They moved into a grove of trees and joined some others hovering around a dim lantern.

"Quantrill and his riffraff, they are killing everybody," said one of the shadows.

"Why?" asked Eugenia.

"They see this as a center of the anti-slavery movement, and they think the authorities are responsible for the deaths of their relatives who had been arrested as sympathizers."

"They had to round them up," said another. "They were giving aid to the Raiders. It is unfortunate that the building where they were being held collapsed."

The sound of horses, and a shout pierced the night. "There's another bunch just ripe for killing."

The horsemen converged on the clustered group and dismounted.

"Wait," said one as he strolled up to the frightened group holding a lantern. "They are all women. Maybe a little satisfaction will give us revenge over what they did to our own women."

"My dear sister Josephine died when that building fell," said another of the men bitterly. "We need to return the favor in kind."

"It was an accident. The whole community regretted it," said one of the women who summoned up the courage to speak. "The building had problems to start with."

"What happened?" whispered Eugenia.

"They think their women were deliberately killed," responded one of the women in kind. "They were locked up in a building in the center of town. It collapsed. Their wives and relatives were giving aid to the Quantrill and his pro-slavery rabble. They had to be locked up."

"What's going on here?" asked a man who had just ridden up.

"That's him. That's Quantrill himself," whispered the woman.

"We caught these women trying to slip away."

"We don't have time to bother with them," said Quantrill. "Get back and burn the place down, before the Union Army gets wind of this and storms in here."

Quantrill looked over the sparsely illuminated gathering of women and spotted Eugenia in her sleek riding outfit, an incongruous accent to the drab conservative dress of the others.

"You, are you of the local women?"

"No, I was passing through by stage, and there was a problem with one of the horses, so we were forced to stay the night here."

One of the men sidled his horse over to Quantrill's and spoke in words just below the threshold of hearing.

After a response in kind, Quantrill turned once again to Eugenia. "You need to come with us. We may have use for you."

Eugenia's first impulse was to evoke the status of her father, but she quickly shelved the idea. *Can't expect help from that area,* she *thought. All business interests in New York are sure to be identified with the Union.*

Quantrill hoisted her up behind him on the horse and shouted orders to the men. "Now get to it! Scorch the town, and then rally at Hogback Ridge." [14]

They negotiated the slopes of Hogback and stood with a small group of Quantrill's lieutenants watching the chaos of Lawrence unfold below.

"Looks like they have just about finished it" said Quantrill. "Give the signal."

One of the men went over and lit a bonfire prepared in an open space. Minutes passed before they heard sounds of hoof beats negotiating the side of the hill.

"Everybody here and accounted for?" yelled Quantrill.

"Yeah," replied one of the raiders. "That'll teach them bluecoats a thing or two."

"Okay, let's leave this place while there's still time."

Eugenia slumped forward grasping the obstreperous bandit to stay mounted in their tiring retreat. They raiders traveled south through the night and rested in a grove as day broke.

"We should be far enough from the Lawrence now to confuse any pursuit," said Quantrill.

VI

Adrian and Francois Plant the Gold Plates in Palmyra

"Glad to see you both," said Seth as Adrian and Rajulk arrived at the uptime transfer point. "When I heard about your encounters in the Wild West era, I got nostalgic as I recalled your vacation in old Rome."

"I appreciate your concern," said Rajulk. "'Vacation in old Rome' is pushing it. It was no picnic either. It brings home the fact that whatever its faults, this era is fraught with fewer dangers and probably as peaceful as humankind can get. For now we need to get back to Obamapolis and get this silly thing with the gold plates going."

They packed up and traveled the 175-plus miles back to the capital and the lab.

"We didn't have the equipment to fabricate the plates, so we melted down the gold coins with lasers into shapeless blobs and took them down to Metallurgy," said Brant. "They were curious at seeing so much of the stuff all at once and started asking questions about where we got it and what we were going to do with it. I made up some story about its role in the instrumentation of our experiments, which was received with some skepticism, but they said they could do it. They suggested that it be alloyed with a little silver to render the plates less amenable to breakage. I told them we would get back to them if that was necessary."

A day or so later the plates arrived back at the ITR.

"Now, just what do you want put on them?" asked Brant, as they all sat around the table staring at the pristine plates neatly stacked on the floor to one side.

"Well … maybe something frivolous to debunk the sacred myths associated with them," said Francois.

"Too obvious," said Rajulk casually. "Putting something frivolous like *Winnie-the-Pooh* on them would be a basis for dubbing them a fraud, not the 'true' tablets described in Mormon literature."

"Perhaps its best to keep it vague, maybe something undecipherable in the form of random sets of letters in some language," said Brant anxious to expedite the frivolous escapades of Adrian and Francois in order to get on with the task of reconnecting with the other timeline.

"Couldn't they just claim that Smith alone had the key to the cipher, thereby enhancing his claim to be an intercessor to the divine?" asked Rajulk.

"Not if the scientific community declared the plain text of the document an indecipherable string of gobbledygook," said Brant. Then, after further consideration, he continued. "Well, maybe they could. Fervent belief always trumps rational thought. We could go for random number strings. Numbers are more or less culturally neutral, whereas a language implies a specific ethnicity. We would only have to incise numbers one through nine in random combinations although I would point out that machine-generated random numbers are never completely random."

"Yes and if correctly timed, they could be proven random or devised after the Mormons, in the euphoria of discovery of their own version of the "Dead Sea Scrolls,' have declared them the lost tablets of Moroni," said Rajulk seeking to give Brant's suggestion a boost. "The question is, what if they ignore the whole thing?"

"The flock as a whole could very well do that, but when the word gets out, it still might plant a seed of doubt about the Mormon theology, which could coax them to a path more consistent with the secular aims of the Trust," said Brant in an effort to expedite matters.

Francois, who had listened quietly to the esoteric debate between Brant and Rajulk, finally broke in. "What is Winnie-the-Pooh?"

Brant, not quite disengaged from the mode of scholarly discourse, paused momentarily. "Winnie … Oh, it's just a fictional anthropomorphic bear character in a group of children's stories presented as a series of episodes."

"That sounds like a good idea," said Francois.

"I say again, something trivial would be the basis for dubbing the plates a fraud," said Brant with a reproachful glance at Rajulk for mentioning it. "Besides, Pooh doesn't date back to the period of Mormon origins."

"That doesn't matter as far as the gold plates are concerned," said Francois. "The important thing is that they are inscribed on gold plates and are found at a site sacred to the Mormons."

"That might work if the circumstances and peripheral evidence supported it," said Brant, looking for some way to conclude the discussion as a preposterously absurd image welled up.

"Well," said Rajulk, in search of some conclusion to the mounting folly. "What we could do is have Pooh translated into Latin or some other obscure language like Sanskrit and inscribed on the plates. With luck, once the discovery of them is leaked, the Mormon cult will at first be so excited at finding the sacred gold plates, that they will confirm the announcement and be stuck with it. Only after scholarly scrutiny will the true content inscribed on the plates be revealed. They will either have to admit the fraud, or, to profound embarrassment conceal it in the morass of the Church's secrets."

As Brant strained to keep from venting his disgust at the absurdity of it all, Rajulk spoke up, coming to the rescue, "Okay then, we have our work cut out for us. I will see if I can find a copy in the local library. We can have at least one of the Pooh stories copied onto the plates in a language of choice, but resist having an image of Pooh himself to complement it since it would give the whole thing away. From there, we can leave it to Adrian and Francois to do their thing with the Mormons."

Adrian stood with Francois mulling over on their projected venture into the realm of Mormon origins.

"If I can persuade Brant to set up near Palmyra, it is best we visit it not long after Smith's 'vision' in 1820, before the farm has taken on its historic significance," said Adrian. *Or maybe even 1860. It would give me a chance to reconnect with Eugenia.* "Brant is increasingly reluctant to aid us in what he considers frivolous activities, a bit of limp gratitude considering this reality is the result of our intervention in the first place."

"It's still his call, however," said Francois. "Maybe if we push the similarities between the Trust's aims and the ethical strictures of the

ITR, along with our cooperation in maintaining contact with our timeline, he will agree to it."

"Assuming he will, we need to concentrate on where to put the gold plates," said Adrian. "Now, from what Rajulk tells me, the basis of the Mormon faith hangs on their existence. The myth centers around this hill called Cumorah near the Smith farm where the plates were supposedly buried. It is local to Palmyra, New York, where I originally encountered Smith. Now it is now some sort of a shrine, and draws tourists loyal to the faith. Of course, we can't use this timeline's global positioning devices. There are no satellites in that era from which to take readings. I will use a compass and do azimuth readings on two different points within sight of where we bury the plates. When we return, we can convert the azimuth readings into GPS coordinates to pinpoint the burial point and then blab it all over the place, forcing them to do something about it. They may have to poke a little to find the exact spot."

"It's ridiculous, but I don't see any reason to deny their request," said Brant. "I passed it by Frondner, and he gave his okay just to get them occupied and off our backs. I have already told them we were not about to drain the ITR's resources by moving our equipment to New York or any other place for the transfer. They will have to transfer here and travel there by whatever means are available."

"The 1860 date they are talking about is the same period from which they got the gold in the first place and is familiar to us now," said Rajulk. "It will at least give them the early rail system, but transferring from here, they will have to travel from this site to some transportation hub to continue the journey. It is no doubt desolate at that date. The old stagecoach routes ran very much south of here. They would still have a trek just to get to one of them."

"How about we compromise?" said Brant after a pause. "I can get Seth to set up on the outskirts of Kansas City and give them a TR connected to that spot. That's only a little over two hundred miles southeast of here, quite a stretch if they had to do it on horseback from here carrying all that gold, not to mention that we would have to scrounge up some horses in the now of A.D. 2288. I am not sure we could even find any. Some circus or riding club might have some, but we would be hard-pressed to pry them away. In any case, once in Kansas City, they could transfer back to the 1860s and pick up a train going east."

"Kansas City is a really big place, and the terrain is generally rolling prairies with some flat spots," said Rajulk. "Once there, they will have to get the gold to the train station. A primitive cart like we used in the first mission to probe the Gospel would do the job, but I can just hear them complaining. Beyond that, I just hope they will stay out of trouble, so that we won't have to go and rescue them again."

Brant addressed the sullen pair as they settled in the house at the outskirts of Kansas City.

"It's about as close as we could get, and we have an open-ended rental of this house. The real estate agent told us he would put its sale on hold until we finished whatever we wanted it for. Now, since currency is not reliable at this date, you each have a cache of silver dollars for expenses that will add to your burden. As for this location, you are lucky Frondner okayed it. It will be about two miles to the west and center of nineteenth century Kansas City. You will have to walk and pull the cart with the gold unless you can find some other way of transporting it. Also, when you get there, you will have to hustle it on the train as best you can. Even distributed between these suitcases you will have your work cut out for you." continued Brant as he surveyed the four bulging bags holding the plates cushioned by items of clothing.

"If you couldn't get us to the New York area, you could have at least gotten us a little closer to the station," complained Adrian.

"No suitable site could be found to plant you nearer to the station. At least you won't be burdened with the gold when you return," said Brant in effort to put a shine on their dismal quest. "We are still of the opinion that you should leave the Mormons and their aberrant take on Christianity be, but if you insist on going through with it, get it done and get back here so we can concentrate on the greater task of reuniting our timelines."

"Now, Seth will return to this site in a month and power up for your return," continued Brant. "If you are delayed, he will try again the following week then again in successive weeks until you return. We will plant you there in late spring, so you can expect reasonable weather for the journey and the task. Try to avoid the authorities, as we don't need the distraction of having to rescue you. Seth will stick around for a few hours to help set up and make sure your transfer goes smoothly before returning to Obamapolis. Should anything happen, as requested, you have the reserve TR connected to the old barn, but you will have the added burden of getting there in the nineteenth century."

Adrian and Francois stared at the open field as their senses reoriented themselves.

They turned and examined the cart still loaded with the suitcases full of gold. A mist rose randomly in the near distance, and the smell of recent rain was in the air. The settled outskirts of Kansas City had given way to a stretch of flat lands. They panned the hazy landscape that showed the faint outline of an occasional house or barn.

"I'll set up some markers so we can find this place again," said Francois.

"Grab that extension tongue on the outside," said Adrian when the markers were set. "It will be easier if we both pull this thing."

"'My kingdom for a horse,' I read it somewhere in this timeline," said Francois sarcastically as they trudged eastward. "I'm not sure in what context."

"I would settle for a goat … maybe two," said Adrian as they negotiated a mushy pothole in the field.

"How would you connect them to the cart?" asked Francois advancing the conversation out of boredom. "There is only room for one between the tongues."

Adrian did a slow take at the struggling Francois on the other side and responded with silence and wonder at his preoccupation with minutiae. They concentrated on getting to what appeared to be a primitive road some hundred yards to the front.

An increase in houses and random encounters with inhabitants signaled that they were entering the environs of nineteenth century Kansas City. A cluster of buildings appeared in the distance.

"That's the railroad station down there where we can inquire about passage to the east," said Francois.

They approached the ticket-office.

"Sir, we wish passage to the east," said Adrian.

"To what place?" inquired the ticket master.

"Palmyra, New York."

The ticket master flipped through his ledger.

"The closest I can get you is near Buffalo, New York. Take the train there east and get off at Manchester. Palmyra is about eight miles to the north."

"Another eight miles and no cart," said Francois. "How are we going to manage that?"

"We will figure out something," said Adrian. "We only have to get it there."

They boarded the next train heading east. In the early morning of a few days later, they stood in the primitive station at Manchester with the cache of gold laden suitcases piled up to the side. Staring out at the bleak landscape now subjected to a light drizzle, Francois was moved to ask, "Now what?"

"We need to find some means of transport. You stay here and watch the luggage, and I will look around," said Adrian.

Adrian stepped off the platform, circled the station, and scanned the area. A collection of taller structures was visible through a sprinkle of houses and the random growth of trees surrounding the station.

That's Manchester all right, now with railroads but still much like it was when I passed through here on the way to my encounter with the youthful Smith, thought Adrian. *Let's see what's around.*

Joining several of the local citizens most of whom were in wagons or on horses, Adrian sauntered toward the settlement and gazed at the main street bisecting an array of buildings reflecting the range of services offered in the rural town. He spotted a sign identifying the livery stable and moved toward it.

"Sir, would it be possible to rent a carriage for a short trip to the north?" Adrian inquired of the owner.

"Sorry, carriages I have, but no horses to pull them. All are engaged in travel to the spring festival at Shortsville south of here."

Stuck, thought Adrian, as he wandered away from the livery stable. *Guess I will have to improvise.*

Again, he surveyed the main street of the modest town. Spying a vehicle parked unobtrusively at the outer fringe of the town center, he moved toward it. Two horses stood patiently waiting for the next call to service were attached to the coach featuring a quadrangular enclosure with sides of glass.

Obviously a funeral vehicle, thought Adrian appraising the black coffin lying within. *It just might work if we can persuade the owner.*

Adrian stepped onto the slightly elevated walkway fronting the town's central buildings and opened the door to the funeral parlor.

"Sir, I wish to rent your fine vehicle parked outside."

An ashen-faced man dressed in black rose from behind a desk and approached, hands clasped together in a gesture of profound sympathy. "My name is Calvert Bliss. I would be so happy to assist you in this moment of sorrow."

"It is not that," said Adrian. "We wish to rent it for a somewhat unusual purpose, the transport of certain items toward the town of Palmyra. We understand that extra compensation may be required for such an unorthodox use," he added, already sensing a change of mood in the proprietor.

"I cannot possibly let my chariot to the realm of immortality be used for such purpose. I have a reputation to maintain," said Bliss. "How much did you have in mind?" he added after only a brief hesitation. "It must be in advance, of course."

"Ten silver dollars," said Adrian.

Bliss's eyes narrowed as he considered. "Business has indeed been slow. The living just refuse to die on a convenient schedule. I would insist on accompanying the coach wherever it goes. After all, you are a complete stranger and could make off with that which I obtained at considerable expense. What and where are the items you speak of?"

"All including myself will be waiting at the train station in one hour. Here is payment in advance. Please arrive on time as we are on a tight schedule."

"I meet my obligations with responsibility, but must guard my reputation," said Bliss. "The station is more than satisfactory since we will be able to bypass the town and any inquisitive onlookers to reach the route to Palmyra."

"It is settled then," said Adrian. *Now, I must secure some tools for digging and a cart of some sort for transporting the plates to a site easily discovered in the future.*

Back outside, Adrian again surveyed the main roadway. Spying a general store, he moved toward it. *If my crash course on the culture of this timeline serves me, that business should sell everything we need.*

Adrian entered the store and negotiated two shovels and a mattock. Placing them in a tow sack provided by the owner, he inspected the other offerings.

"What is the purpose is that device over there, the one with the single wheel?"

"That … is a wheelbarrow," said the proprietor hesitantly, incredulous that Adrian didn't seem to know what it was.

I guess my orientation couldn't possibly have covered every aspect of this timeline, thought Adrian. "And it works by grasping the two handles, lifting, and pushing it forward?"

"Yes," said the proprietor, at a loss to elaborate further.

"Good. I will take that also along with some rope. Please place all the items purchased in the … wheelbarrow for transport."

Pushing the loaded wheelbarrow, Adrian staggered back to the station and a restless Francois.

"Our travel arrangements have been made and should arrive shortly," said Adrian.

The agreed upon hour passed, and Bliss pulled up at the train station with the wagon.

"This is all that was available," said Adrian, preempting a sardonic riposte from Francois. "Now, how should we do this?"

"Yes, how will we all fit in or on the vehicle along with the suitcases?" asked Francois. "There is barely enough room for two up on the driver's perch."

"One of us will have to ride inside," said Adrian without further comment.

"There's barely room for the luggage scattered around and on top of the … the coffin," said Francois, a farcical image lurking just below the surface of consciousness.

"Hmm" … mused Adrian who turned to Bliss. "Could we possibly return to your place of business and remove the coffin to make room for my colleague here?"

"Certainly not," replied Bliss. "I would not want to advertise the aberrant use of my vehicle by parading it through town bedecked in such a way. We must depart discretely from here, advantaging the routes which bypass the town."

"Then I guess we will have to go with what's available. Francois, would you mind—"

"I think we should let the vagaries of chance decide who rides within the vehicle," said Francois. "Perhaps the toss of one of our silver dollars will produce a random result."

"Fair enough," said Adrian taking a coin from his cache. "Indicate your choice, the lady, or the eagle."

"The eagle," said Francois as Adrian flipped the coin.

The sparkle of the tumbling silver flashed for an instant before the coin hit the ground.

"It is the lady," said Adrian with feigned sadness.

"Wedge something under the lid," said Francois as he slid inside the coffin, "I don't want to smother in here. Otherwise, I could use a nap."

Adrian slid the coffin lid slid almost closed, piled the tow sack and suitcases around it, and tied the wheelbarrow atop the enclosure. With all secured, they set out for Palmyra.

"We are here," said Adrian, lifting the lid.

"Wha … what? Oh … I guess we must be there … uh, here," said Francois as he slowly emerged from slumber.

"We are close enough," said Adrian, out of earshot of Bliss. "We are in the middle of nowhere somewhat short of Palmyra itself, but I recognize this as the area of the Smith farm. Rajulk briefed me on what he remembered of Mormon legends. The Hill Cumorah should be somewhat south of the farm, which is up ahead, although various factions of the Church have disputed the location of the farm itself. If we can plant these plates, then whatever else they stir up, it should at least settle once and for all where the hill was."

Adrian approached Bliss. "We have reached our desired destination and will unload the luggage. A friend is to meet us here for further transport. We are grateful for your service. Have a safe trip back."

With a look around at the somewhat desolate landscape, Bliss gave a shrug, a nod, and urged the horses back in the direction of Manchester.

"Now what?" asked Francois.

"We need to find the Hill Cumorah since it is where the plates are supposed to be buried. Here is a rough map I drew from memory that we can compare to this modern topographic one," said Adrian taking a folded sheaf of papers from his jacket and spreading them out.

"There is only one mound of that description in sight, and it is over there," said Adrian pointing. He then referred back to the map. "I remember passing it on my first visit. It's that elongated bulge in the terrain, which extends almost out of sight back toward the way we came. Its highest point is right there, close to us."

They stood for a moment taking in the sight. The glint of early flowers accented the green canopy, which enshrouded the most prominent landmark in sight, the Hill of Cumorah.

Adrian considered. "We can unload the plates over there behind that abandoned shack, and leave the suitcases there while we truck the plates to the hill in the wheelbarrow. Stay here and guard the rest while I muscle the first load over."

"How about we catch our breath?" said Francois as they ferried the last of their cargo out of sight.

"Okay, you rest while I start unpacking," said Adrian who seemed to have boundless energy, enhanced by a residue of guilt the *schadenfreude* of Francois's temporary confinement in the coffin. "We can wrap the plates in the tow sack and bury the whole thing. The sack should be completely decomposed or in an unidentifiable state by the time they are discovered. The plates, being gold, may gather a few surface stains from reacting with hostile trace elements, but they should last indefinitely."

After another ten minutes, and all was ready. The gold was securely wrapped in the tow sack and placed in the wheelbarrow with the tools piled on top.

"You take the first shift with the wheelbarrow," said Adrian. "The land is flat here, but it slopes up at the base of the hill. I will take it from there."

They urged the wheelbarrow to the base of the hill and paused.

"I'll take it now. About half way up should do it," said Adrian. "There is a primitive path over there. We might as well take advantage of it."

Adrian forced the wheelbarrow up the bumpy slope for about fifteen minutes and paused to rest in a grassy area relatively free of growth. He looked back the way they had come. The tops of the trees they had encountered at the bottom of the hill could now be seen somewhat below.

"We should be high enough. Over there where the grade temporarily levels out is a good place," said Adrian.

They struggled the last few yards and unloaded the suitcases and tools.

"I'll start hacking, and you shovel the dirt away," said Adrian as he sized up the mattock. "A couple of feet down should do it."

It was late afternoon when they finished and sat down to rest. A few minutes passed and Adrian said, "If we have recovered from this unaccustomed exertion I need a few minutes to figure out a way let this location be known to those who might be concerned with it in the future."

"I will take two azimuth readings for this place," said Adrian. Then, in the future era, taking some subtle hints, they can back-azimuth from those places to find it. "Let me see … one point for sure is the high point of the Cumorah ridge, which is visible from here. Adrian sighted along the collapsible accessories appended to the compass and wrote down the results. "Got it," he said. "Now, we need another point."

"How about the Smith farm you talked about?" asked Francois. "It would not only serve to orient back to this point, but also would also carry some weight symbolically."

"That's a good idea, since it is historically preserved in the future. Now, can I spot it from here?" asked Adrian.

He scanned the lands to the north. "Hmm … It is fortunate that there are only a few structures to choose from. Yes, there, that's it all right," he said, pointing. "At this date, it has been fifty years since I encountered Smith, so the family is probably not there, but no matter."

He repeated the process and wrote down the results.

"It will be dark soon. We should depart this area before someone who owns it stumbles on us and asks what we are doing here."

"What should we do with the wheelbarrow and tools?" asked Francois.

"We can wheel them down to the road and leave them. The trip back downhill minus the gold will be much easier," said Adrian. "Unfortunately, we will have to walk back to Manchester."

"That's okay," said Francois. "We have set it up and have only to get back up time to plant the seed. Maybe we can at least purge the Mormon movement of its mythological underpinnings. Beyond that, if as Brant says they are an asset to the community, perhaps we shouldn't pursue it further."

"Perhaps you are right, but let's see what happens first," said Adrian. "The Trust never intended for our mission to result in anything so bizarre."

They retrieved the suitcases and began the trek back to Manchester in unaccustomed silence, with Francois's idle talk meeting increasingly diminished responses.

Adrian was finally moved to engage the subject that was dominating his thoughts.

"When we get to Manchester, I am going east to try and reconnect with Eugenia. You need to return to Kansas City, transfer back uptime, and pursue the Mormon issue without me—at least for now."

Francois responded to the news with silence.

It was dark when they arrived back in Manchester. Adrian addressed the stationmaster. "Sir, can you tell me when the next scheduled trains travel, both east and west?"

"The next train traveling toward Buffalo is tomorrow morning at 8:00 a.m. If you wish to go east, the next train will not pass through until 4:00 p.m. in the afternoon. In which direction are you going?"

"I am going eastward, and my associate is going west," said Adrian.

Francois finally made the decision to comment on Adrian's surprise change of plans. "You said nothing about this extended mission before we started out."

"I am sorry, but this is the best opportunity I may have to reconnect with Eugenia. It is the reason I did my best to lobby for this date," said Adrian.

"I obviously missed the seriousness of your relationship."

"It took me by surprise also—how it grew so quickly. After all, we were only there for a few days, but our bond was instantaneous. Maybe there is some exotic lure in women of other eras."

"There may be something to that. There was that woman Mary in Judea and now this Eugenia."[15]

"Ah yes, Mary. I was drawn to her and distressed to leave the era so abruptly," said Adrian. "But back to what we are here for: to pursue the aims of the Trust even though the colony itself is in state of flux. See if you can maneuver the discovery of the gold plates, which will at least throw some doubt as to the foundations of the Mormon Church. If we can achieve that, I think we can leave them alone. I will try to rejoin you some time in the future, but if I become permanently involved here, I expect you to carry on."

"I will do so as long as possible," said Francois, still shaken by Adrian's new plans and anxious at carrying on without him.

"I will be off this afternoon," said Adrian. "You can sleep the night at the local hotel and be off in the morning."

Francois watched as the train carrying Adrian disappeared out of sight. The next morning, now unencumbered by the cache of gold and carrying only a suitcase, he picked up a train traveling westward to Kansas City.

He thought it over. *It will be two days until Seth makes his weekly power up at the uptime transfer point, but I will transfer immediately and wait for him. Better to be in an era of adequate transportation than here.*

Making his way back to the transfer point west of town, he located the markers, activated his TR, and again found himself in the rented quarters west of town. On schedule, Seth showed up two days later.

"Where is Adrian?" asked Seth.

"He is okay, but he decided to travel to New York on a personal mission," said Francois.

Convening once more in Obamapolis Francois attempted to explain Adrian's absence.

"Personal mission—what personal mission?" asked Brant when he got wind of Adrian's frivolous wanderings.

"I will bet it has something to do with that woman he met when we went after the gold," said Rajulk.

"You didn't say anything about this before, said Brant."

"I thought it would pass," said Rajulk. "Francois tells me Adrian seems to get entwined with natives of the female persuasion in each of the eras he visits."

"Well, I can think of someone else who succumbed to the charms of a bygone era," said Brant.

Rajulk resisted a futile impulse to rant that Meriam, his beloved wife from the biblical era, was an exception.

"Let's hope I don't have to travel to the New York of that period to retrieve him," said Rajulk, changing the subject. "At least it is not Rome, Judea, or any other of the dangerous eras we have visited."

VII

Brant and the Others Attempt to Rendezvous with the Trust Envoys

Brant, Rajulk, Lila, and Francois convened for an update.

"I hope you got done whatever you wanted to do," said Brant, unable to hide his disgust. He continued before Francois had a chance to chronicle the whole saga. "We need Adrian to concentrate on forming a permanent link with your timeline. As far as Adrian is concerned, he will be tromping around in an era he knows little about. Let's see, what was going on in America at that time?"

"The war and the contentious time leading up to it," said Rajulk.

"War, what war? We saw no evidence of a war," said Francois.

"At Palmyra, you were too far north to feel the rumblings of it. It mostly involved the south and the issue of slavery."

"Slavery—we were aware of it in Judea, but figured it would be long gone in this era of enlightenment," said Francois.

"That time, four hundred years ago, was not yet this time and not too enlightened over that issue in particular. It was, at least for the south, an agonizing decision," said Rajulk. "Its economy was based on it."

"Well, it throws a kink in our plans. We need him for the contact with your timeline," said Brant. "We will assume that their envoys are already looking for us. We have only to zero in on the agreed-upon rendezvous time and place and go search ourselves."

"You don't really need him for contact. I will go," said Francois. "I planned to all along. I can recognize the Trust people as well as Adrian, but first I must address this issue of the Mormons and any other distortions of our efforts to promote the values of the Trust. At least for the Mormons, we have the gold plates in place on the side of the Hill Cumorah. Maybe some anonymous posting in the press will tweak the community interest."

"To hell with the Mormons! You can pursue that afterwards," barked an increasingly frustrated Brant. "That gold will be there when you get around to doing whatever you plan to do with it. Surely the Trust itself is now more occupied with survival and consolidating the enclave's resources than nitpicking their thrust into our timeline."

"A fine lot of appreciation, considering this timeline wouldn't exist had it not been for our introducing Adrian as Jesus," whined Francois.

"That's like holding a kid hostage to parents who sired him," groused Brant. "We are here; that's that. The one little piece of strangeness we haven't figured out is what makes one event singular enough to initiate a new timeline, whereas other seemingly equivalent events do not. If they do, we are unaware of it. The fact is, we have two separate realities accessible to each other through points downtime their point of diversion. The more we learn of each other, the more we can guard against mutual deficiencies and eccentricities."

"What deficentricities?" contracted Francois awkwardly.

"Oh, what deficiencies," Brant sang mockingly. "How about the loony Xerjinko that took me captive and the wacky Garuletzsky that rescued me? And don't think I haven't noticed the preference you have for this timeline, having maneuvered yourself into the Vatican."

"All right," said Francois after a huff and a pause. "If we can resume contact with the Trust, I want your cooperation on this Mormon thing and any other distorted results of our introducing Jesus into this timeline. I must research the numerous cults which seem to have sprung from our efforts."

"Deal," said Brant anxious to get on with it. "Though I doubt you will be able to suppress them all."

Brant conferred with Frondner.

"LeBrust says he will go. Adrian is off on some harebrained quest to reunite with up with someone he met during the trek to get the gold. He was in the same time window and decided to take advantage of it.

Rajulk filled me in. We should have guessed he was up to something when he lobbied for that date."

"All right," said Frondner, pausing to think it over. "If Adrian has not shown up in real time by the time we resume contact, we should at least check on him. We have important things to resolve. See if you can connect, wind it up, and get some kind of permanent agreement with the Trust's timeline about contact. Besides the fact that I have to manipulate the budget allocations to favor the ITR, we still have the problem of secrecy. We were lucky to have neutralized Bromfsted and his cronies at US Intelligence—for now at least. I have a feeling we have not heard the last of him. Another slip could bring it all out in the open. Now, have you decided on who is going?"

"Well, other than LeBrust, Rajulk and Lila for sure," said Brant. "I want to keep it tight. Rajulk has pinpointed this old town of Pelusium as a target and will set up outside of it. It corresponds to the general location of the Alcon settlement described by Adrian and is the only city of consequence in the area at that time."

"How about the Egyptian Government?"

"We will use the same ruse we always have: scientific experimentation. It always works because science and industry are strong lobbies, and they strive for reciprocal cooperation."

A few days later, Seth informed Brant that everything was in place. "The portable unit is ready to go. We have left the site in Kansas City active. If Adrian wants to transfer back from wherever he went, he will have to travel back there."

<hr />

At the airport in Cairo, they packed up the equipment in a rented van and traveled northeast. Standing before the ruins of Pelusium, they watched as a crew of archeologists systematically probed the site in a network of cordoned-off squares.

"We'd better move a little away from this spot and find some place to set up," said Brant.

"All right," said Seth, "inland or toward the sea?"

"Maybe ... toward the water, " said Brant. "We will have natural protection on at least one side. No telling what hostile elements are roaming around here at the 60 B.C."

"There, how about that jut out from the shore," said Rajulk after they had walked a half hour. "If we set up our base there, nobody in the uncertainties of 60 B.C. can rush us except from one side."

"Yeah, and we can even take a dip if it gets too hot," said Lila.

Seth stayed busy setting up the transfer perimeter while the four travelers put on garments appropriate for the target period.

"I guess the only way to get into this *thobe* is to pull it over the head," said Brant, sizing up the full-length, off-white dress.

"It opens just enough for you to step into to it and pull it up," said Lila as she donned her *jillbab* and headscarf.

"Okay, now we can top it off with these pre-wound turbans and *Albas*," said Brant as he busied with the unfamiliar garments. He finished and looked around at the others who had just finished the process themselves. "This looks like a scene from one of those old movies."

"Yeah, one of the comedies," said Lila.

"The transfer perimeter is set up and we are ready to go when you are," said Seth, laughing.

"Anytime," said Brant. "Let's get on with it. It is still early in the day and you have set the parameters for the same time sync downtime. We can don our packs after we transfer."

The familiar sensation of disorientation accompanied the transfer, but an environment of pure water suddenly replaced the dryness of the simi-desert. The change of venue caught all unexpected.

Rajulk was the first to surface, choking out some water. He looked around just as Lila's head broke the surface. A thrashing from behind signaled relief that they had all survived the unexpected event.

"What the hell!" gasped Brant as he treaded water, struggling against his unfamiliar clothing. "I didn't take into account that the shoreline may have changed in over two millenniums."

"It's not too deep here where I am. My feet occasionally touch bottom," said Rajulk.

"Well, mine don't. I'm making for shore," said Lila. "Where's Francois?"

"Here," said LeBrust thrashing about several yards away, already in a dog-paddle toward shore.

"Lila, you and Francois go ahead and try to corral our supplies, which look like they've washed toward shore in the ingoing surf," yelled

Brant while treading water. "Give us a minute to sight some landmarks, so we can pin down this place again, otherwise we could spend forever trying to find it."

"Swim over here," said Rajulk, breaking in. "I'm standing on a slight lift in the sea floor. You can either share it with me, or I can get off it while you look around."

A few strokes brought Brant to where Rajulk was. He could now just stand as he braced against the ever-changing surge of water. He surveyed the shore nearby.

"There," he said, pointing. "We are in luck. That rock there, just above the tide line is unusual enough for us to recognize. I judge we are about … twenty five yards from shore. We can't put out any stakes to delineate the transfer perimeter, but we can eyeball this location from the rock and find it after a few tries. All we need is some reference to find the rock itself when we return here."

By the time they reached the shore, Lila and Francois had fished their packs out of the water.

"We are all soaked, but it is hot, and we should dry out quickly," said Brant as he looked around. "We can retrace our steps."

He pointed. "Pelusium is back that way."

They moved inland and gradually encountered natives, all headed toward or away from a point not yet visible beyond the gently swelling landscape. Topping a low rise, the stark reality of ancient Pelusium stood shimmering in the desert sun.

"That's it, all right, a far cry from the near-nothingness of the ruins we saw before we transferred," said Brant after a breathless moment. "Okay, Francois, it's up to you now. You are the one most likely to recognize the Trust people. I only had contact with a handful when I visited the Trust enclave. Chances are that none of them are among the emissaries."

Brant and the others stood before the gate of Pelusium. A detachment of Roman soldiers was just exiting the city. After a moment, he gave the go-ahead nod, and they all plodded in.

VIII

The Envoys Connect

Dolf and Kara awoke in full daylight locked in an inadvertent embrace. Dolf uncurled his body and reached for the nearest suspending limb of the tree. He swung down and looked up at Kara now, awake and peering down at him through interstices of the net.

They sat silently munching on some temporary rations.

"We can take vigil near the city gate, watch whoever enters, and look for anomalies in dress and behavior," said Kara. "There are also many natives bringing foodstuffs in and out of the city. We shouldn't have any trouble adding to the modest fare we brought along."

The day progressed and waned.

"No sign of any travelers who don't fit in," said Dolf as the sun was setting. "We should make for our tree-house and try again tomorrow."

The next day they again took vigil outside the gate of the city. About midday, three men and a woman drifted past amid the flow of natives going in and out.

Kara nudged Dolf who had already locked in on the trio as they paused briefly before the gate. "What do you think? Did you recognize any of them? They certainly look like they are foreign to the city. They stopped to consider before entering?"

"Yes, that may well be them, but the *gutra* covered most of their faces," said Dolf. "A good look should settle the matter if Francois or Adrian is there, but I am leery of entering the city again. The natives we zapped will take out their wrath on us if they see us again. After all, it's only small city, nothing like the size of the Trust enclave."

"Well, what choice do we have? If we try to wait until they come out again it could only be when they give up on finding us and exit the city," said Kara.

"Maybe and maybe not," said Dolf. "They can't speak the local language either, and all transactions are probably done by bartering. Unless they have something to trade, they will be at the same disadvantage as we are."

"You are right on most counts," said Kara. "But from the reports about Francois and Adrian, the language of the Roman conquerors is known to them."

"That may give them some advantage but at the same time, could pose even more danger than from the locals," said Dolf.

"I say we should chance it," said Kara finally. "The Trust sent us out to make this contact. We should go before they are too far out of sight. We still look like beggars and are unimportant to all but the few locals we did in."

"I suppose you are right, but I hope we don't incite the whole town," said Dolf. "We don't have enough charge in our stunners to anesthetize everyone."

They cautiously approached the town gate. The same pair of listless soldiers manning the entrance gave them scant notice as they moved slowly through along with the parade of itinerants.

"Do you see them?" asked Kara.

"No," said Dolf, slowly panning the busy square. "Wait—there, clumped together on the other side, it's them—if it is them."

"Quick, let us move closer. If it really is them, we can cut short this frustrating open-ended search."

They made their way through the crowded expanse of the square. About half way across, a shout rang out. Dolf and Kara turned to see two burley locals closing on them in a run.

"It's the servants we did in yesterday," said Dolf as he frantically groped for his stunner.

Kara had managed to retrieve hers, but managed only a peripheral blast as the two charged and overran them. The one receiving a partial dose staggered against Kara and knocked her to the ground before Dolf could bring his stunner into play. At the same instant, the second servant charged and toppled Dolf, pinning him with brute force.

Brant and the others entered and paused inside the walls of Pelusium.

"Francois, any suggestions?" asked Brant.

"No, not immediately, the dress conventions in this culture make it difficult to recognize—"

Suddenly, they heard a loud outcry from one of the natives. They turned and watched from a distance as two locals charged and overran two beggars.

"A couple of natives were up to no-good," laughed Lila. "Those two hulks should be quick to bring revenge for whatever transgression there was."

"One of them looks a little drunk. That won't help when the debt is paid," said a sympathetic Rajulk.

"They are headed in this direction," said Brant. "Let's move a little. I don't want any extra scrutiny, especially from a bunch of irate local toughs."

Half dragging them, the two servants ushered their captives toward the maze of low structures ringing the square. The light flashed briefly on one of the unfortunates as they passed by, still struggling against the restraints of their captors.

Brant started suddenly and then suppressed a whisper. "I think I recognized one of them."

"What, Who?" asked Rajulk.

"I could swear that was Dolf Barret, who was captive with me in the Trust timeline," said Brant. "We bonded under the harsh conditions of our captivity by the Xerjinko."

"But they looked like all the other beggars that inhabit the square," said Lila.

"As strangers in a hostile land, what better way to hide," said Brant.

"Let's go after them," said Lila.

"Wait," said Rajulk. "We must at least get them in a setting more private than the streets of Pelusium. There are Roman soldiers all around. It's similar to the situation we had in Rome where there were just too many to mow down."

"Okay, we will follow them and see where it leads," said Brant.

They waited until the burly duo and their captives disappeared between two buildings then hurried after. An arched egress was outlined at the end of the shadowed passageway, which brightened as they reached it and gave entrance into another sunlit square, this one nearly vacant.

"Hurry, we need to keep them in sight. There may be some grievance we don't know about, and those ruffians are taking it out on them," said Brant cutting off, hesitating to voice his fears of retribution in this barbaric setting.

At the far end, the retreating natives disappeared with the captives into one of the mud-baked structures typical of Pelusium.

"We forgot our invitations, but I don't think they will mind if we crash the party," said Lila, who had now shuffled into the lead.

Lila pounded on the door. After a moment, a surprised servant opened it, but before he could express his displeasure at the intrusion, Lila flattened his nose with a lethal karate chop.

Blinking in a cauldron of pain, he staggered back with a mournful yelp before Brant's stunner mercifully reduced him to a heap. They saw a short stairway, which connected the entrance with the living areas of the house. Walled on one side and open on the other, they started toward it with Lila in the lead, but the commotion had drawn the curious from the recesses of the house.

Brant yelled, "Lila, be careful! Let Rajulk and—"

Belatedly accessing the situation, a retinue of beefy retainers charged down toward the invaders. Rajulk leaped up the stairs ahead of Lila, yelling, "Look out below!" Ducking low, he met the first of the on comers, who sailed through the air as his momentum was augmented by Rajulk's levered judo heft. On came the second, third, and fourth in a jumble of robed bodies trying to reach the source of action but were restrained by the narrowness of the stairway. Lila reached under and past Rajulk, grabbed the ankle of the second servant wielding an improvised club, and pulled. The servant fell backwards upsetting his fellows crowding in behind. Rajulk flattened himself against the sidewall as one tumbled headfirst down the stairs, and his cohort fell off to the side. Brant sprayed the lot with his stunner, and all was quiet again.

They looked up toward the way their adversaries had come to see the frightened owner in the doorway several feet away, standing transfixed at the demise of his retainers. He backed off and disappeared into the inner chambers of the household.

"We should grab him before he raises the alarm. We don't know how intimate he is with the authorities," said Brant. "First though, we have to find the captives. I could swear that was Dolf I saw but hope we aren't on a wild goose chase."

They hurried up the short stairway and explored the rooms of the house.

"Here," said Lila.

Dolf lay in a corner with bruises and other injuries while Kara, still showing fear, was tethered to a bed of sorts.

"It's them," said Dolf weakly in Anglo.

"Dolf, are you okay?" exclaimed Brant.

"I'll mend," he said as Rajulk helped him to his feet. "Please see to my colleague Kara. They almost had their way with her. We couldn't unlimber our weapons quick enough to stop it."

"Kara!" exclaimed LeBrust. "I knew you were in the mission pool, but I am still surprised they sent you."

"I was chosen because I could recognize you. Several of the others were compromised in one way or other when the enclave was overrun."

Lila busied herself loosening Kara's restraining bonds.

"I'm told you speak Anglo, our second language," said Kara.

"Yes, your Gallogermanian is opaque to us. It appears to be a mixture of several in our timeline," said Lila. She smiled refreshingly relieved that in her time shifts she could still occasionally deal with those of her own sex. At the same time, she wondered why the Trust would rely on a woman of seeming delicacy for such a mission.

"What has happened at the Enclave? Did everybody escape?" asked LeBrust.

"Most all of us got out and fled south to join our sister enclave at Alcon," said Dolf. "But we stress the urgency of this contact because the Alcon enclave is at capacity in terms of the ability of the local community to supply its needs. They have embraced us temporarily, but have requested that we find another place for settlement."

"Okay, we can sort it out later," said Brant. "Dolf, can you walk? We need to gather ourselves together and get out of here. The owner may already have slipped out to summon the authorities or some other kind of help."

The group, now augmented to six, made their way back to the entrance of the house. Brant peeked out of the door. All was quiet except for the random stroll of several natives in and out of the square.

"Let's go," said Brant.

They strode across the open area, reentered the shadowed passageway to the main square, and headed for the city gate. All appeared normal as they started across the square. Suddenly, an attachment of Roman soldiers burst through the gate. The horses milled about and stomped in restless complaint of an arduous journey in progress, yet, they knew through some equine intuition, not yet done. In full battle regalia, the soldiers barked instructions to some officials who had come out to meet them.

Brant, in the lead, gestured to the others in the universal "hold it" signal. "We don't want to get too close. They are here for some reason." He turned to Rajulk. "Did you get any of that?"

"Some of it," said Rajulk. "They are looking for some service personnel to augment a battle contingent. This may be related to the Battle of Actium which is about to happen, in which case they could be heading north to rendezvous with other forces. It starts as a sea battle accompanied by land skirmishes. The sea part reaches a stalemate until Antony bolts the scene to chase after Cleopatra and part of the fleet, leaving Octavianus's forces to achieve the upper hand against the remnants of Antony's forces."

"Well, that's a bit of history that didn't stick," said Brant with a chuckle. "It's always good to have a historian along on these missions. In any case, we don't want to get caught up in it."

They waited until the detachment had dismounted, corralled the horses, and retired to the recesses of the town, leaving only a small contingent and one officer to stand watch. The leaders converged on a house at the periphery of the square.

"That must be the seat of government here, such as it is," commented Brant.

"Quite likely," said Rajulk. "We should rid ourselves of this place as quietly as possible before something unpredictable happens."

"Let's split into two groups and join the outflow so that we are less likely to attract attention," said Brant. "Lila, Dolf, and I will go first and you and the others follow."

Brant and his group approached the gate followed by Rajulk with Kara and LeBrust. They were halfway across the square when another squadron of soldiers escorting several locals disturbed the normalcy of the square. A sudden hail from the leader made Rajulk stop.

"Keep going," he force-whispered to the others. "I think they are recruiting local forces and are focused on me. I will rejoin you as soon as I can."

LeBrust and Kara first hesitated but continued onward to join the others while Rajulk turned with a sigh to greet the oncoming soldiers.

"We better do as he says," said Brant reluctantly. "He still has his weapons, and even without them he is far more able to defend himself than any of us. He knows where the transfer portal is. We can leave it activated until he can escape."

IX

1860

Adrian Attempts to Reunite with Eugenia

It has been a long and difficult path, thought Adrian, now alone and pondering events that had led him to this time and place. *At least we got the gold plates buried.*

He boarded the train going south and settled down to read a local newspaper someone had left on the empty seat next to him. Each rhythmic clatter of the train seemed to coincide with some fleeting remembrance of his efforts on the part of the Trust mixed incongruously with his whirlwind encounter with Eugenia. He awoke with a start, his reverie jarred by the clang of the car door and an announcement by the conductor.

I must have been more tired than I thought.

The paper had slipped from his grasp and lay in a heap at his feet, and he now sat facing another man. Emerging from the fog of sleep, he appraised his fellow traveler. Middle aged and graying, the man looked up from the book he was reading.

"Oh, I see you are with finally with us. You slept all the way through stops in Syracuse and Albany."

"Your pardon," said Adrian. "My previous activity involved much travel and some strenuous physical activity. My descent into the oblivion of coma was my body's subtle message."

The man blinked, sensing his first appraisal of the disheveled Adrian was off the mark. "So where are you off to?"

"New York, in search of a person of prior acquaintance and of important to me."

"Are you familiar with the city?" asked the stranger.

"Not at all, I will have to improvise when I reach there."

"It is my home. Perhaps I can be of assistance. My name is Claven, Booster Claven."

"That is so kind of you Mr. Claven," said Adrian. "My initial quest is to find the residence of the Winthrop family."

"Such a name is common and embraces many classes. Can you give some specifics?"

"Of course. I wish to locate Miss Eugenia Winthrop, daughter of Edgar Winthrop. I made her acquaintance during a trip to the west."

"I may know that family. I have had business dealings with a Mr. Edgar Winthrop. I think he has a daughter."

"This is a stroke of good fortune," said Adrian. "I would appreciate knowing how I might contact the Winthrops when we reach New York."

"I will consult my personal log and should come up with something. Where can I contact you … Oh, I forgot—you probably have no idea where to stay in New York."

"I should be able to find a hotel or similar accommodation."

"I would suggest the Westchester Hotel on the Bowery. It is reasonable, and I shall be able to contact you there."

"My thanks for the suggestion," said Adrian.

The next day, Claven himself stopped at the Westchester. "Yes, I checked, and the Winthrop family lives at 2870 on the Old Post Road. You can certainly hire a carriage to take you there, go by horseback, or take the New York & Harlem Railroad Company horse-car for a great part of the distance."

"The latter should be within my means," said Adrian. "I thank you for the information. Had it been necessary for me to ferret it out from scratch, it would have taken time consuming efforts."

"The least I could do for a stranger visiting our great city," said Claven.

———

The sun was about to set as a weary Adrian stood before a formidable house on Old Post Road.

Impressive, he thought. *Eugenia's family must be among the more fortunate.*

He sighed, took a breath, and knocked on the door. After a pause, the door opened. "Can I be of service to you sir?" said the man.

Obviously a servant, thought Adrian.

"I would like to speak to Miss Eugenia Winthrop, if it is possible. I am an acquaintance by prior association and was told to make contact should I ever visit the area."

The servant blinked and hesitated, weighing Adrian's somewhat disheveled look against the simple eloquence of his request. "I shall have to refer you to Mr. Winthrop for matters concerning Miss ... Miss Eugenia," said the servant hesitating ominously. Mr. Winthrop is in the midst of dining. I will show you to the drawing room and inform him of your somewhat disturbing request."

Now what could he possibly mean by that? thought Adrian as he was led to a paneled room lined with bookcases. *I hope the ritual of the end-of-day meal is brief in this timeline.*

Winthrop appeared after only a moment, followed by his wife.

"You were inquiring about Eugenia?" asked Winthrop, his voice tinged with uncertainty.

"Yes, and if she is available, I would very much like to see her. She may have told you of our pleasant encounter during her trip to the west."

After a short pause, Edgar spoke. "Eugenia was due back from her trip west by now. We have not seen or heard from her since her last letter in June from California, indicating that she had concluded affairs relative to the family estate and was poised to return. "The carrier responsible for her transport has informed us that several of the coaches linking the remote areas to St. Louis had been intercepted, and that some coaches had not reached Kansas City," said Edgar. "The fate of their passengers is unknown. We fear she has been abducted or worse. When was your encounter with her? It may help point to the time of her disappearance and to her fate."

"This is distressing to hear," said Adrian suddenly drawn into the anxious atmosphere that hovered over the Winthrop household. "I can only tell you that our brief but rewarding association was subsequent to your letter," said Adrian. "It was in the town of Dodge in Kansas. I believe the month was August. At the time, she had been delayed by an unfortunate incident along the route and was waiting for transport eastward to the rail hub in St. Louis. So, it seems that between Dodge and there something happened."

"You have given us new information. It is possible that our beloved daughter was among the victims of some malevolence. We can now narrow down the location and time window of her disappearance and revive the stalled investigation."

"Let's see …" Winthrop went to a cabinet and rummaged through a container of rolled-up maps. Choosing one, he brought it to the table and spread it out while Adrian and Mrs. Winthrop looked on. "From what you tell us, she had cleared the area of mountains, which so inhibits travel to the far west … so she was here," he said, pointing. "Dodge City, that's where you last saw her?"

"Yes," said Adrian.

"Then most likely, somewhere between Dodge and Kansas City is where something happened," said Edgar pointing to two points on the map while stroking his neatly trimmed beard.

He is right, and only in afterthought when all the facts are in place can such history be written. Quite likely, any details of mischief by Rogue elements have not yet become public knowledge, thought Adrian, extrapolating from what was known. *I must return uptime and research the history of that period.*

"I will have to draw upon other sources to refine the data on the danger spots on the route," said Adrian. "I will get word back to you later after I learn more. For now, I must depart and consider the path forward."

"It is late," said Edgar. "Perhaps you will stay with us the night before you proceed with this mission so dear to us."

"You are right. I accept your offer and will start afresh tomorrow," said Adrian.

After the night stay, Adrian left the Winthrop residence and headed for the railroad station, deep in thought. *The time and projection of her travel seem to point to some unfortunate event en route. The stage route passes through Kansas City—a fortunate coincidence. Maybe I can persuade Brant to leave the portal there open. I must first get back uptime and take a chance that I can zero in on the incident of Eugenia's disappearance. I can't judge Brant's displeasure at such a side venture, but to intercede in events, I must convince him to project me into the time window just after I left Eugenia.*

After two days, Adrian reached Kansas City and made his way to the abandoned site representing the future location of the rented house. He located the markers, activated his TR, and held his breath.

"Oh, there you are," said Seth who made his weekly trip to see if Adrian had shown up. "We had just about given up on you."

"I was delayed," voiced a sullen Adrian. "I must get to Obamapolis as soon as possible and try to persuade Brant to transfer me again from this very place but in the period of our previous visit to Dodge City."

Seth's eyes flicked upwards with a weary shake of the head. "Okay, I will call Brant to see if he will agree to this new venture, whatever it is. Pending his okay, we will leave the transfer setup in place here. In the meantime I will go back to Obamapolis with you."

X

Brant and the Others Return Uptime

Having made contact with those of the Trust's timeline, Brant, Lila, Dolf, and Kara traveled from Pelusium to the transfer point minus Rajulk.

"There, that's the rock we used for reference," said Brant. "If we swim straight out about fifty yards, we should be in the transfer perimeter. We will leave it open for Rajulk. I still feel uneasy leaving him to the vagaries of the historic schism between Antony and Rome."

"I feel he will take care of it and get back," said Lila, herself with some misgivings at leaving his fate hanging. "Now, why don't we use that log over there to hang on to and float it out to the transfer point. That way we won't get separated with some of us transferring and others outside the periphery left behind."

"Good idea," said Brant.

They managed to drag the log into the water where it floated, then walked it out to where the water deepened.

"A few more strokes, and I believe we are there," said Brant as he turned to eye the reference points. "Good," he said finally.

Here goes. He activated his TR and the group, log and all, found themselves on dry land in the transfer area.

"Get this thing off me," said Lila as she struggled to extract her leg from under the log. "Quite naturally, the thing transferred with us. It's a good thing the sand acts as a cushion. That thing is heavy."

Now in the uptime transfer base near the Pelusium ruins, Brant called in to Frondner.

"We made contact with the Trust reps, but Rajulk got sidetracked by some over-enthusiastic Romans who were recruiting for some sort of encounter. I feared it was that rumpus with Mark Antony. He signaled us to go on, so we expect he will sneak away when he can. For this, we will have to leave this transfer point open and send Seth to man it."

"That would work, but Seth is now manning the Kansas City point," said Frondner. LeBrust has returned without Adrian, who is sidetracked by his quest to find the woman he met on the trip to get the gold. He has asked to keep the Kansas City point open to facilitate Adrian's return. The question is, 'Should we continue to use our limited resources to indulge his whims while we are saddled with other priorities?'"

"Maybe we should," said Brant on consideration. "If we can get it resolved, we can concentrate on the central objective of our time streams—to establish a permanent link. However, it makes two of our crazy family who are flailing around in time. At least Rajulk was forced into it, but Adrian is wandering around like an orphaned lamb.

"We are coming back to Obamapolis," said Brant after a pause. "In the meantime send Seth over here to Pelusium to man the transfer point and watch over the equipment. It will be dormant for a few days, but if Rajulk is free to return during that time, he will understand the delay and wait. I will return to Obamopolis and deal with Adrian when I get there."

Adrian himself showed up in Kansas City a few days later.

"There you are," said Brant as Adrian appeared within the transfer perimeter.

"Yes, I must get to Obamapolis and consult maps of nineteenth century America," said Adrian. "Sometime after I left the period, Eugenia may have been abducted en route to her home in New York. I must research it and try to find out what may have happened to her."

"Good, because I need to get back to the lab and stop babysitting while you resolve your personal problems," said Brant sarcastically.

Adrian was silent, ignoring Brant's barb and concentrating on the task at hand. Back in Obamapolis, he settled in at the map room of the main library.

In the window of my visit, this is where she must have been, he thought as he traced the route tracing with his finger on the map spread out before him. *Given the stage's route and its speed of passage, it should have almost reached Kansas City. The date would be more or less at the end of August in 1863. So, something must have happened around … here.* He stabbed the town of Lawrence with his finger. *Most of the war has been far to the south and east except for a few rogue groups with mixed sympathies. I must talk to Brant.*

Brant, Lila, and the others, back from their sojourn in ancient Pelusium, arrived in Obamapolis and met with an anxious Adrian.

"Adrian, do you really have to do this?" asked Brant as Lila looked on.

"You are just assuming that the incident Eugenia got caught up in involved this bunch called Quantrill's Raiders."

"My research strongly suggests it. The timing is right. It was a major historical incident. The town of Lawrence was sacked and burnt then by Quantrill. There was little else going on along her route around that time," said Adrian.

"Also, I remind you of both our mandates and those of the trust regarding harming those of target periods," said Brant pressing forward.

"I don't follow you," said Adrian. "How does the fate of Eugenia enter into the equation?"

"Well, we entered the time stream and altered events involving Eugenia," said Brant. "Had we not done so, her future from that point might have been quite different, even worse, if I am to believe Rajulk's account of it. The bandits would have had a free hand to do as they wished."

"We don't know that," said Adrian. "It is likely they were interested only in the gold. The fact is, we did intervene."

"You are treading in the misty area of cause and effect and its interaction with time travel. The same questions can arise if you try to interfere with the Quantrill gang. Many historic figures of the period were associated with Quantrill. You might … do in somebody," said Brant, his voice trailing off.

"All right," said Brant after a pause. "This is the downside of having so few of the ITR in on the actual use of time travel. I will have to go to the Kansas City transfer point myself because Seth is going to the Pelusium site to wait for Rajulk. So, I would prefer that you also wait until Rajulk is available to go with you. As you know, time is not pressing when you can insert at will, anywhere in the time stream."

"Perhaps that is so, but I feel a subjective urgency that trumps the scientific reality of time travel," said Adrian.

"Maybe I could go with him," said Lila. "I could take Vanora with me."

"A formidable team, I admit," said Brant, calming down as a tendril of subliminal humor surfaced at the idea. "You must remember that firearms are prevalent in that period, so your skills would not be as effective there as during the Roman era."

"Effective enough," said Lila. "Even in the early west, there was a certain code when using firearms face to face, and women don't seem to be involved in the lore of the gunfighter."

"Okay, there's safety in numbers," said Brant after a pause. "Go with him and, yes, take Vanora if you like. But a question remains, what will you wear? The feminine getup of that period would restrict movement along with the fact that Vanora would look ridiculous in a full-length dress. For Adrian it is no problem, but if you wear the things that make you comfortably mobile, you will look masculine and be treated as such."

"I have some ideas along that line," said Lila to a skeptical Brant.

"The other thing is exactly when and where to transfer you," continued Brant. "We certainly can't send you to arrive in the middle of the raid itself or, for that matter, too long after. The Raiders would have scattered to the wind. The Kansas City portal is some thirty miles from Lawrence. It will take you most of a day to reach there by horseback. First, you will have to deal with the locals to get some horses. I will send you at least a day early, but I caution you to stay away until the day following the incident. Ask around about the Quantrill bunch, where they hang out, might go, and so on."

They traveled to Kansas City and went to the rented house with the equipment Seth had set up for transfer.

"Settle down for a bit while I check everything out," said Brant as he inspected the transfer perimeter laid out in the largest room of the house. *Everything seems to be in order,* thought Brant. *We have taken a chance leaving this site unattended for extended periods. Some local yokel could slip in here and tear it all up.*

"Everything looks okay. Any time," said Brant as he scrutinized Lila,

Vanora, and a sullen Adrian. "You two look like the cowgirls in those old movies. My take is that no women dressed like that back then; it was just a fantasy of the film industry."

"No matter," said Lila. "I went to considerable trouble to have something made up to fit Vanora, and I kinda like this hat, this kerchief, and these chaps. How about you Vanora?"

"I like," said Vanora, resorting to her as-yet sparse English. "Miss armor and sword but will use weapons nearby if needed."

After a lingering inspection of the two, Brant shook his head and rolled his eyes. "I have set the transporter for early morning, so you are not likely to be observed when you appear out of nowhere."

"Let's get on with it," said Lila, impatient as always for some new action.

The three arrived in the misty field outside Kansas City.

"Where are the markers we left on our previous transfer?" asked Adrian.

"They wouldn't be here yet," said Lila. "We need to put down new ones"

"Oh that's right, we have arrived before we did last time," said Adrian.

"In any case, somebody owns this land, and we shouldn't be surprised if any markers are come upon and removed. That makes it even more important to have a backup plan to locate the transfer area," said Lila.

"We can do it with azimuth sightings like Francois and I did with the gold plates on the Hill of Cumorah so that with suitable hints, they can be relocated," said Adrian.

"Okay, get to it, so that we can get on with it," said Lila. "Lawrence will be chaos from the raid last night. First, we need to go into the Kansas City for some horses and then, make for Lawrence and ask around."

The horse reared up and sprang forward, jolting Lila backward.

"Whoa! Oh, you are dead meat!" she shouted as they trotted along. "This horse is a bit spirited for my taste. It keeps breaking stride and bobbing its head. She pointed to Adrian's mount as he kept laughing. Why couldn't I have drawn that old grey mare you have?"

"Be nice to horse, and he be nice," soothed Vanora reflecting an undercurrent of humor.

"That's it," said Lila as they topped a low rise. "That cluster of burnt out buildings and the shroud of smoke clinches it. We should use care in entering. Any surviving natives will be suspicious of strangers. Let's go this way."

They circled the town and cautiously approached from the south.

"We should check in with the local authority before asking around, if there is one," said Lila.

A shot rang out. Adrian slumped in the saddle. Lila raised her hands with Vanora following suit as several men emerged from one of the few intact structures.

"Hold it right there!" shouted a man holding a shotgun who seemed to be in charge. "I suppose you have come back to find out what is left of this place. Well, that's your mistake—"

"Them's women in men's clothes!" interrupted another. "Septin that ter hombre what we shot. Ain't never heared of no women ridin with the Raiders."

The leader paused and then asked, "Who are you and what are you doing here?"

"We are after the Raiders ourselves. They have taken someone known to us, and we want her back," said Lila.

"Yes, a woman," said the leader. "Our women tell us there was one who was taken, a stranger here. We are told the whole batch escaped to the south where there's more sympathy for the Confederacy."

"We first need to care for our wounded comrade," said Lila returning to the present. *This is all we need. One of us is hurt … we may have to abort the whole thing.*

"My name is Larson, sheriff here in Lawrence. "You all took a chance coming here. We are suspicious of everybody, especially strangers. Beyond that, I can't see how a couple of women can do anything to persuade that rabble to do anything unless … perhaps they offered some services … uh, if you know what I mean."

"We will meet that problem when we catch up with Quantrill."

"So you know who they are," said the man, his suspicions rekindled.

"Yes, we heard they were in the area, and now it seems they chose Lawrence to promote their mischief and cause," said Lila as she dismounted and went over to Adrian who was bleeding from the shoulder.

"Let me help you down. We have to look at that."

Adrian slipped from the saddle and lay down. Lila examined wound while Larson looked on.

"It is painful but nowhere near as bad as that ordeal on the cross," said Adrian. [16]

"A religious man, I am elated by such courage, and so sorry that a grievous mistake has put him in this situation," said Larson.

Lila worked hard to suppress a laugh at the irony of Larson's remark even in the urgency of caring for Adrian. The idea that the Jesus of history was there in such a mundane setting transcended even the most bizarre extrapolation of the bible story.

"Why yes," said Lila picking up where Larson left off but hesitant to overdo it. "He is almost as virtuous as Christ himself."

Lila spoke softly to Adrian. "Looks like it went straight through. We have some antibiotics and painkillers in our kits, but we need to get you back uptime and have that looked at for complications."

"Give me those. I can make it back to the transfer point. You see if you can catch up with Quantrill and his gang."

"Are you sure?"

"Yes, if you are successful, tell Eugenia to continue her return home to New York, and I will meet her there later. Tell her … that I love her."

Lila turned to Larson. "He says he can return to Kansas City for treatment at the hospital. He has requested that we continue with our mission."

"All right," said Larson hesitantly, now in a state of total confusion at the seemingly impossible task confronting Lila and Vanora. "They were heading south. Track them as you wish, but I urge you to notify the nearest Union post if you do find them."

Adrian doused himself with the antibiotics and pain killers and made it back to the transfer point.

"What happened to you?" said Brant as Adrian appeared subdued in the field, his shoulder covered with makeshift dressings.

"A little accident in the field," said Adrian. "I need to get to a hospital and have it checked out."

"Let me look at it. That looks like a gunshot wound!" said Brant as he unwound the makeshift bandages. "I warned Lila about poking around in an era of firearms. Are she and Vanora all right?"

"They were fine and trying to catch up with the Quantrill Raiders, who were reported to have traveled south with Eugenia. I got this wound from the local militia. They thought we were mixed up with the outlaws."

"The nearest hospital is here in Kansas City," said Brant. "We'd better use that rather than lug you back to Obamapolis. I will get you there and then return here to wait for Lila's return. "Dammit," said Brant, talking to himself as much as to Adrian. "Rajulk is stuck in post-Ptolemaic Egypt and Seth is in Pelusium waiting for him. This is the downside of having such a limited staff fully involved in time travel activities. Now I am stuck here waiting for Lila and Vanora. I should never have okayed the rescue, but I will just have to trust that they will have things under control."

"Hopefully it will work out," said Adrian, now subdued and showing signs of faltering under the stress of his injury.

A taxi deposited them at the Kansas City hospital. Brant made up an elaborate story about the gunshot wound that seemed to satisfy the doctors.

I am glad they didn't have a bullet to do ballistics on, thought Brant. *Coming from an antique weapon, the thing would have raised all kinds of questions.*

Lila and Vanora headed south and by sunset decided to call it a day. Queries of locals on the way indicated that Quantrill's Raiders had passed that way. After spending the night beside a road and refreshing the horses with the aid of locals, they resumed their pursuit of Quantrill.

At the end of the second day, they entered a town. A crude sign read "Joplin."

"It's somewhat of a city uptime, but it appears a little shopworn at this point," said Lila, looking around for some type of transient quarters.

"We camp out in open again?" asked Vanora who had said little on the quest, which to her was somewhat enigmatic.

"Let's look for something better. That building there, which looks like a bar is promising. The second story may have transient rooms. It is probably the nearest thing to a hotel we can find. I could use a bed for a change, and maybe we can find something to eat."

They entered the premises through swinging doors. A desk stood opposite with a bar to the side exposed through a wide opening. The men sitting around slowly looked up from cards or casual drinking and took in the scene.

Lila approached the desk. "We would like rooms for the night."

The clerk looked up, at first confused by the man who stood before him who was obviously a woman, accompanied by another of similar dress but of substantial proportions.

"Well … uh, we have rooms for one silver dollar a night."

"That will do nicely," said Lila. She paid and accepted the key. "Is it possible to get something to eat here?"

"Sure, the bar can serve you," said the clerk.

They moved to the bar under the scrutiny of all the patrons who stopped their activity and gaped.

A somewhat sleazy woman approached and asked, "What can I get ya?"

"What's good?" asked Lila, not knowing what kind of food such a place at such a time would have.

"Well, we've got good ribs fresh cooked from slaughter and corn bread fixed with taters and gravy. How's that sound?"

"Sounds great," said Lila, not wanting to dwell on the deficiencies of nineteenth century cuisine.

As they sat waiting for the fare, a couple of the locals slowly got up and approached.

"Now what's two nice ladies like you doin wandrin round dressed like men? Maybe you should join us on the trail for some 'man stuff,'" said one to the laughter of his cohorts and the others sitting nearby.

"We are on the trail of Quantrill and his men," said Lila in a friendly tone while sizing up the stranger for possible action. "Perhaps you can help us."

"What do you want with Quantrill?" asked one of the men from a table nearby.

"He has with him an acquaintance of ours who was taken by mistake. We wish to secure her release."

"Yes, that woman, I think I know who you are talking about. My name is Anderson. I am here to get supplies. I can take you to him. He is camped south of here and will keep going."

"Look here mister, we was talkin to the ladies and don't need no stranger butn in."

"Sit down if you know what's good for you," said Anderson who then drew a pistol.

"You wouldn't shoot a man what ain't got no gun, would ja?"

"I will if you make trouble," said Anderson. "You ladies finish your grub, and we can catch up with Quantrill."

Lila approached the desk. "We won't be staying after all," said Lila. Here is your key.

The clerk took the key and grudgingly refunded their money.

Anderson loaded a packhorse with provisions for Quantrill's men, and the three left traveling south.

A tired Lila and Vanora pulled into a glade at dawn with Anderson in the lead. Most of the men were still wrapped in blankets, snoozing. Quantrill himself was out in front of a makeshift tent talking to another man.

"Anderson! Your timing is good. We are out of everything. Give the—" He paused, for the first time noticing Lila and Vanora. "Who are they, and why are they dressed like that?"

"I met them in Joplin. They are trying to find that woman we took during the raid on Lawrence. I guess they are more mobile in those pants and chaps."

"She's still sleeping in that tent over there," said Quantrill. "I was talked into bringing her along because of her aristocratic demeanor and Yankee connections with the idea that she might be useful as a trade in some situation. I now suspect other motives. In any case, she has been a distraction. It's been all I can do to keep the men away from her. They are loyal and unified when it comes to our cause, but as you know they get deprived of certain … things, when on the move," he added with a glance at Lila.

Lila spoke for the first time. "We would be glad to take her off your hands."

Quantrill looked around and then turned to focus on the two. "See if you can get her out of here without rousing the men."

Lila and Vanora approached the tent and looked inside. Eugenia was sleeping but woke at the intrusion. Still clad in her now dusty and disheveled riding clothes, she sat up to face them with a fearful look.

"We've come to free you. Quantrill seems to be okay with it if we can get out of here without rousing the rest of the gang."

Recognizing the treble voices of her sex, she rose and faced the two. "Who are you? Why should I go with you? I might be in worse trouble in your company than here."

"Your reprieve from the ravages of this unruly bunch is running out," said Lila.

"My name is Lila, and this is Vanora. In time, we will explain who we are, but time is pressing. Come with us. Adrian said to tell you he loves you and is anxious to be with you."

"Adrian? Wha—what do you know of Adrian? He said that? I did not expect to see him until I reached New York where he promised to visit me in the future. Where is he? Is he alright, and why should he send such strange emissaries to convey this message?"

"All will be explained when we get you out of here." *At least part of it,* thought Lila. "Adrian suffered an accident in Lawrence where we first went to find you. He had guessed that you must have been caught up in the chaos there. For now, he has returned to his ... his base to recuperate from his wound."

"And where would that be?" asked Eugenia, now wide awake."

"That would beee ... revealed later," said Lila, not wanting to commit to any future for Eugenia beyond her rescue. "Now, let's see if we can sneak out of here without rousing the men."

Lila peeked out of the flap of the tent. *It's about as quiet as it is going to get.* "Let's go."

They left the tent and sauntered toward where Lila had tied up the horses. A shout broke the languid flow of early morning.

"Where are you going with our woman?"

Quantrill responded as forcefully as possible under the circumstances. "They are relatives and have come to fetch her home."

"Not if the rest of us have anything to say about it," said the man. "We been ridin solid since Lawrence. This is the first time we ain't dead tired. And who are those two other ... Why, they're women too," he shouted joyfully now joined by several of his roused mates. I think it's time we are due a little relief from all our work."

"They're out of control," said Quantrill. "Let them have their way and they will probably let you go."

Lila and Vanora stood quietly and Eugenia shrank back behind as the men approached.

The first of the group reached out to touch Lila and found himself momentarily airborne before crashing into a tree behind. Vanora moved forward toward two follow-ups who paused to regard the dispatch of the advance guard. Too late aware that something else unexpected might come their way, the closest received, mid face, the full weight of Vanora's fist. Staggering back in the throes of blinding pain, he instinctively reached for his gun, which in the fog of early morning arousal wasn't there. Two or three others advanced to join the fray, while others, including Quantrill himself, watched with fascination. Lila waded in, giving a lethal chop to the next in line as another approached from the side encapsulating her briefly in his hairy arms. With an elbow to his face, she managed to relax his grip, and a kick to the groin sent him staggering backward, doubled over.

Three of the men lay moaning while the one with the altered face stood in a nebulous stupor, still feeling around for the gun that wasn't there.

"Enough," Quantrill intervened, himself in a state of shock at the easy dispatch of his men by two unarmed women. "Get out of here before somebody gets shot," he snapped.

Lila, Vanora, and Eugenia backed away from the scene as the men stood uncertain as to what they had just witnessed. They quickly mounted, Eugenia behind Lila on her horse, and galloped away before the transfixed rebels could react.

Eugenia was quiet for a long time as they moved quickly to escape possible pursuit by the disgruntled raiders. Finally, after several miles, they moved off the primitive road to rest.

"Joplin is just ahead, we can get something to eat there and rest the horses," said Lila.

"I am familiar with horses," said Eugenia. "If we can get another, it will take the burden off the one that brought us here double-mounted."

"A good idea," said Lila, who reassessed the jewel-like Eugenia, somehow intact in spite of the near miss. *Tougher than she looks.*

They reached Joplin in late afternoon and spied the hotel-saloon they had visited before.

"Should we try that place again?" said Lila as the others looked on.

"Men not got manners there," said Vanora in an economy of words.

"Maybe we should at least get a room to rest," said Lila. "I prefer to avoid the bar. We can try to have some food sent up."

Lila went again to the clerk's desk and asked for a room.

"So, you are back. Are you going to stay this time?" he asked sarcastically.

"Yes," said Lila, nearing the end of her patience. "Can you have some food sent up?"

"Yes, for extra charge," said the clerk as he turned and pointed. "On the board there is the special of the day."

RIBS FRESH COOKED FROM SLAUGHTER
WITH
CORNBREAD
TATERS AND GRAVY

No hors d'oeuvres or aperitifs, thought Lila. "Well, send up enough for three people. I'll pay in advance."

They piled into the room. A high-backed bed decked with patchwork quilts and flanked by buffalo rugs occupied the center of the room. Mounted steer heads and crossed sabers decorated the room along with other signatures of the period. Rough-hewn boards encased the space, which in spite of its crudeness offered welcome to weary travelers.

After a short wait, the food arrived.

"It's either not bad, or I am so hungry I will eat anything," said Lila to the snickers of Eugenia, who had begun to bond with the weird pair of strangers.

Having achieved a place of relative safety and satisfied their hunger cravings, they succumbed to the fatigues of the day. With a momentary respite from the perilous activity of the day, Eugenia flopped crosswise across the bed and immediately took refuge in sleep. Lila sighed and did likewise while Vanora curled up on the thick buffalo skin rug, which lay on the floor beside the bed.

Lila awoke first as sunlight flashed through the open window. "Let's get rolling," she said as the others stirred. "There must be something like a general store here. We can pick up some more food and eat it as we travel. We have at least two days' travel back to Kansas City."

Delayed by floods and bad weather, it took three days for them to reach Kansas City.

"Here are funds for the continuation of your travel. Do as I suggest," said Lila, handing over some silver dollars from her stash. "Return home and await contact from Adrian. You may want to stay the night in a local hotel to freshen up before going forward."

"You have presented me with a series of obscured and conflicting facts," said Eugenia in an explosion of pent-up emotion. "I am grateful for your help and friendship but still have no idea who you are, what your relation to Adrian is, and why you would involve yourselves in his affairs in the first place. Take me to him. He needs me and my help."

Lila took a deep breath and responded with a sigh. *He obviously has told her little or nothing about who he is and what he does.* "Adrian is involved in a mission of wider scope than he has revealed to you. It is up to him to inform you or not. Unfortunately, we are unable to take you to him at this time. We have enjoyed your camaraderie in adversity and hope the future brings us together again. If not, may the pleasant memory of it always linger."

With a smile and a nod, Lila and Vanora left the still-troubled Eugenia. Traveling to the outskirts of the city, they again located the transfer point.

Brant had returned to his vigil at the house in the Kansas City suburbs. To his relief, Lila and Vanora appeared in the transfer perimeter within the next two hours.

"We are bushed. I assume Adrian made it back and has taken care of his wound?" asked Lila.

"Yes, he is in a hospital here in Kansas City for observation," said Brant, relieved that they were intact. "I am happy you have put my mind at ease by promptly getting back. It is convenient and reassuring that we can insert and reinsert at convenient times, but it is yet to be determined what sort of catastrophe occurs when one returns to a point before one left. Fortunately, our TRs are programed to warn us before such a situation occurs. Unfortunately, though, the priority of our contact with the other timeline has precluded any systematic investigation of such paradoxes. As soon as this contact issue is resolved, we must get a handle on these issues."

"Okay, okay," said Lila. "We can talk theory later. For now, we both could use a shower and some food."

"We can go to a restaurant when you rest up, but for now, there are some frozen dinners in the fridge," said Brant, opening the refrigerator door. "Let's see … Oh. This looks good: beef ribs with mashed potatoes and gravy."

"What! No cornbread?" said Lila. "Please, let's find a health food restaurant."

"Cornbread?" asked Brant tentatively.

"Inside joke," said Lila.

A week later, Adrian left the hospital in Kansas City and returned to the lab in Obamapolis.

"It's still a little sore, but the doctor said I would be as good as new in a week or so. I would like to rejoin Eugenia as soon as possible."

"Okay then, moving forward, we will leave the Kansas City portal open since you may wish to return for some reason of other," said Brant. "That settled, Lila has something to say about your relationship with Eugenia."

"Yes, indeed," said Lila. "Adrian, you must be aware that you, LeBrust, and all those we have brought back to the present of this timeline have left their original periods under duress and been exposed to this one first-hand. Without that experience, the reality of this uptime environment cannot be easily explained and could be mistaken for, at best, an overactive fantasy, at worst, the illusions of a lunatic. This is the problem of engaging the subject with Eugenia. We don't know what plans you have for her. You may want to bring her to this era, but that has problems of its own. She may be perfectly happy in her own time window and not so anxious to escape it. It is up to you to do as you see fit."

"I know this," said Adrian with a sigh. "The choice for me is whether to continue, or to pass on the mantle of the Trust's aims to someone else and settle down in her era. I am worried that my skills are for the most part useless there."

"Joining her there is certainly one option, and I understand the issue of your skills, but you can't go on pushing the aims of the Trust forever," said Brant. "The elders can pass on the mission to someone else. You have seen that the result has been overall successful. So if your feeling is that strong, do what your heart tells you and let Francois carry on."

"I will get together with her and work it out. The issue of the Mormons will resolve itself one way or another," said Adrian.

XI

Rajulk Is Drafted in the Roman Service

Separated from Brant and the others in the square of Pelusium, Rajulk listened as the recruiting officer briefed the hodgepodge of reluctant conscripts.

"We are assembling those of you who seem qualified and worthy to the service of Rome. Please join us for the glory of the empire," said the soldier who seemed to have some kind of rank.

That's his ritual recruiting spiel. Is this déjà vu of our first mission or what? He doesn't even know if I understand him, thought Rajulk.

Rajulk responded with a timeless gesture: palms up and shoulders shrug.

"No matter," said the officer, motioning to his troops. "You'll learn enough of our language along the way."

Rajulk was corralled with several others from the town and herded toward the town headquarters, he turned and gave the go-on signal to the others standing anxiously just inside the gate. He and the other recruits were escorted out of the city and westward. The gentle slope of the land gave way to a more abrupt separation from the sea. Masts of Roman *biremes* appeared amid scattered palm trees. A flurry of activity greeted the retinue, now somewhat wary from the forced march. The recruiting officer addressed another at the docks and pointed to his charges. After another exchange, the officer returned and escorted them to one of the ships.

Shades of the Ostia-Judea jaunt, thought Rajulk in recollection of the frantic pursuit of LeBrust in a previous mission. [17]

The recruits were divided into three groups. Two burly specimens were immediately sent to the hold to supplement those unfortunates manning the oars while another trio was sent to load cargo of weapons and food, leaving only Rajulk and another Pelusium captive at the mercy of Roman caprice.

The officer was consulting with the ship's captain.

Not of centurion rank, thought Rajulk. *No indication of it in his dress … Probably a trierarch slated to meet up with a greater command later*

Rajulk appraised his fellow captive.

Tall and muscular, the man stood with a sardonic expression on his face. His *thobe* and turban were clean and neatly arranged, signaling a somewhat better class than the others. Rajulk took a chance. "Sir, do you speak the Language of Rome?"

He focused on Rajulk for a moment and responded in Latin: "Yes, I was under the impression from your encounter with the officer in charge that you did not."

"I was playing the fool in hopes of not getting caught up in this fiasco," said Rajulk

"You either have some foresight denied the rest of us, or you are a pessimist of the first order," said the stranger, his tone now matching his sour expression.

"Have you no fear that they will thrust us into some conflict of their choosing?" asked Rajulk.

"The Romans have full control of the lands bordering the Mediterranean now. What possible force could rise to challenge them?"

Not surprising that news doesn't travel fast in this age, thought Rajulk.

"I have heard," said Rajulk after a pause, "that there has been a revolt within the ranks of the Roman high command. Part of those loyal to the central authority have defected to another."

"How so?" asked the stranger, distracted from an express disdain of his captors and now fully engaged in the exchange.

Rajulk spoke carefully, hesitant at saying too much. "I don't know for sure, but it is said that Mark Antony has broken from the Roman establishment and joined in revolt against it. The confrontation may take form of a naval engagement which is the reason for our summons to this place of embarkation."

"How could you know this?"

"Abundant rumors of the schism have surfaced of late."

The stranger paused to consider and then spoke slowly. "If so, it puts our conscription in a new light. We could even be drawn into the conflict if there is one ... I am called Thoth," he added in a relaxed tone. "Your name would be?"

"Parzan Rajulk Petrov. Just call me Rajulk."

"Such a name is strange in sound and makeup," said Thoth.

"Where I am from two names are the norms. The first may be compounded with another and is sometimes referred to as a middle name. The third name designates a larger clan, with the first two reflecting our individuality within it. In my personal interactions, I am known by my middle name, Rajulk," said Rajulk realizing he had overdone it.

"Well—Rajulk, we are thrown together by fate. If what you say is true, our involvement is more than I first thought. Perhaps we can pool our wits and stay free of the worst that may come."

Not a bad idea, thought Rajulk in the silence that ensued. *I certainly know more of what is going to happen, but he is sure to be more up on the uncertainties of this period.*

A command broke their reverie.

"You two join the deck crew," said the captain. "We must hoist sail and be underway. The future of Rome is about to be decided." He gave instructions to the first mate who shouted below, "Hold port! Starboard, back it down!"

My best guess is that this will be part of Antony's force, thought Rajulk. "They are rotating the ship to get underway. How many days sail to Actium?"

"About three days," said Thoth, and on second thought asked, "Why Actium?"

"Well—I heard one of the crewmen mention it in passing and thought it might be where we are going."

Thoth eyed Rajulk for a moment and then turned to the ship's duties.

Rajulk considered. *We are sailing into a chaotic situation. There are different versions of how it develops, but all of them have in common that the forces of Octavian prevail. The only solution is to make sure we don't reach the battle scene. I will have to disable this ship somehow.*

Rajulk joined in the crew's preparations and looked for the ship's vulnerabilities. *I could fry the mainsail, but for this ship, which looks like a single masted bireme, they probably have replacements … I must wait until dark.*

Darkness came as the ship moved northward in a light wind until land was out of sight. Rajulk, along with Thoth, partook of the meager rations available to the overcrowded ship. The gentle flap of the mainsail synchronized eerily with the ship's rhythmic surge forward.

The oarsmen are already at it. Glad I am not back down there tugging away, thought Rajulk in recollection of the travails of a previous mission. *I can't sink or immobilize this ship on the open sea … The most I can do is slow it down to keep it from reaching the site of battle.*

Thoth broke his reverie. "We are reduced to sleeping out here in the open."

"Barring bad weather, it's better than down below," said Rajulk.

The wind picked up as the evening progressed, giving respite to the men laboring at the oars. The deck became quiet, with crew and soldiers snoozing in clusters or makeshift nooks. The heavy breathing of deep sleep brought counterpoint to the now familiar sounds of the ship. Still in thought, Rajulk reclined against the main mast and soon he himself gave in to slumber.

A spritz of salty wetness brought him to consciousness. *Guess I didn't dream it,* thought Rajulk.

Sitting up, he peered over the rail toward the sun just peeping over the horizon. The rest of the deck was stirring as a sleepy-eyed Thoth wandered over and crouched down beside him.

"Neither of us wants to get involved Rome's internal dispute," said Rajulk deciding to reveal his plans to disable the ship. "We have to find some way to keep the ship from reaching the scene of battle."

"And how do you propose to do that?" asked Thoth.

"I'll let you know when I figure it out."

The day progressed with a favorable wind pushing the ship ever northward.

With the oarsmen's extra push, we should reach the Actium battle site in another three days, thought Rajulk.

Nightfall brought respite from the labors of the day. Rajulk waited until all was quiet on deck and slipped over the port side of the ship near the stern. An ornamental shelf ran lengthwise just above the top tier of oars. A slow but steady rhythm came from the swish of oars in the lower tier, the token group on duty for the night. Rajulk balanced on the shelf and brought out his laser. Holding on with one hand, he set the laser to a tight beam. One by one, he severed those oars lifted out of the water at rest, leaving the small contingent still at work untouched. The smell of burnt wood quickly dissipated in the night air.

That should slow things down a bit, thought Rajulk as he slid back over onto the deck.

Dawn broke. On cue, confusion and an ensuing uproar came as the crew was roused and orders were shouted into the hold. Confounded by the erratic lurch of the ship, the captain leaned over the side and saw the nubs of the oars frantically gyrating as the portside oarsmen probed for some aqueous counter force to their efforts. The starboard oarsmen tugged away, sending the ship in a preposterous circle until the enraged captain called a halt. He and the rest of the deck crew lined up on the port side and studied the enigma of the missing oars.

Better join the party, thought Rajulk. *Don't want anyone to think I am less surprised than anybody else is.*

"What happened?" asked Thoth as he came up beside Rajulk.

"I did a little damage to the ship. Let's see what effect it has," said Rajulk.

Thoth looked over the rail to where the oars were supposed to be and gasped. "You did that? How—?"

"Shh," cautioned Rajulk. "It will slow us down, but it may not be enough to sideline this boat."

The captain spoke to his first officer just under the ambient sounds of the ship. "For some reason, the gods are displeased. We must watch our actions to see that it does not happen again. Detach the useless oar stubs and replace them with a balanced number taken from the starboard side of the ship."

After several hours, the ship was again underway, though at reduced speed.

I will have to try something else, thought Rajulk. *He is going to reach the scene of battle if it kills him—and it probably will.*

Nighttime came again and Rajulk slipped below. Most of the oarsmen were snoozing in place. Others were still manacled, but loosely enough to find space for an improvised repose in any empty recess available.

Rajulk stepped over several of the sleeping men and made his way toward the front of the ship, which was separated from the rowers' section by a crude door. He slipped through and examined the enclosure, which tapered to a point some three yards away.

The floor here is still suspended above the bottom of the hull below, thought Rajulk. *There, that trapdoor should lead down to the ballast housing.*

Closing the door he had just passed through cut off the snores of the crew and left Rajulk in a cocoon of silence, the first he had experienced since his conscription into the mission. He slipped down through the trap door, closed it behind, and activated the emergency LED light he and all members of the mission carried.

This ingress is surely only for servicing, thought Rajulk as he looked around. *The bulk of the ballast must have been packed in here through a larger opening on the deck before Thoth and I were drafted for the voyage. What do we have here? ... Weapons ... Figures, they are heavy and useless until we reach the site of battle ... kegs, probably wine and—these long logs, timber ... The ship is probably in commercial use when not in battle. Now just a little ...*

Burning a small hole just below what he judged to be the water line, the water started seeping in, dousing the small flame caused by the laser. *That should slow us down a bit. By the time they discover it, this place will be pretty much inundated with water.*

He returned to the deck and his duties as shouted out by the first mate.

A little after midmorning, the ship stood perceptively lower in the water. A shout came from the hold. The captain descended to where the slaves tugged away at the oars and emerged fuming. This time, he said nothing about the whim of the gods, but looked around at everything and everyone with suspicion. He focused on the deck crew.

"All deck crew go below and help bale out."

They entered the area where the oarsmen, now reduced in number, tugged away, with the bottom tier now sitting just above the water line.

The ballast hold must be completely flooded, thought Rajulk. *I hope I didn't overdo it.*

A bucket parade formed, stretching from the open trap door to the deck.

"Is this some more of your mischief?" asked Thoth, more amused than annoyed as they labored side by side in the queue summoned to bale out the hold.

The water level gradually lowered due to the efforts of the crew, but the hole in the hull, the source of the problem, was still submerged and undiscovered. The captain appraised the situation and finally gave orders to steer southwest.

Rajulk looked at the sun. "I would judge, from the direction we are sailing, we may be headed for the port of Alexandria. The captain can recoup, make needed repairs there, and be off again to the battle site. I, or perhaps the both of us, can possibly escape—if you are agreeable."

"Anything to keep from getting drawn into some internal dispute between the factions in the Empire," said Thoth. "You think Alexandria?" he asked off hand. "I have often visited the library there."

"You have?" asked Rajulk, caught off guard as his scholar's instincts surfaced. He recalled his brief brush with the historic city during a previous mission. "What is its state now? I mean, is it definitely there?"

"It is definitely there, but somewhat in neglect. The Roman conquerors are distracted by other problems."

"If we dock there, perhaps we can slip away during whatever they plan," said Rajulk reluctantly returning to the present. "From here, judging from the time we have been out, it should take more or less the same time to reach Alexandria."

Another night passed as they approached the city, and by the midday following, the calm protected waters of Alexandria's bay came into sight.

"There, that's it," murmured Rajulk to nobody in particular as he focused on an elaborate building close to the water. *It's the library all right. The last time I was here with Brant, it was A.D. 60, and the thing had been long gone.*

Rajulk and Thoth joined in docking the ship, which had struck anchor some hundred yards offshore. The captain and another officer prepared a small hand-propelled boat for the trip to land.

"They will probably negotiate repairs and reload supplies, which should put us here at least two days," said Rajulk. "If we are going to do it, we should look for an opportunity to escape tonight. Can you swim?"

"I trust in your judgment, and yes, I can swim," said Thoth, ever confident that the enigmatic stranger he had chanced upon knew what he was doing.

Darkness fell once again, and all was quiet on deck. Rajulk regarded the watery expanse separating them from the shore. *I had better do a little tailoring on this thobe. A wet covering like this will hamper any response to an emergency.*

Using a knife from the emergency kit he carried, he severed the portion below his knees. *It doesn't look too much different from a Roman tunic now, albeit a designer version.* He started to discard the cut- off portion, but hesitated. Making a cut in the closed circle of remains, he laid out the material, rolled it up lengthwise, and secured it around his waist. He then took out the compacted vapor barrier sheet designed as a blanket but could serve a variety of other uses. He tightly wrapped his stunner and laser in it, secured it with ties, and left the remainder of it loose.

He sidled over to Thoth and whispered, "It's almost time. I will slip over the side first and wait for you. I have sequestered a few essential things in the nucleus of this collapsible blanket I carry that will protect them. Its trailing remnants will capture air and be buoyant enough to assist should we falter in our efforts to reach land."

The captain had returned from shore, and all was finally quiet. Rajulk made his way to the rail and slid over into the cool waters. Holding on to one of the idle oars, he waited. Seconds stretched into minutes. *Maybe he decided not to come.*

A shout followed by the splash of a body jarred his reverie. Rajulk followed the sound of churning water, dragging the blanket with him.

"Thoth, is that you?" he force whispered as he heard the splatter sounds of a swimming body.

"Yes," said Thoth answering in kind. "I was discovered just as I was about to launch."

"Make for shore before they get it together and come after us," said Rajulk. "I don't know what they do to deserters in this situation—maybe make an example of them or kill them on the spot."

They stroked in tandem toward the shore while shouts and the splash of a dory signaled that the captain was wasting no time in pursuit.

"There, my feet just touched the bottom," said Rajulk, breathing hard. "Keep moving toward shore. We both should be able to wade the rest of the way."

As the pursuers' dinghy foundered in shallow water, three crewmen were over the side in pursuit while the captain secured it. Rajulk turned to see two almost upon him as he reached the sandy beach. Instead of continuing his flight, Rajulk surged to the right, forcing the duo into a single file as they continued after him. He slowed as they continued to close in. Suddenly, Rajulk swept the still loose remnants of the blanket into the path of his pursuers. The nearest became tangled in its folds and went down. Cursing humanity, the one following scrambled around the jumble of plastic and charged Rajulk. Dropping the small compact scrap of the blanket containing his weapons, Rajulk grasped a handful of sand with his left hand and flung it into the eyes of the hulking crewman, following up with a right hook. The blinded adversary's head snapped back as the sweep of Rajulk's leg rendered him face down in the ankle-deep water. The one tangled in the blanket had just recovered when Rajulk's foot caught him in the side of the head.

Unaccustomed to physical violence, Thoth, already captive of the remaining crewman, was being dragged back to the dinghy. The captain, now aware that things were not going well, yelled at Thoth's captor and pointed. Hesitant at whether to keep hold of his captive or take on Rajulk, he released the squirming Thoth. The two closed on each other in a dreamy slow motion slog through the surf while Thoth, now free, watched the confrontation as he again waded toward shore. Closing to arm's length, the crewman reached out. Rajulk grabbed his arm and twisted it clockwise forcing him to turn, at the same time levering it to a painful position behind and up. A sharp cry signaled his discomfort as Rajulk continued to apply pressure. Released, the wary crewman backed away toward the dinghy nursing his wrenched arm him to a withering dressing down from the captain.

The duo advance guard was slowly recovering as Rajulk moved past them and rejoined Thoth. To the fading shouts of the captain, they made their way into the innards of the city.

"We can't stay around here for long. The Romans may have severe penalties for the sort of insubordination we showed them," said Rajulk.

"We can travel back east, then south to the city of Ineb Hedj. I have friends there who can help us," said Thoth.

That is probably Memphis, thought Rajulk in effort to sort out the geography of ancient Egypt. "That's too much out of the way for me. I must return to the vicinity of Pelusium to … to finish my purpose here."

"I wish to return there too, but Pelusium is too far away to achieve without food and shelter on the way," said Thoth.

"We must travel the most direct route if possible, so we will have to do as best we can," said Rajulk. "We have around 150 to 200 miles to travel back to Pelusium, which on this terrain, should take at least ten days. I have on me a small packet of food for emergencies, but we cannot rely on it for survival. We must look for food on the way and will have to rely on some natural sources. "You are more familiar than I am with what grows here and is edible."

"If nothing else, we can eat roots of papyrus, which seem to be abundant, but perhaps we will be fortunate enough to find some figs or grapes," said Thoth.

"Well, keep an eye out. I would probably pass them by without realizing it."

With Thoth in the lead, they left the city and traveled eastward to where the great river had splintered before emptying into the great inland sea to the north. For the first two days, they crossed the marsh-like terrain with numerous rivulets. On the third day, they came to a halt. To the front was a stretch of still murky water dotted with patches of reeds and an occasional dead tree partly submerged with others tilting plaintively toward their watery graves to come. Rajulk regarded the way forward with a leer y eye.

"I don't see any way around it," said Rajulk. "We need to move across it with care to that dry land over there covered with trees. From here to there, there is no telling what lurks under that layer of muck. I will go first."

Rajulk slipped into the mucky water followed by Thoth. The knee high water gradually deepened to waist height as they moved forward. Small wavelets of their passage radiated outward in ever-decreasing strength compromising the overwhelming tranquility of the scene.

A splash, a floating log came to life, to the side, another.

"Crocs!" yelled Rajulk. "Move faster!"

Suddenly, the tranquil waters trembled with agitation. Each innocuous bump in the lazy aquatic setting seemed to move. They had progressed several yards from the shore when a monster reared up to challenge their advance. Rajulk moved sideways to where a tree had already surrendered in its relentless battle with the swamp. Cracking off a piece of limb, he motioned Thoth to stay behind him. The crocodile veered and advanced from the side. As it closed on the pair, Rajulk waited for the precise moment of attack. At the instant when the croc's tightly closed mouth opened, Rajulk jammed the limb as far in the croc's mouth as he could. Still braced against the limb, he was knocked over backwards by the forward motion of the croc. He struggled to right himself amid the thrashings of the now compromised reptile. Thoth overcame his fears and came to the rescue, lifting Rajulk from the sludge and dragging him toward the shore. The two reached dry land just as several of the reptile's colleagues made tentative lunges. They retreated further into the brush away from the hostile domain of their reptilian nemeses.

Covered with mud, the two regarded one another. As if by common impulse, they burst out laughing, signaling a bonding from shared adversity.

"I hope we won't have to repeat that little drama," said Rajulk to the silent assent of Thoth. "We have come no closer to the coast as we have traveled directly eastward. I suggest we head to the coast and follow it even though we will have to cross numerous tributaries of the Ni … that is, the great river flowing from the south." *I don't know what they call it now or even when the name 'Nile' finally stuck.*

Rajulk and Thoth washed off as much of the gunk as possible and veered north, now moving more cautiously after their reptilian encounter.

"We are lucky at not being in the season of flood. Much of the land we have covered would have been under water, making it even more dangerous," said Thoth.

After several days' struggle and detours, they settled into a trek beside one of the tributaries of the great river carrying the waters from the highlands of mid Africa. Numerous settlements began to appear.

"Best we skirt these clusters of habitation," said Thoth. "You never can tell if they are friendly or will take a dislike to you because you are a stranger."

"Easy to say but hard to do," said Rajulk. "We keep encountering them. That grove of trees probably conceals another of them. I see smoke coming rising above the foliage." He pointed, "This way."

Rounding a cluster of reeds bordering another of the endless stretches of water, they stopped abruptly. A small girl stood sideways to them transfixed. A snake of considerable length was coiled only inches away.

"Stand back," said Thoth. "It's a deadly serpent."

A black cobra, thought Rajulk. *I had better try something quick. I don't know what can be done for such a bite in this age.*

The girl turned toward them terrified, but immediately focused again on the snake.

Rajulk pulled his laser from his tunic and aimed. *I hope that flop in the swamp with the crocs didn't disable this thing.*

The snake's head disappeared in a puff of smoke and a frying sound. Absent a cranial command center, its sinuous remains flopped lazily to the ground.

"That takes care of that," said Rajulk as he hid away the laser.

Thoth, who had focused on the girl and the snake, turned to Rajulk as he was pocketing the laser. "Is that some of the magic you used on the ship's oars?"

"Yes," said Rajulk, although it's not exactly magic."

The girl, still frightened and oblivious to the fact that the reptile had been neutralized by something beyond the scope of her imagination, moved away as quickly as possible with but with an odd gait.

"She seems to be limping," said Thoth.

"Yes, she's favoring the right foot, placing most of the weight on it as she moves," said Rajulk. "That shoe, if you can call it that, on the bad foot is completely worn through where it drags on the ground."

There is a blank in my knowledge of kids in antiquity, Egypt in particular, thought Rajulk as he watched the frightened little urchin scampering away. *For orphans though, if that's what she is, the prospects are not good. She looks to be around six or seven. How she even could have survived in the wild is the question?*

Rajulk watched as the child disappeared into the reeds; then he sighed and followed after. After a few strides, he overtook her as she paused on the edge of a pool of water. He stood watching as she pried a plant from the mini-jungle of vegetation, rinsed the roots in the tepid water, and chewed on them. Rajulk shifted, causing the snap of a twig. The girl looked up again in terror and again began to scamper away. Rajulk stepped forward, reached down, and touched her shoulder. She turned to confront her assumed nemesis. Cold black hair framed an oval face dotted with smudges of earth, reflecting the imperatives of her existence. The child's body itself was intact except for the damaged foot, but the fright of before changed and now focused on survival from yet another unknown danger.

How many times has she met this before? thought Rajulk, who somehow sensed that any movement would precipitate an explosion of maneuvers, which to that point had served her. He continued staring at the girl and slowly knelt down to one knee. Thoth had come up behind and watched from a distance as Rajulk and the girl faced off.

Reaching into his improvised tunic, he retrieved what little was left of the emergency supplies. Feeling through the selections without taking his eyes off the girl, he retrieved a packet of dried fruit and a small bar of chocolate, and held it out. The tableau lingered as if frozen in time before the girl took a tentative step forward and then another as Rajulk slowly placed the items in the ground, rose, and backed away a few steps. She picked up, tore open and ate the packet of fruit and then turned to the chocolate, never taking her eyes off Rajulk

After a moment, Rajulk again knelt and put out his hand. After another endless pause, the girl slowly limped toward him and placed her hand in his. He rose, towering over her. Together, they moved back toward where the mesmerized Thoth stood.

They moved slowly eastward in silence until Thoth finally said, "That which empowers you is a mystery."

Rajulk ignored the comment and pondered the enigma of the girl. *I wonder what language she speaks, if any. Considering this region, she possibly picked up some Demotic from earlier years, if she ever had any nurturing at all.* "Hopefully she was exposed to some language. There are dire results and bizarre examples of language deprived children."

"I cannot imagine where you would have come upon such knowledge," said Thoth.

Again leaving Thoth's retort hanging, Rajulk said, "Maybe you can test her on a couple of the local ones when we stop for a break. In the meantime, it would seem that she could not have been on her own for long. At her age survival in the wild is tenuous"

"At any age in this unpredictable land," said Thoth.

Even at a slow pace, after several hundred yards the child began to falter.

"I had better take a look at that foot. I can't tell if it's a deformity or something else."

He sat her down and lifted the foot. *There ... what is that? It's raised like a callus, but it looks infected, so it's not surprising she is limping. I can try some antiseptic agent from my kit, but she may need more aggressive treatment than I can give her for now.* Rajulk reached down, took her up in his arms, and trudged forward. After a tense few seconds, some instinct from a forgotten infancy took over. She slowly relaxed, encircled Rajulk's neck with her fragile arms and dozed silently, soothed by the gentle rhythm of his stride.

Having bonded with Rajulk, it took some time for the somewhat aloof Thoth to gain the trust of the child, but now they shared the burden of transporting her.

After another day on the trek north, a channel of the river loomed before them, slicing diagonally to the south. Boats of various sizes plied the waters, harvesting the fruits of nature the various gods of vogue deigned to bestow upon them.

"The wind-driven boats all seem to be going south," said Rajulk.

"It's very handy. It blows in that direction," said Thoth. "The river itself flows north, which makes that direction easier for oarsmen."

"How do we get across?" asked Rajulk, figuring that Thoth would know better than he would.

"I suggest we continue north to some village on the shore of the great sea. Maybe we can get a boat there to take us across. In any case, we need to stay away from the river's edge. That's where the *crocodillus* live."

"Yes, the Crocs," agreed Rajulk. "I think we have had quite enough of them. As to the river, its tributaries slant to the west. Following them will take us out of the way, but it is a trade-off. Our chances of finding passage across are better as we near the great sea."

"Yes," agreed Thoth. "We are sure to come upon numerous riverlets resulting from the splintering of the river flowing from the south, and once there, we can barter for passage at any of the settlements we should encounter."

The girl, now in the secure keep of Rajulk, listened intently to the exchange between Thoth and Rajulk. In one of the silent spaces she spoke softly just above the ambient sounds of nature, "Crocodillus."

Rajulk turned and looked at the girl and then at Thoth. "Is she just repeating what I said, or is it a familiar word that she has heard somewhere before? I can try some Latin on her—something simple. I will rely on you if we need to test a local language."

"Uh ... iniuria," said Rajulk, pointing to her foot, which brought no response. *Too complicated,* he thought. Rajulk again pointed to her foot. "Pedis."

"Pedis," said the girl hesitantly. He pointed to the sky "Caelum."

"Caelum," repeated the girl, pointing to the sky as Rajulk mouthed it. Inferring from the drift of the exchange, he pointed to the river. "Aqua," said the girl.

"She must have picked up on the Latin sounds as we talked, and inferred some of the context," said Rajulk. "I wonder where she learned even that much Latin."

"She could have been the child of a Roman servant who incurred disfavor for one reason or another," ventured Thoth. "How she fell into or has even survived in such an existence is a mystery."

"Well, it's something to build on," said Rajulk as they moved slowly along.

On impulse, he turned to the child, pointed to himself and said, "Rajulk."

Then he pointed to Thoth and said, "Thoth."

The child stared as if mystified.

"Maybe she has no name, or it was implanted when she was so young that she has forgotten it," said Thoth.

"Strange she should have experienced language without retaining a label for herself," said Rajulk. "Well, we will just have to give her one. Let's see. We found her confronting a cobra … an asp. How about … Aspira?"

Rajulk turned again to the girl, pointed to himself, and said, "Rajulk." He pointed to Thoth, and said, "Thoth," and lastly pointed to the girl and said, "Aspira." He repeated the word, "Aspira."

"As … pira," repeated the girl tentatively, reflecting a vague understanding that she now had a denotation to distinguish her from the countless things in her experience.

"It sounds fitting enough although I cannot fathom how you would come up with such a name," said Thoth.

With a chuckle, Rajulk ignored Thoth's remark and concentrated on the journey forward. After another day's travel, they reached the coast. Already in an area of copious vegetation, they partook of the occasional fruits and other edibles that grew wild along their tentative route.

At last, the Mediterranean, something I can at least reference. Now to veer eastward, thought Rajulk as they spied the expanse of blue water in the distance.

Thoth pointed. "There, that cluster of structures at the edge of the river is what I hoped to find. They are merchants used to itinerants and likely to be less hostile. Many of the products generated along the river end up here for transshipment."

"Let's give it a try. You better do the talking."

They approached one of the buildings where locals were coming in and out.

Sunbaked brick, noted Rajulk. *It figures. There are few lumber-grade trees here for construction.* He settled the ever-clinging Aspira on the ground, and they passed through the door.

"We request passage to the other side of the river," said Thoth.

"Such is possible for a small remittance," said the local. "What do you have?"

Barter, thought Rajulk, getting the gist of the man's response to Thoth's query. *What do we have? Some Roman coins from the original packets provided us ... How will he react to them?* He groped inside his robe, but Thoth produced a set of rings, removed one, and gave to the man.

Ring money, thought Rajulk. *It Looks like bronze or copper—too much patina to tell. The guy is prepared for anything.*

Rajulk and the others held onto the sides of the flimsy boat as the solemn boatman lazily dipped his oar in the murky waters of the river. Ominous bulges in the churning flow appeared and disappeared. A sudden bump suddenly broke the oarsman's orderly stroke. He raised high the oar and brought it crashing down. The mischievous reptile received the affront with indignation, thrashing briefly but drifting away. They reached the far shore, happy once again to leave behind the uncertainties of the river.

Rajulk lifted Aspira from the boat. *If my recollection of the delta geography serves me, we may have to repeat that little act a few more times before reaching Pelusium.*

They moved ever eastward, negotiating in similar fashion the three remaining branches of the Nile.

Rajulk devised an improved shoe for Aspira's damaged foot, so she could move somewhat better under her own power, but she now seemed to relish the comfort of Rajulk's embrace when negotiating rough terrain.

"We have been lucky, being able to live off land. The vegetation is thinning out now. Hopefully we will soon see some landmark we recognize," said Rajulk as they approached the last of the tributaries fanning out from the main stem of the great river.

"I know that settlement ahead," said Thoth suddenly as they stood looking at the adobe-like structures just across the water. "It's Domyat. I did business there several times. Between here and Pelusium; however, the sea enters the land. Only scattered islands lie on the direct path there. We will have to detour south then east around it."

"Okay, I trust your judgment," said Rajulk.

They skirted around the bay-like incursion of the sea and approached the arid expanse, which signaled the end of the river's domination of the land. Topping a sandy mound Thoth stopped. "There, it's Pelusium at last."

"I will continue a short way with you, but I need to veer toward the sea to ... to rendezvous with friends there."

"Will they be waiting after all this time, and what about the child?" asked Thoth.

"They will be waiting one way or another," said Rajulk deceptively. "As for the child ... I will take her with me."

"I hope you will visit me when you again travel to Pelusium," said Thoth with sadness. "You have shown character and skills far beyond from those of my experience, not to mention the mysterious devices you employ, which I have not before even heard of."

"I cherish that we were thrown together by chance and will remember it always," said Rajulk, matching Thoth's ardor.

Rajulk bid farewell, and then he made for the seashore carrying Aspira.

Now where is that reference rock? he thought as they approached the water. He looked up and down the shore. *That way,* he decided. They rounded a rise in the land that had obscured the way forward. *There, yes, that has to be it. Now, how can I get Aspira out there? Rescue is one thing, but all her survival instincts will come out if I just plunge in carrying her with no explanation. Besides, I need my hands free to manipulate the TR.*

He sat Aspira down and surveyed the surroundings for something to float as she looked on. "Hmm" ... *Nothing but scraps washed up from the sea ... maybe.*

He started gathering small pieces of driftwood, branches, twigs, anything lighter than its displaced volume of water. Removing his *thobe*, he made a transverse cut below the place where the arms were attached. Filling the arms with the woody gatherings, he sealed them off at the cuff and the upper extremities of the arms by threading through strips of dead papyrus lying about. He stood back and surveyed his work.

If I can balance her on the flaccid cloth in the center, it should have enough buoyancy to get her out there.

Rajulk turned to his wide-eyed charge who had watched his antics in wonder, some amusement for the first time breaking through her childhood innocence. Eying once more the reference rock, he took her hand and waded out to where the water was up to Aspira's chest. He positioned the flotation device behind her, reached down, and swept her legs backward from under her. After a brief panic, she realized the makeshift device kept her from going under. He hesitated briefly before grabbing a piece of the dismembered thobe. Wading out to where the water was too deep, he swam further outward a few strokes. *This should be about far enough.* He let go of Aspira, rolled over on his back, and activated the TR.

The warmth of dry sand cushioned his back as the sound of Seth's voice pierced the rushing of the surf. "I had just about given up on you. Oh— who is that?" he asked, suddenly noticing Aspira still partially enveloped in her Rube Goldberg pontoon device, which was now somewhat askew, lacking the buoyancy of water to keep it in place.

"Just something I picked up along the way," said Rajulk. Aspira righted herself and sat staring at Seth dressed in his bizarre twenty-third century garb.

Rajulk removed the tangle of his handiwork from Aspira and brushed some wet sand from her face. *The rest will fall away as we dry off … I hope she can shed the wild child syndrome and adapt … Better get her something more fitting for a little girl … Meriam can help me with that. First, we need to see about that infected foot.*

Seth broke into his musings. "I'm glad you finally showed up. Some stuff has happened since you got stuck back there. Brant is busy with Francois. He finally returned from a trek to upper New York State to plant the plates made of the gold you guys brought back from Dodge City."

"Okay, I will check in with him and get the latest on that. For now, give me your cell. Meriam must be crazy that I didn't return with the others after I told her it would just be a casual jaunt downtime."

"Where have you been?" asked Meriam when Rajulk connected. "You said it was just a routine trip to make contact with the other timeline."

Accented of course, but I can't believe how she has absorbed the English language, thought Rajulk.

"Sorry, but there were a few complications," said Rajulk not wanting to detail it with so many other issues pressing.

"I have brought back someone, a child, a girl," he ventured cautiously not knowing how she would react. *We could put her up for adoption. She would be infinitely better off than before*, Rajulk thought wistfully.

"Good," said Meriam after a short pause. "She can be an older sister."

"Okay, said Rajulk with relief which was cut short by a sudden dawning.

"You don't mean—?"

"Six months, more or less, make sure you are here. I mean both time and place-wise when it happens."

"Well, I'll be damned."

XII

Adrian Returns to 1861 to Reunite with Eugenia

Adrian once again stared out over the foggy landscape of the Kansas City transfer point. *Gloomy and dismal,* he thought. *Does the sun ever burn the fog off here? Maybe I should try this particular transfer later in the day.*

He fingered the stunner and laser he had decided to bring. *Don't know why I still carry these things. It's not a particularly dangerous period. Still, this timeline always presents uncertainty when one least expects it.*

With a sigh, he started the now familiar trek into the city and the train station. This time he had an ample supply of gold eagles he had pried out of Brant over his objections that it was making a dent in the ITR budget. Negotiating the fare and itinerary to his final New York destination, he settled down to the lazy, sensual input of the journey. The Missouri landscape passed by in frames as presented in the panning rectangle of the train's windows while the train's metronomic click on the track presented an oddly repetitive lullaby.

Two days went by, and the conductor's call "New York," signaled he was near his journey's end. Alighting from the train and unlimbering stiff members, he once again took the horse car to Old Post Road and made for the Winthrop residence. He knocked on the door. *Let's hope that after all that has transpired she is home and safe,* thought Adrian. Once again, the same servant of his previous visit greeted him.

"I wish to inquire once again—"

"Mr. Beike, we have been expecting you," said the servant. "Please, come in. Miss Eugenia is in the garden with her parents. I will inform them you have arrived."

A few moments later, there was a rustling of footsteps and the muted din of animated talk as Eugenia burst in the room and rushed into Adrian's arms as Edgar and Sally Winthrop who stood watching from the doorway. The tableau lingered until finally the Winthrops retired to the drawing room to wait for the two lovers to resurface.

After an extended period, the couple rejoined the Winthrops.

"I have come to this place for an indefinite period to reunite with Eugenia," said Adrian speaking formally. "Since my presence here is uncertain for practical and … other reasons, I may have to pursue other options for the future. Hopefully these will include Eugenia, if she may so wish." *That should cover it should I decide to whisk her off up time.*

"First, I must find some sort of employment to justify my presence here."

"I may be able to help you there," said Edgar. "We always have entry level positions in my financial firm."

Sounds quite dull after the Jesus role and the latest Mormon tangle, thought Adrian. *On a practical level, I could be caught up in a compendium of deficiencies relating to my limited knowledge of this timeline's conventions.*

"That could work," said Adrian politely. "But I would be starting from scratch."

"I was never exactly clear what your previous employment activities were," said Edgar in a tone matching Adrian's civility.

Now I am really stuck, thought Adrian. *I will have to spin something.*

With only a slight pause, Adrian held forth. "As Eugenia has now doubt told you, we first met in the desolate west. I had gone there under the auspices of … CEITA," said Adrian, pausing to correlate the fictitious entity of his tale with its alphabetic equivalent. "CEITA stands for Committee for the Embrace of the Indigenous Tribes of America. "Having only modest success at prodding the reluctant primitives to accept the values of our European-based culture, I abandoned the task and was returning to the east when I met Eugenia."

"So, your work was of a philanthropic nature," said Edgar.

"Yes, and considering that, I have thought of exploring some aspect of the ministry, should such an opportunity present itself," continued Adrian as the idea seemed to spring out of nowhere.

"You would probably have to ally yourself with one of the established denominations and go from there," said Edgar.

"What if I wanted to establish one of my own?" asked Adrian, silently building on the thought. *Yes, perhaps I can justify my presence in this timeline and continue to promote the values of the Trust even as I phase out my official connection to it.*

"An unusual question," responded Edgar hesitantly as he sat back to appraise Adrian anew. "It would depend on what you had in mind. We are a Christian nation. You are fortunate the Winthrop family is uncommonly secular in this age of ardent faith, even though we, as many do, regularly attend church services to keep up appearances. After all, the ethics and morals of Christianity do help stabilize the populace no matter who advocates them. As to your proposal, such thoughts could be considered irreverent in some quarters."

"Even if they promoted an ethical society?"

"Well, yes. Those on the extremes regard any stray from the fundamentals of the faith as a threat. Any such movement could be considered a cult, of which there are many. Often, such mavericks are associated with witchcraft and dealt with harshly."

"I plan no such ventures into the occult and wish to give it a try anyway."

"You would need to recruit followers and persuade them to support you financially. This might take some time, should you be able to do it at all. Do you have sufficient funds to sustain yourself in a period of growth?"

"I have some resources, but they are limited," said Adrian

"You are invited to stay with us during your period of trial. Should you not succeed, I would suggest you take a more conventional path by accepting the offer with my firm."

"There is another matter of concern to Mrs. Winthrop and myself. I assume, from your efforts to get here and your obvious affection for my daughter that your plans include marriage."

"Yes, that is the proper thing to do," said Adrian.

"To facilitate, I will arrange a civil marriage devoid of excessive religious connotations, so we can get it out of the way."

Eugenia listened to the exchange in silence interspersed by frequent furtive glances at Adrian. After dinner, the couple settled in the living room while Edgar attended to some leftover business matters, and Sally supervised the servants in the post-meal cleanup.

"I must ask you, Adrian," said Eugenia, her head leaned against his shoulder and her arm interlocked with his. "Who were those women you sent to rescue me from the bandits?"

This will be difficult, thought Adrian. *Anything I say will only elicit more questions.* "A pair of exceptional women I met in the course of my travels. They possess extraordinary skills and are eager to employ them in the service of justice."

His explanation was met with extended silence.

"But ... they took on those men and bested them on their own terms," said Eugenia finally. "What kind of environment would produce and even sustain such activity without its becoming common knowledge? Also, they told me that you were involved in a mission of greater extent than you have told me. Just what is it?"

"All I can say is that they are willing to respond when the need is made clear to them," said Adrian, now feeling some guilt at deceiving his beloved. "Maybe someday they will appear again. You can then ask what their motivation is. As to the mission, I know I have given you only the broad details. For now, I beg you concentrate on what is most important, that we are, at last, united."

A few days later, Edgar sat with Adrian looking at the ad appeared in The New York Times.

> *Minister seeks followers for the establishment of a new Church to support a faith based on the fusion of science and the spirit. The first meeting will be held at the Communal Meeting House on Park Place, Aug. 3rd, at which time the future home of the church will be decided. Those interested please reply to P.O. Box 324, Main Post Office.*

"It's a little vague. Every misfit or malcontent may come out of the shadows to answer it," said Edgar in a voice full of doubt. "But let's see what happens."

A few days later, Adrian emptied out a box full of letters onto Edgar's desk.

"I guess the world is always looking for something new," said Edgar, more amused than surprised at the response. "Let's see what they have to say."

Edgar went through the stack and sat back. Choosing one from the pile at random, he read:

Dear Mr. Beike,

Perchance I stumbled upon your ad in the Times regarding the establishment of a new church. Having recently come in conflict with the influential laymen of my usual Sunday haunt, I may be interested in supporting your efforts. You may count on my presence at your suggested meeting place.

Sincerely,
Norman Calhoon

"This one seems to be typical of the others, except a few inquiring about the commitment to the traditional Christian idea," said Edgar as they both gazed at the heap of opened mail. "Since you had not mentioned any Christian basis of the Church, I am astounded at how few references were made to it in the letters."

"Perhaps they either assumed it, or it wasn't an issue," said Adrian.

"Possibly," said Edgar. "In any case, in your interest I will attend your first meeting and observe the audience."

It's only about half full, thought Adrian as he gazed out over the disparate group of attendees. *Still, that's not bad considering the vagueness of the offering. Let's hope I don't have a repeat of the scene with St. Paul at Iconium where Francois told me things really got out of control.* [18] *Here goes.*

Adrian stepped to the podium.

"My friends, we gather here out of common desire to seek certain truths which seem to lie just beyond our reach. What is our purpose here on this planet? How are we to live in harmony with our fellow man?" What state of mind most effectively supports this end? My new Church will attempt to answer these questions and chart a path forward. First, we must find a more appropriate place for our meetings that encourages an atmosphere conducive to the consideration of these weighty matters. I would call upon you to be generous with your contributions to this end."

A member of the audience stood up. "I would be glad to offer an appropriate space in a building of my ownership which contains an abandoned theater. Pending satisfaction with the details of your movement, I would ask: will your church be bedecked with the customary symbols of Christianity?"

"Only if it is in a tune with the congregation's consensus," said Adrian, uncertain as to the reason for the man's question.

"What will you call your new Church?" asked another as the previous issue remained unresolved.

"I have tentatively given it the name, 'Church of the Enduring Trust,'" said Adrian.

A collection was taken, and the meeting ended.

Adrian and Edgar sat tallying the take.

"Not bad for such a vague offering," said Edgar wryly. "You will need to hone your message to suggest ultimate rewards, either earthly or in the hereafter, and to organize social events. Eugenia should be able to help you with that. Oh yes, and guard against an occasional radical who might spark internal disputes, which have caused the demise of many a Church."

"Advice taken," said Adrian, again in recollection of Francois's experiences in shoring up the work of St. Paul.

XIII

General Bromfsted Probes the Government Science Institute

Bromfsted groused just above the threshold of hearing as his aide, Lieutenant Jebbia Defoe, shuffled files in a nearby cabinet. [19]

"What was your take on that farce of a celebration concocted by the GSI about some fundamental breakthrough in penetrating the time barrier?"

His trim assistant turned with a sheaf of papers in hand.

"I couldn't cut through it, sir, but something was not quite right about such a disparate assembly of people," said Defoe. "It's my guess that the format of the party, a costume ball, was devised to conceal some perverse aspect of the get-together. That hoopla about a breakthrough in their research and the celebration itself may have been a ruse to throw us off the track."

"Yes, I agree," said Bromfsted, stroking a nonexistent beard. "There are too many anecdotal hints about their progress in time travel to dismiss. On the other hand, they figured right. We could look like fools if we made unsupported claims or accusations. And Onsley, what the hell was he doing there at the so-called celebration? How did they even know enough about him to invite him in the first place? I don't like to be reminded that his shadow operation to follow Van Croizen to Israel turned out to be a disaster. [20] At least, that is the impression we were left with. I wonder if it has anything to do with his leaving the service."

"They may have spotted Onsley on your staff listing," said Defoe.

"True, it is probably nothing, even though he was my aide before you got here, and he was suited for the oddball mission I sent him on to follow Van Croizen. However, there are still some unresolved mysteries about his disastrous trip there. I understand he is engaged to someone he brought back from Jerusalem, which doesn't exactly fit with the tale of being waylaid by some ruffians there. When did he even have time to form a relationship? I wonder if he told us everything that happened when he followed Van Croizen. Do you have any ideas?"

"Not about Onsley sir. As far as the GSI is concerned, we could try to plant a mole in there. Also, there's always that reporter who floated the snippet in the Midland Tribune on the GSI involvement in time travel," said Defoe. "Where did he get it from in the first place?"

"The mole is out, but we can certainly ask that reporter about the time travel malarkey. At the time, it was only one of several bites in the media suggesting there may be something to it. Do you have the Tribune article handy?"

"Just a second ... here it is," said Defoe as she pulled a sheath of papers out of a file cabinet.

"What's his name again?"

"Bryce Carter."

Bromfsted examined the clipping.

Unconfirmed sources have revealed that a division within the Government Science Institute has succeeded in devising a way to travel in time. The GSI's penchant for secrecy may be delaying revelation of this remarkable breakthrough for a variety of items from historical eras have appeared in the 'now' of 2289 A.D., suggesting that the efforts to link with the past have borne fruit.

"He couldn't have just pulled this out of the air," said Bromfsted. "We will pick him up, scare the crap out of him, and see where it goes."

Bryce Carter was just leaving the Tribune building when two men sidled up to him and flashed a badge.

"Please come with us," said a stoic officer.

"Who—what's this about?"

"We just want to ask you a few questions."

Carter was wedged in between the two beefy agents as the car made its way to the Federal Building. He was hustled into a room with only a table and two chairs. Bromfsted entered and sat staring at the now anxious reporter.

"Where did you get the information on the time travel bit which appeared in the Tribune?" he asked finally.

"Uh … from an employee at the GSI," responded Carter nervously. "I got him drunk and loose-mouthed. He told me about some stuff that had appeared in one of the research facilities. The objects as described seemed to be from another period in history, so I concluded that they must have had some success in moving through time."

"What was his name?"

"Lenny, Lenny Barre."

"Thank you very much. You have been most helpful. You can go," said Bromfsted, straining against his cantankerous nature.

He conferred with his aide. "Not much new from Carter, but we have the source of the leak in the GSI. His name is Lenny Barre."

Defoe consulted the government directory. "Here he is, sir, assistant to the GSI director, Gerald Frondner. He's probably at a desk job, not connected to the scientific wing, although what happens there probably passes by him."

"That would imply that the head of the GSI was in on any deception regarding time travel. Makes sense," said Bromfsted, looking off into space. "The ITR is a subdivision of the GSI and depends on it for funds."

Bromfsted and Defoe stood behind one-way glass regarding Lenny as he sat nervously in the austere room Carter was interrogated the day before.

"I might lose it with the kid. He looks ultra-sensitive. You see if you can get something out of him."

Defoe entered the interrogation room with an icy smile and sat down.

"Now, Mr. Barre, just what did you tell Mr. Carter regarding the time travel activities at the GSI?"

So that's what this is about, thought Lenny. *I had better do some damage control.*

"If you are talking about our encounter at the bar, I was looped out of my mind and have no idea what I blabbed about."

"Come now, Mr. Barre, such thoughts don't just come from nowhere."

"I assume you have been talking to Carter. I still don't remember what I said."

"As he reported it in his paper, he spoke of a breakthrough in the ITR, and that certain items had already been brought back from historical eras.

"If he says I said it in one way or another, I probably did. But ... Well, that was a little sexual folly on my part. I thought he was coming on, and I was probably trying to impress him with some kind of wild tale."

"That pansy showed more spine than Carter," beefed Bromfsted. "We didn't get anything specific from either of them, but my impression is reinforced that at least Barre may be hiding something. The other one looks like a trick of opportunity. As far as the GSI is concerned, we don't have enough to charge in and take over in the name of national security."

"We could always try to get a mole in there sir," said Defoe.

"Not likely, I'm sure they vet the staff thoroughly before hiring."

"Then, what we might do is make a courtesy visit to the ITR lab ourselves, rave about the party they threw, and extol the accomplishments of penetrating the time barrier. We could look around in the clutter for some hint, some suggestion that there is more than they have revealed, carelessly left lying around."

Bromfsted did a take at his attractive aide and sat back. "Not a bad idea. Trouble is, neither one of us is an expert and wouldn't pick up on any scientific anomaly in the setup. Still ... I need something more substantial to justify action. A premature move would bring us into another conflict with the libertarian sector of society, but a casual visit might give us insight as to how to move forward in the investigation. Yes, yes, set it up."

XIV

Brant Pursues Permanent Contact with the Trust Timeline

Frondner sat in the single armchair occupying the improvised lounge section of the lab. Lila sat on a lab table, while Rajulk leaned against the food dispenser incongruously infringing on the space. Brant stood, mulling things over.

"I heard from Bromfsted's office," said Frondner. "He wants a visit to our 'marvelous facility.' I have set up a tour to keep him off our backs, but we need to focus on things that are more important."

"I'll take care of him and give him the deluxe tour," said Brant. He's not likely to pick up on anything.

Good. Now to important matters: We have indulged our friends in the Trust to show our good will and to assure their cooperation. LeBrust and the emissaries from the Trust's timeline are safely here, and although it may be somewhat tenuous, we have established a link with it. The only thing dangling in this quest for clarity with the Trust's timeline is Adrian. That he is off on a some where and when romantic quest seems benign enough. God forbid that he introduces some anomaly jolting himself into a new timeline where we can't reach him. But pending his attempt to contact us, we will let him do his thing in the 1800s."

I have taken those here now who are from the Trust's timeline under wing to get them used to the eccentricities of this timeline," said Lila

"Good," said Brant. "Now to the matter at hand, Dolf has told us that the enclave has only temporary settlement at the Alcon enclave. Should we leave them to fend for themselves, or help them figure out something? After all, in the surviving pockets of advanced scientific capability in their timeline, they are the only ones who developed time travel. They need some place to settle and start over. If they are starting from scratch, it could take them some time to develop the capacity for time travel again. Now, we at least have the Pelusium-Alcon link. It will serve the purpose, even if it is somewhat cumbersome to use, given the Egyptian authority's constant nosing around the installation at our uptime end."

"I would suggest keeping the Trust enclave within its own timeline but moving them to this hemisphere," said Frondner.

"I was leaning that way too," said Brant. "The only thing is that we know little about conditions on this side of the Atlantic in their timeline. "As they told it, the northern part, which they referred to as 'the great double continent to the west,' is uninhabitable for some vague reason. That would be the America and Canada, but as far as we know, South America is still unaffected. We could consider moving them there. Then, to reestablish contact, we will have to travel to our timeline's geographic location of the Trust's settling place, establish a bounce point below the intersecting node of the timelines, and link with them by probing, like we did at Pelusium."

"Won't that require the consent of some South American authority, whoever it turns out to be?" asked Frondner.

"Yes, but we will cross that bridge when we come to it," said Brant

"If we can get them to go along with the idea, we could then mount a transatlantic exodus," said Frondner. "We have no idea of the difficulties of moving that many refugees to this hemisphere in their timeline, or even what kind of seagoing or other transport is available."

"There must be some sort of interaction between continents," said Brant. "The Alcon establishment can inform us what the options are. However, time is pressing for the Trust enclave. Rajulk is tied up with the pending birth of his first child, so I will have to go myself and take Dolf since he has the TR pertaining to that timeline, and he knows where the transfer point is."

"I won't be tied up forever," said Rajulk. "I can stand by if things get hairy."

"I'll go with you," said Lila. "Bad things can happen if you are alone in that age."

"All right," said Brant slowly with a wary look at his volatile soul mate. "Let's get on with it. To now, we have encountered a barely controllable set of complications in our probes. We will go after our soiree with Bromfsted this Saturday."

———————————

"He is in the foyer with his moll," said Lila.

"Show them in. Let's get it over with," said Brant, looking up from some charts.

A moment later, Lila conducted Bromfsted and Defoe through the maze of equipment to where Brant was standing.

"General, it's such a pleasure to welcome you and your charming aide," said Brant. "I remember you in that striking costume at the celebration," he added evoking a subtle wince from Bromfsted. [21]

"Lila, please," said Brant turning … *Now where did she go?* "Uh … I will give you the standard tour of our junky lab and explain the highlights of our efforts. First, I am sure you would like to see the chamber from which we dispatched the specimen of Americium a few seconds back in time. It's over here."

Brant showed them what could have been construed as such and went on to explain the various banks of instrumentation scattered about the lab.

"What is that space over there, enclosed in the array of metal stakes?" asked Bromfsted, pointing. "It stands out because it is free of the clutter."

"That is … or, rather represents our efforts to ramp up the size of the specimen," said Brant, annoyed that the actual transfer space had attracted undue attention.

Bromfsted and Defoe sauntered over, entered the space, and looked around.

He turned to Defoe to say something. It happened all at once. The hum and glow of the transfer field came to life, and the couple dimmed and disappeared. Brant turned wide-eyed toward the lab control room, the only place that could have activated the transporter. Lila was there behind the soundproof glass waving with a sardonic grin on her face. Brant rushed to the control room as Lila sauntered out.

"What did you do?"

"Fixed the old goat for good."

"Wha—where did you send him? We must retrieve them and explain, or at least … try to," said Brant his voice trailing off.

"Now how can we do that? He now knows we can do it and will infer that we have done it many times. If I set the parameters right, he resides not too far in the past. He will pass on before he is born so that, god forbid, we won't have the paradox of a duplicate Bromfsted."

"To when exactly did you send him?" asked Brant straining for calm in the face of an irreversible event.

"Let me see … to precisely 2010," said Lila, consulting the instruments and responding in her most obnoxious businesslike voice."

"That's before Obamapolis was even here! He and Defoe will end up in a vacant countryside!"

"The interstate runs not too far to the south. He can get his bearings by quizzing the locals and make his way back to Washington or some other place his background might serve him."

"What about Defoe?"

"They can become a couple," said Lila gleefully.

"Oh, how romantic," said Brant in his most sarcastic tone. He scanned the lab in quick flicks hoping that some phantom might appear to tell him what had just happened didn't really happen. "I must tell Frondner about this and prepare some damage control if there is a big hoopla about their disappearance."

XV

Bromfsted and Defoe Stand Ensnared in a Time Transfer

Bromfsted and Defoe stood wavering as the landscape took form.

"Where in hell are we?" groused the still dizzy general as he and Defoe scanned the surrounds.

"It looks like Conjular and the ITR crew did a number on us," said Defoe, self-contained in spite of their radical change of venue. "They had gone much further with time travel than they admitted, and they concocted that ruse of a celebration party dramatizing a miniscule advance to throw us off the track."

"It's that holier-than-thou attitude of the scientific community. In any case, they are trifling with the government and jeopardizing national security. They will pay dearly," said Bromfsted who had not quite come to terms with his predicament.

"That may not be so easily done," said Defoe at once the realist. "From what I can surmise, they have put us somewhere in the past. We have to figure out the period they have put us in and how to survive before we even try to find some way to return to our original era."

"There's a country road over there that looks somewhat up to date," said Bromfsted, slowly coming to grips with reality. "Let's trudge along it. Maybe a car or horse and buggy will come along. If we are still located at the same point we were sent from, we should be in northern Kansas."

They set out along the road. In the distance to the left, a barn with a silo appeared.

"Looks post-Columbus," said Bromfsted with sarcasm, still teetering between the rational and mad-dog syndrome. "What's that coming toward us?"

"It's an automobile for sure, a small truck," said Defoe.

"Well, at least we are in the era of the internal combustion engine," said Bromfsted as he hailed the oncoming vehicle. "Now, just what should I say to this Neanderthal?"

"Better update your exchange a few thousand years," said Defoe, for the first time complementing her frosty exterior with an undertone of humor. "I don't think you can fashion an automobile out of rock."

Bromfsted waxed sarcastic. "How about, 'Excuse me sir, but I have just come from the future, and I need some orientation for this era. Could you direct me to the nearest center of civilization, so that I might assess its features?'"

"That should go over great," said Defoe as the car slowed and stopped.

"Howdy," said the driver as he rolled down the window. "You folks need a lift? I'm headed south to Cawker City."

"Thank you," said Defoe as Bromfsted stood by quietly in an effort to contain himself.

They squeezed into the front seat with Defoe in the middle having to move her knees each time the driver shifted gears.

"How'd you folks come to be out here in the middle of nowhere?" asked the driver.

Bromfsted remained in a silent, stubborn, stupor while Defoe scrambled for some reasonable explanation.

"Uh … well, we were flying over this part of the country and had to ditch our plane. We barely escaped alive."

Bromfsted did a slow take at his creative partner.

"You folks part of the military?"

Bromfsted was suddenly aware that their garb, however sparse, was unmistakably a uniform.

"Yes," said Bromfsted, curtly coming to life.

"Fort Riley is about a hundred miles south of here. You can probably rent a car somewhere or hitch another ride to connect with the military down there."

"Thank you," said Defoe, breaking the ensuing silence to preempt any perceived barb by Bromfsted. *Riley is as good a place as any, since we are more familiar with military culture than the uncertainties of civilian life.*

They arrived in Cawker City and hitched a ride south. After two more lifts, they were drop off at the entrance of Fort Riley.

"Now what?" asked the continually flustered Bromfsted, having given the initiative over to Defoe.

Defoe scanned the soldiers and civilians going in and out. *Maybe this was not such a good idea after all.* "Our uniforms are out of date—not in the usual antiquated sense, of course. We might be considered kooks doing military dress-up. On the other hand, the rank insignias haven't changed much through the years, so ours may be generic enough to pass as some specialist branch of the service. In any case, we are entirely without resources and must go with what we know. We have to chance it.

Bromfsted was having the same thoughts. They nodded to each other and strolled toward the base entrance. The two soldiers at rest gave a cursory glance and salute, which Bromfsted briskly returned as he passed through the gate, affecting his most superior bearing.

"That's a mess hall over there," said Bromfsted. "If you are as hungry as I am, we should visit there first."

They filed in with Bromfsted returning several salutes of individual soldiers exiting. He motioned to the right. "That's the officers' section over there." They sauntered up, took a tray, and joined the cue.

The standard military food filled the need after a stressful day. Speaking in undertones, Bromfsted, now more contained and suddenly aware that they were locked together by a bizarre set of events, reassessed their situation.

"In the near term, we are both tired and need some place to billet. We can find some temporary quarters and look for a way forward tomorrow. I am not sure we can fake our way here indefinitely."

"Okay, there should be women's quarters somewhere. I will see if I can worm my way in. We can meet here at breakfast tomorrow and plan ahead," said Defoe giving her gruff superior a warm smile.

Don't tell me there's a real woman behind that ice, thought Bromfsted as they parted.

The next morning they met, revived by the freshness of day.

"I think I can use my expertise in military security to our advantage, but I will have to bluff my way through it," said Bromfsted. "Few challenge the credentials of a general officer. Looking around, I don't see any women as adjutants to the brass. They are all men. I will divvy up some transfer orders, needle my way into the IG, and get an office. I will crank up some paperwork to get you on in some clerk position. It will probably get lost in the abyss of army bureaucracy and nobody will think of looking closely at it. " From across the table he took her hand. "We are in this together. At my rank, I can design my own uniform, but we need to get you some civvies. The local Post Exchange should do it."

Defoe's frigid countenance softened as she again favored Bromfsted with a smile.

Bromfsted had just settled in when a corporal knocked, entered, and saluted.

"At your convenience, General Sneed requests your presence in his office sir."

Better get it over with, thought Bromfsted. Waiting the required interval consistent with his perceived status, Bromfsted wandered over to Sneed's office.

Concluding the ritual formalities, Sneed sat at his desk and stared at his newcomer. "Frankly, I was wondering why Washington needed to overload the IG at this time. We have no extraordinary security threats here."

"It's a pilot program," said Bromfsted, reviewing what he remembered about the history of the US military. "The pentagon got a wild hair and started getting creative. [22] I'll chip in and take some of the load off your paperwork and report back in accordance with the directive." *That was vague enough … maybe too vague*, thought Bromfsted. *Let's see how it plays out.*

"I would like to see this directive," said Sneed.

"I'll get you a copy, and you see if you can make sense out of it," said Bromfsted stalling. *Maybe he will just forget it.*

Three days later, Bromfsted was in his office when an attachment of soldiers showed up.

"We have orders to conduct you to confinement," said the sergeant in charge.

"By whose authority," said Bromfsted in his most official tone.

"Base commander General Norman at the request of General Sneed, sir."

Bromfsted remained quiet as he was handcuffed and paraded through the assemblege of transfixed office personnel of the IG. He caught Defoe's eye as he passed by her desk. She gave a faint nod realizing that their luck had run out and wondered if and how long it would take to link her with the now discredited Bromfsted?

For the alert Defoe, the day passed without further incident, except for endless office gossip about what had taken place.

Defoe considered. *Authority is so compartmentalized here that* **A** *doesn't know or particularly care what is going on with* **B**. Waiting a day, she ambled over to the stockade.

"I would like to visit General Bromfsted."

The bored noncom staffing the entry responded by handing Defoe a clipboard with a form. "Here, fill this out."

Defoe looked over the form and paused at an entry, Relationship to the Incarcerated: Spouse, Relative, Friend. Spouse ... *Spouse—too close, I could be implicated in whatever charges they have in mind for him,* thought Defoe. *On the other hand, depending on which way he wants to take it, as his wife, I could reinforce whatever strategy he has in mind.*

She handed the form to the noncom and was conducted to visitor's area. A row of windows with perforations to permit the passage of sound separated the visitors from the prisoners.

Bromfsted settled in the chair opposite and gazed at his anxious aide.

"I'm glad you came. I thought you had abandoned me," said a relieved Bromfsted.

"Not a chance," assured Defoe. "I wanted to wait till the base hoopla about a fake officer settled down. At the prelim hearing, how do you want to play it?"

"Haven't decided. The truth is out, of course. I barely believe it myself."

"How about you go the loony route? I can back it up. I put myself down as your wife."

Bromfsted's stony countenance softened perceptibly before responding. "That may be the easiest way out. Given my age, and the fact that I am to all intense and purposes, a civilian, there's not too much they can do to me."

"Okay, I'll back you up. We can be out of here, and ... take it from there," said Defoe.

A hearing was held two days later. Defoe who identified herself as his wife was called to testify.

"Yes, I wondered what he had been up to," Defoe told the panel. "He has had so much time on his hands having retired last year that he is living out some unfulfilled fantasy of being in the military."

"He sure had me fooled," said General Sneed when he took the stand before the panel. "We could fine him for trespassing on the base, but he seems harmless."

After receiving a dressing down by the presiding officer, the MPs ushered Bromfsted out, accompanied by Defoe.

Deposited outside the entrance to the base, they looked at each other, for the first time relieved of the tensions of their deception. By common impulse, they burst out laughing.

Bromfsted managed to speak through the lingering atmosphere of mirth, "I still have a bit of cash from the temp pay, which they seem to have forgotten about in their haste to get rid of me. Let's grab a bite and try to figure out something else to survive."

"You probably have skills of your own relevant in the civilian world, like weapons procurement for instance. We only have to find and exploit them," said Defoe, yet again favoring Bromfsted with a generous smile and determined not to leave him dangling. "In the meantime, I have secretarial knowhow and should be able to get a job someplace to tide us over."

Bromfsted, momentarily silent in the face of their subtle shift of roles, spoke up. "Then we'd best migrate east toward Kansas City and make our way to Washington. We can disappear into the bureaucracy and find more opportunity there. There are numerous civilian advisors to the military, and I have a storehouse of info to lean on. I will have to get some civvies' to blend in, since my uniform has no relevance in this era, but for now, in transit, it will be a plus. My recollection is that the army has held a measure of respect through the years, except in that era of the Vietnam War where soldiers were spat upon due to its controversial aspect."

"We should bunk together to save the few resources we have—if it's all right with you," said Defoe to a hesitant nod from the straight-laced Bromfsted.

XVI

Plans Made to Relocate the Trust Enclave

Brant, not quite recovered from the unscheduled dispatch of their nemeses, Bromfsted and Defoe, arrived along with the others at the transfer point near the Mediterranean.

"The transfer point is set up inland a few meters higher now," said Seth. "You shouldn't have any problems at the downtime relay point. Since its original purpose was only to make contact with the Trust's timeline, it is more or less dormant now."

"Okay, let's get to it," said Brant. "The situation with Bromfsted will have to sit for now, but we will need at least to check on them when things clear up. For the immediate task, we have some emergency subsistence supplies with us, but we may have to improvise later."

After the familiar disorientation of the transfer, they stood looking at the blue Mediterranean in the near distance and the now familiar simi-desert of ancient Egypt. Fleeting glimpses of ancient Pelusium loomed in the distance.

Dolf hesitated a moment and motioned. "This way, I recognize the landscape and dead trees."

They walked a half an hour or so before Dolf signaled a halt. He sighted the marker s that he and Kara had put down to delineate the bounce point into the Trust's timeline. Retrieving his TR, he activated it. The temporary Trust lab in Alcon sprang to life as the retinue of time travelers appeared.

Binzing and the techies of the Trust approached and surveyed the disparate group from the alternate timeline. Brant, Lila, and Dolf stared back.

"Glad you are okay," said Binzing. "We were worried since we had not heard from you since you transferred."

"We ran into some trouble in ancient Pelusium," said Dolf. "After some confusion, we finally connected with our friends from the Christian timeline. Just as we were returning, some Roman soldiers on a recruiting campaign sidetracked Rajulk, but we expect him to worm his way out of it and show up later. Kara stayed in their timeline as backup for the contact. They have discussed the plight of our enclave, and Brant has suggested moving it to the great double continent to the west, which they call the Americas. If this has the agreement of the Trust, we need to send a delegation to find some promising place to settle. We can consult with the Alcon leaders about what mode of transport may be available to take us to this new land."

"That seems like the best of an assortment of bad alternatives for a fresh start," said Binzing after a pause. "Due to the chaos of the Flood, uncertainty lies in the states to the north, and even small portions of the land there are probably already claimed.[23] This place to the west, how would you suggest getting us there?"

"We offer our services to that end," said Brant.

"All right, on the condition we find a suitable place to settle, we will go," said Binzing. "The Alconian fathers may know something about how to get there."

Informed of the reappearance of Dolf and the others, Marzin appeared to greet them.

"The jump off place for travel to the double continent to the west is called Anfa and is located to the south of the narrow straits separating the inland sea from the vast ocean which extends westward," said Marzin. "Anfa is more than two thousand miles away. You can reach it most quickly by taking air transport, by balloon, from Alexandria some fifty miles from here. There are numerous shuttle boats on the coast to get you from here to Alexandria."

Alexandria … at least that is familiar, but Anfa, thought Brant visualizing Africa's Atlantic coast. *It is probably some ancient name for Casablanca that stuck because its history is doubtless different in this timeline.*

"It sounds like a long way," said Binzing. "I will need the permission of the Trust leadership, but the enclave is depending on me to find a viable place to settle. I hope the Alconians will put up with us until it is resolved, and that we are not embarking on the quest for a raving boar."

"We would say 'a wild goose chase' in the English variant of Anglo we speak," said Lila over Brant's snicker and echoed by Binzing's own.

After the hop to Alexandra, the balloon to Anfa took three days.

"Glad to be off that thing and the rat-tat-tat of the engine if you can call it that," said Lila.

"Now to gain passage to the west," said Brant. "I am a little leery of these balloons, but the folks running them seem to take the uncertainties in stride."

An agreement on the schedule and price for the trip was hammered out, and the travelers settled in the balloon's primitive quarters for the journey. After several days, the balloon moored in the tropical city of Blairton.

"Let's see what kinds of accommodations are available," said Brant. "The flora and fauna here are tropical, so we appear to be on the northern coast of South America. Aside from some settled areas near the coast, it is sparsely populated. Blairton is the name the captain kept throwing around. It wasn't familiar, but we may be in what is called Fortaleza in our timeline."

"In any case, we are now starting from scratch. We should first let Binzing try to do his thing with the Trust enclave's stash of gold."

Brant scanned what passed as the urban area of the settlement. "That saloon or … maybe better, that church-like building over there seems to be good place to inquire.

There is probably some sort of overseer there, and we are not likely to get into trouble with the clergy. They may give us a clue as to who owns what around here. In the meantime, the rest of you see if you can find something resembling a hotel."

Lila and Dolf left in quest of lodging while Brant and Binzing passed through the portal into the dimness of the modest building. A few devout parishioners sat in silent meditation. A figure entered from a side door and stood in appraisal of the interior's arrangement that only superficially resembled that of a church. He strode over to a lectern and shuffled the pages of a book, but looked up when he noticed the newcomers. Not wanting to violate the somewhat dubious sanctity of the scene they stood quietly as the man approached.

Frustrated by the linguistic barrier presented by this timeline, Brant took a chance that the man may have some knowledge of Anglo. "Sir, we inquire as to the availability of a generous plot of land in order to settle our comrades who will travel to this place from afar."

To Brant's relief, the official of the temple responded in kind, in heavily accented but understandable Anglo. "You may be in luck. A local rancher has decided to relocate to the south. He will transport his livestock, but will dispose of his land and other assets. I can direct you to his villa, if you wish."

Binzing broke in. "Yes indeed, we will be anxious to view the property and talk with the owner, but we are on foot and need transportation, at least temporarily."

"A livery stable is only two blocks that way," said the man with a nod. "They can supply you with a carriage or horses."

Binzing mounted the driver's seat of the carriage and motioned to Brant. "Let me see if I can manage these animals. We used horses intermittently in our interaction with the Garuletzsky."

They followed the directions of the official and soon encountered a well-kept pathway bordered by an ordered set of palm trees. In the distance, a white villa of considerable size peeked through the array of tree trunks as the way forward curved to the right. Scattered around the complex were mounds resembling pillboxes, which were dotted with numerous small openings.

"Those look like some sort of defense structure," said Brant pointing as they pulled up in front of the house. A servant came out to greet them.

"We would like to speak to the master of the house on business," said Brant, in Anglo, chancing he would be understood.

"One moment," responded the servant in kind. "Mr. Longton is in the garden with another client."

They waited for half an hour before two men strolled through the foyer. The older and crustier of the two was saying, "I will consider your offer, but it falls far short of what the property is worth."

When the visitor was gone, Longton turned to the newcomers and remarked sarcastically, "Are you interested in the property, too? What kind of miserly offer do you have?"

"Whatever you think it is worth," said Binzing without missing a beat.

Somewhat taken off guard at the absence of haggling, Longton hesitated.

"Well ... considering the going price for land, and the intact structures, and amenities I leave behind, the equivalent of fifty thousand Drakes in gold is fair in my opinion."

"Pending a thorough inspection of the property, I can give you a goodly sum in the form of gold in advance, but the balance must await the arrival of the courier from overseas, which will take at least two weeks depending on the availability of *wavant* communications in this area."

"Such can be found at the town's communication center," said Longton. "In the meantime, I will give you a preliminary tour of my holdings."

"I am impressed," said Binzing after they had completed the tour. "I was wondering what the mounds arranged around the main house were meant to protect against."

"Local Indians, who see us as intruders on their traditional turf," said Longton. "They harass us frequently with primitive weapons, deadly if one happens to become the victim of one."

Shades of the Garuletzsky, only in this case it is serious; not play war, thought Binzing.

"It's more than we could have expected," said Binzing as they left the Longton compound. "As for the Indian threat, they can't be much worse than the Xerjinko—in intent, that is. Historically, at least, they may have some claim on the land, but given it is a fait accompli, they may be more open to some sort of accommodation."

A pensive Brant looked off in to space. "With the Drake as currency, the use of Anglo widespread, and Longton a big land owner, I'm getting the impression that the Anglo-Saxon presence in this hemisphere is dominant. What ever happened to the great Spanish Portuguese sweep west with the Christian message? The Moorish influence in this timeline must have remained dominant in the Hispanic realm to deter it. I guess we should not look for any of the familiar place names on this or the off-limits North American continent. I wonder what they call all the great cities to the south like Rio de Janeiro and Buenos Aires."

"Never heard of any of them," said Binzing. "It points out the divergent paths our timelines took after the split."

The first envoys of the Trust arrived ahead of schedule.

"Fenart, we are glad to see you," said Binzing. "What is the status of the Trust? Are the Alconians getting impatient with our presence?"

"Somewhat, but they are sympathetic with our plight, knowing that invasion by rogue forces could uproot Alcon, too," said Fenart, surrounded by several of the Trust security. "We have the funds in gold you requested and have alerted the whole compound to prepare for transport to this continent. Due to limited space, transport by balloon is feasible only for an advance guard essential to the establishment of this new colony. For the bulk of the enclave, including what technology we managed to save, we will travel by sea making the passage in two convoys."

"Good, we need to close with Longton before he has second thoughts," said Binzing. "Do you have any information on just what sort of vehicles they have for travel by sea?"

"They combine a number of seagoing modes including sail, hydrofoil, and screw propeller drives, depending on the conditions en route," said Fenart. "They get weather reports by *wavant* from the continual passage of balloons."

"That's a relief," said Binzing. "It eliminates some of the uncertainty."

"The citizens of the Trust enclave are waiting for word of what's next," said Fenart. "We will signal them to organize the armadas and start immediately."

"Things are under control," said Brant. "If you think you can handle the logistics of getting the Trust populace here, we will return to our timeline and start the process of creating the link in this hemisphere. We do not need a continuation of the convoluted process of contact through the Alcon locale and making the journey here. Hopefully, the uptime local government will be as pliable as the Egyptians were when it comes to establishing facilities on their territory. Assuming all goes according to plan; we will establish a new bounce point near Blairton at the usual 40 B.C. date and wait for your envoys. Dolf is known to us, so send him and perhaps another. Arm them both for extra cover. We have no idea who or what hostile elements may be at the bounce point at that time."

"We will be on alert for that too," said Binzing. "Give us a year or so to settle the Trust populace and set up for contact through the 40B.C bounce point you suggest."

Brant and Lila took the next balloon transfer back to Casablanca and onto Alexandria. They alighted from the shuttle boat and looked around. Brant pointed. "The Pelusium transfer point is over that way. It will be a relief to finally get back."

"Ditto on that," said Lila, with a lilt reflecting fatigue from prolonged encounters with the unfamiliar.

Taking out the TR linked to the Christian timeline, he looked around before activating it.

"Is the whole time travel club here?" asked Brant playfully as they assembled in the lab back in Obamapolis for an update.

"It's a boy!" said Rajulk with excitement, preempting Brant's pronouncements on the growing complications about contact with the Trust timeline. "Aspira is already playing big sister to him in the crib."

"That's great," said Brant. "It brings a warm feeling that once again something tangibly positive has come from these time travel escapades. Now, the issue at hand is to cement for good, a link with the one timeline we have contacted, that is, a more direct link that replaces the awkward Pelusium-Alcon pathway. For this, we must first establish a transfer base on the northern coast near Fortaleza. I have started talking to Brazilian authorities about it, in general terms of course. They haven't the slightest idea what we are really up to. In any case, there appear to be no obstacles since we have good relations with them. Just as we did when we linked with Alcon, we will jump to the agreed upon bounce point of 30 B.C. for that location, and once again await reps of the Trust with the TRs connected to their timeline. We must go prepared. It is long before there is much detailed knowledge of the indigenous tribes of the area. God knows what's at the bounce point to create trouble."

"At least we will be far away while that Anthony and Cleopatra mess is going on at Actium," said Rajulk.

Six months later, Frondner managed, through diplomatic, channels to obtain permission to establish a base for research near the city of Fortaleza.

"The equipment is in place for the transfer," said Brant. "Seth and I have been tinkering with it for three weeks, and it is up to speed. I hope the Trust itself is on schedule."

IN THE TIMELINE OF THE TRUST

The officer in charge of communications hurried into the Trust's command center in Blairton. "It's a *wavant* from some unknown source claiming they have the ships of the second armada in seclusion and are demanding ransom."

"It may be a hoax, but the balance of our enclave citizens is overdue," said Binzing.

A tattered sailing ship staggered into the port at Blairton. A tired citizen hurried off the boat with his arm in a sling.

"What happened?" asked Binzing his voice fraught with alarm. "You are late, but we thought it was weather related."

"The bulk of the ships was hijacked and taken south. Ours is the only one that got away. Lenyon, our leader, was captured along with the others," said the Trust citizen.

"Can you tell us more?" asked Binzing as they settled into the makeshift hospital with Danbro and others of the Trust.

"Only that the men spoke Latin, of all things, and were dressed in monk's robes," said the citizen, wincing as the med examined his arm. "I heard mention of some place they called Portsmouth,"

"Probably their base," said Binzing.

"It's most likely situated in a natural harbor. Even with our superior weapons, this may be more than our forces can handle," said Danbro who had joined Binzing and the wounded citizen at the clinic. "We need to contact the Christian timeline and ask for help."

"I will go but I will still have to return to Pelusium to make the contact," said Binzing. "Even though we are ahead of schedule here to link in this hemisphere, we can't just show up in the Christian timeline in some uncertain location without some coordination with them. Once I am in Pelusium, I can transfer uptime, connect with Brant by phone, and tell him of our situation. Luckily we shared all that equipment early on."

––––––––––––––

"It's a Mr. Binzing," said the lab assistant.

"*What is he doing here in this timeline,* thought Brant. *Something must have happened.*

"Daner, what's up? The time of our linkup in this hemisphere is still months away."

"Yes, it is ahead of schedule and will be up soon, but for the moment, lacking it, I had to return all the way to Pelusium and transfer to its uptime site to link with you," said Binzing. "The situation is this: The second of the armadas bringing the Trust contingent was intercepted by pirates and taken south. We have is little info as to who they are and what they want, but it is probable that they have taken refuge in some natural harbor. Also unknown is what lies south of the Trust's new enclave in general. Longton mentioned moving south when he sold out, so we can eliminate his presumably civilized site from the choices."

"As far as the pirates are concerned, the locals in that hemisphere probably know something," said Brant. "We need to question them, even if it means going once again by that circuitous route to get there. I'll talk it over with Rajulk and the others to see if we can do anything about it. The upside is that we are ahead of schedule with the link in the Americas."

"I'm not surprised there is such mischief in the seemingly untamed southern continent of their timeline," said Rajulk as Brant consulted with him. "We at least need to investigate and see if there is anything we can do. We know little of what lies to the south of the Trust's new enclave, but the locals in that hemisphere probably know where the riffraff hang out. It's unfortunate that this has happened just as we are both just about ready for the new link. My suggestion is that you return to Fortaleza and wait for the contact to materialize."

XVII

The Timelines Establish a New Linkage

From the edge of the transfer perimeter of the Trust's improvised lab, Binzing surveyed the jumble of equipment needed for the transfer. "Rather primitive compared with the first one in the Trust enclave, but as long as we can keep it up and running, we will have a link to the past and hopefully, to the other timeline."

"It's been only six months, and it's in place ahead of schedule," said Danbro. "Fortunately, we have been able to establish a stable economy and relations with friendly elements in the area, and we can still produce unique products for exchange in spite of our still compromised community. The trauma of our displacement will be long in dissipating. The hostile elements we were warned of have yet to appear, but there is evidence that we are being watched. At this point, they are deterred by the unfamiliar course of our activities. But if they still covet this land as a traditional right, we may yet see trouble."

"I agree, but unless they mount some kind of attack, we need not worry about them," said Binzing. "For now, we need to concentrate on the contact. And when the time transfer equipment is up to speed, we can head off trouble by exploring conditions at the downtime rendezvous point before linkup."

"For the contact itself, I think myself and ... perhaps one other person will be enough."

"Volunteers?" asked Danbro addressing those assembled.

"I'll go," said Dolf from the front row.

"That didn't take long," said Danbro with a laugh.

"All right, make sure you have your supplies and weapons. No sense waiting any longer," said Binzing.

After a moment of disorientation, the two found themselves in thick jungle.

"There you are," said Danbro as he moved aside a subtropical shrub. "We could use one of those, what do you call them, machetes. We didn't foresee ending up in such a thicket, so we will have to hack our way out of it some way."

"I can burn away a path out of here with my laser to make it a little less confining," said Dolf.

"Good, the charred foliage will also give us a way of finding this spot when we return. Also, since this will be the relay point into our timeline, we need to dress it up a little," said Danbro.

"Okay, I will burn a circle and we can clear it off and maybe put an identifying object here to mark the spot. If we are lucky, we have hit the rendezvous date on the nose and will not have to wait long. The temperature is moderate, too. That helps."

"Yes, we won't have to fight the elements, but the insects are already eating away at my exposed —"

A spear thudded into a tree to the side of Dolf and Danbro.

"Where did it come from?" shouted Dolf.

"I don't know, but we'd better take cover," snapped Danbro.

"Over there," said Dolf responding in kind and pointing as he hit the ground.

Another spear flew overhead.

"Stay down while I see if I can reduce the surrounding foliage with this laser," said Danbro. "We can't stun them until we can see them."

He sprayed the nearby growth, causing howls of distress and the rustle of their fleeing nemeses as they escaped.

Dolf pointed. "It's fairly clear in that direction, but it's still too enclosed the rest of the way around. I'll burn away all but a sliver of it. We will need some cover ourselves while we rig something more permanent."

Several minutes passed as Dolf sprayed the circle, leaving only a leafy wedge-shaped woodlet.

"The tip of my forest sculpture now more or less points to our transfer point," said Dolf surveying his work. "A fortunate byproduct of this encounter, not permanent, but it will do as a marker for now."

"We need to build some kind of structure for protection," said Dolf. "The trees here are soft wood but will suffice until we can figure out something more durable." He pointed. "You keep watch on any movement those larger trees there, while I check them out."

Dolf started to make his way through the pie-shaped growth cover, but was summoned back by his dumbfounded colleague.

"What do you make of that?" asked Danbro as he stared across the burnt out, open space.

Several natives were slinking forward, heads bowed, with arms extended holding items. Bare to the waist, they had covered their bodies with an assortment of symbols of incomprehensible meaning.

"That looks like an inventory of their pantries and handicrafts," said Dolf. "We are in luck. They seem to think we are gods."

"I think you are right. We must rise to the task, but with benevolence," said Danbro. "Let's just hope they don't confuse it with weakness. I will break out some goody from our supplies as a peace offering."

The two emerged from cover and approached the natives. One excessively adorned native crept to the front with a primitive vessel of pottery.

Danbro accepted the vessel and presented a sweetened high protein wafer in return. He took one, bit off a chunk, and chewed it as the native watched. The native seemed to understand and did likewise as the others looked on.

"We are not likely to understand a word, if they start talking," said Dolf.

"Right," said Danbro. "But we have broken the ice. I wonder if we fried anybody with that laser sweep."

"I was wondering the same," said Dolf. "We should do a quick once-over of the attackers. A little first aid will go a long way toward cementing good relations."

In the rear of the rustic phalanx, several of the natives had received varying doses of the laser sweep. They shrank back as the two approached.

"Let's start with that one," said Dolf pointing. "He seems to be the worst off. It's like a bad sunburn. Hand me some pain-killers and moistening salve from the pack."

They tended to those most affected by the laser, and finally convinced the natives to retire.

"I hope that ends it, and that we can concentrate on the contact," said Dolf with a sigh.

"If we have the date right, they can't be far," said Danbro. "Brant knew where we were on the coast here. He cautioned us not to get too close since neither of us knew what sort of paradox would result if two transfer points leading to two different timelines overlapped. Now, we just have to wait it out."

In the Christian Timeline

"No sense waiting," said Brant as he, Lila, Rajulk, and LeBrust sat in the improvised lab at Fortaleza. "I hope the Trust has it together on their end and is either there or will be soon. Unfortunately, we have to thread a needle on the rendezvous date. In any case, it's time to go. Thankfully, we had no trouble with the Brazilian authorities in setting up, and they haven't been nosing around in suspicion that we are doing something against their national interests."

"Yes, and I was lucky to get off from my job at the university," said Rajulk. "Meriam is okay with it too since the kid is doing fine. We named him Mark Vanor Petrov in deference to the duo we brought back from the Roman jaunt." [24]

"That's fitting," said Brant. "Every time I look at him, it will bring back memories of our venture there—the good ones, not the close calls."

"How do we actually make contact when we get there?" asked Lila, returning to the present.

"Ah," said Brant craftily. "I have a bunch of weather balloons definitely out of sync with the prehistory age we will be probing. Such an anomaly will doubtless attract the attention of the Trust reps. Now, all set? Okay, Seth will send us along to the agreed-upon date."

The instant change from a dry environment was dramatic. They emerged in the open to a driving rain whose rush competed with the surf bathing the shore a short distance away.

"We need to find some cover till this blows over," yelled Brant over nature's cacophony that muted any manmade sound.

Lila's voice lifted above the din. "How come we end up in water half the time?"

"Don't exaggerate," said Brant, only half-serious. "The only other time was near Pelusium. That was our fault for not realizing the coastline could change. This time it is the weather. Try to change that! At least it is warm here. I will put down a temporary marker, but as a backup, we all need to memorize where we are from points on the surrounds. The rest of you make for that grove of palms over there and wait for me."

Assembling in the grove, they huddled under the largest specimen while Brant drove a stake of dead wood in the ground.

"These ain't oaks," griped Lila as the water dripped off her nose.

"Better than nothing," said Rajulk with a laugh.

Brant joined them. "We have no idea how long this soaker will last so we might as well try to build some sort of shelter. Let's see … those four palms over there are close enough together to form a rough rectangle. Eyeball the distance between them and cut a couple of lengths from the palms on the periphery. We can notch the ends, and with some of the twine in our kits, attach them on two opposing sides—one about six feet up and the other slightly lower for a sloping roof. If we can get this done, we can shove enough trunks on top to make a slanting roof and pile the fronds on top. That should give us some relief."

Wielding the lasers, several of the tall *Arecaceae* came swishing down in a cloud of smoke and the sizzle of charred wood. The zany structure gradually took form. At last done, they retired to its interior.

"I'm soaked," said LeBrust as they crammed in, drenched, but for the moment out of the torrent. "Lousy luck that we landed in the most resource-free area of the coast. I wonder if the Trust folks are in the same situation."

"They have to be or at least, I hope they are. Otherwise it could mean they are far away," said Rajulk.

"Okay, it has to letup sometime," said Brant. "We just have to wait it out."

THE TRUST PROBES FOR CONTACT

Dark clouds rolled in signaling an impending storm.

"We've hit the rainy season," said Danbro. "Maybe our newly befriended natives will give us some shelter. They disappeared in that direction, so their settlement can't be far. Let's mosey over there and feel them out."

As they approached the cluster of grass huts, spritz of rain bathed the camp. Several of the natives retreated to escape their recognized nemeses while others ran towards what appeared to be a centralized point. A well-adorned Elder emerged from the hut and stood resolute and unbowed as the newcomers approached. "That's the chief," said Danbro. "He has undoubtedly heard about us, but is determined to show courage in the face of the unknown. What have we in our kits to offer him?"

"How about a pocket knife," said Dolf. "They surely have knives of sort, but the novelty of a folding one may grab him. Best not show too much deference as his tribe, whom I see watching, might interpret it as weakness."

With a truncated bow and a brief nod, Danbro took out the knife and held it out for the chief to see. He then opened the main blade and showed it again. He then closed it and handed it to the chief.

The chief took it and puzzled over the primitive manipulation needed to render the knife functional.

Danbro slowly retrieved it, held it out, and moved closer. Placing his fingernail in the groove of the blade, he again pried the blade open. Once again closing it, he handed it back to the chief, who, to his obvious pleasure, mimicked Danbro's action.

"I think the ice is broken," mumbled Dolf. The chief made the universal 'come with me' gesture as the rain started really coming down.

They followed the chief into the hut and sat cross-legged around a fire. A kettle tended by a woman of the same vintage as the chief sizzled away in a corner.

"Probably the wife or one of them," said Dolf

She ladled a portion of the primitive gruel into a trio of hollowed out gourds and handed it to Dolf and Danbro.

"Should we?" asked Dolf.

"Hasn't killed them … yet," said Danbro, appending the qualification after a slight hesitation.

He took a sip and shrugged, "At least as good as our rations. I don't want to know what's in it. After the ritual of contact here, whatever here is, we could use some shelter until this storm blows over."

As if sensing the stranger's plight, the chief conducted them to a nearby hut, rousing some of the natives from a primitive game involving the random fall of tossed animal bones. Dolf and Danabro spent a restless night in the hut as the hubbub of the village came diminished to silence.

For those from the Christian timeline, the rain continued through the night, and dwindled to droplets at dawn. The sun rose and baked the soaked landscape. A crystalline blue sky formed the backdrop to a landscape dotted with palms, other fauna, and the now visible surf rolling just beyond.

"It's all but stopped," said Brant. "Anybody still damp will soon dry out. Let's head for the beach and launch a balloon."

The others arose from a collective stupor, shielding their eyes from the brilliance of tropical daylight.

"There. That's good open space," said Brant pointing.

Brant took out a balloon and started blowing it up manually. "I feel a little light headed," he said as the balloon, still somewhat limp, swayed in the breeze coming from offshore. "In any case, just a little bit more will do it. It will expand as it gains altitude. We have to balance its buoyancy with the low altitude we wish it to settle in to attract attention. Too high and it would be almost invisible or mistaken for a bird. We'll have to wing it."

The first try landed the balloon in a palm as a rush of wind swept it out of Brant's grasp.

"It's hopelessly snagged up there," said Brant as he took out another balloon and inflated it. Waiting until there was a lull in the fickle breeze, he launched it and watched as it cleared the palms, moving east.

"Good. If they are anywhere nearby and spot it, they will know it is us," said Rajulk. "We must stay here and maybe start a smoky fire."

For the Trust envoys, the rain finally tapered off and patches of brilliant blue began to appear in the cloud breaks. Dolf and Danbro emerged from the hut. A group of the natives rushed to the chief's hut as the balloon floated lazily across the village clearing at some two hundred feet.

"It's them. It has to be," said Danbro.

The chief emerged and pondered the mysterious omen, the second time in a day coping with an anomalous occurrence disrupting the ordered state of the tribe.

"It is floating east, so it came from west of here. Let's make for the shore and look for them."

"There they are," said Dolf excitedly as they spotted the fire and those lolling around it.

All stood and waved as the Trust envoys came forward in a brisk walk.

"It is a relief to see you," said Brant. "The vague parameters of the connection scheme always left us with a degree of uncertainty. Now, in order to have unencumbered access to each other's timelines, we need to accurately mark our insertion points and at least get an idea of their positions relative to one another."

"Yes, we ended up about six hundred of your meters in that direction," said Danbro pointing. "We have a temporary scheme to pinpoint the location by sculpting the local fauna with our lasers, but we will need something more permanent. We also met and tamed some of the local natives, at least for now."

"We can fuse some of the soil in both locations and with periodic contact, always be able to reference the transfer points," said Brant. "How is it going at your uptime terminus in establishing the Trust colony in this hemisphere?"

"It is practically done—at least half the Trust contingent has reached our new home. We are near self-sufficiency and have goo d relations with the neighbors," said Danbro. "We must concentrate on the future."

"Okay," said Brant. "We need to exchange TRs and familiarize ourselves thoroughly with each other's transfer points at this bounce time.

Then, aside from routine communications, let them go dormant until some issue arises, important enough to call for interaction. At such time, we will take problems as they arise and make a judgment as to whether we should intervene and, if so, determine if we have the resources to do it. For now, I cannot see anything, which might require major attention. But considering the unpredictable aspect of human nature, we should never rule it out. The important thing is that two distinct timelines, each with its unique history, are now in contact. I hope we are not making a mistake."

"I share your concerns," said Danbro.

After they each made a fix on both transfer points, they prepared to go their separate ways.

"I will return to the Christian timeline," said Dolf unexpectedly. "Not only will my presence firm our relationship with them, but Kara is there. During the mission, I confess we developed a bond of devotion, and I long to be with her."

Ah, the power of love, thought Brant.

XVIII

Rajulk Checks on Bromfsted and Defoe

Arriving at the uptime terminus, Brant, and the others prepared to return to America.

"I will leave some faux monitoring instruments here and tell the Brazilian authorities we will monitor them by remote, but for appearances send Seth for an onsite check of them periodically. For now, I will be glad to get back to the lab humdrum of Obamapolis and deal in some way with the dispatch of Bromfsted and Defoe."

"Why not just let them bask joy of 2010?" said Lila still captive of the humor of her mischief.

"We can't just leave them to their own devices," said Brant wincing and coming as close as he could to censoring his soul mate. "You knew it was against the ethics we agreed upon when we started this enterprise. We have to do some damage control. I will research the period and see if they turn up somewhere, but it has to be soon. They're sure to abandon the desolate Obamapolis site immediately for some inhabited place."

"Put Rajulk on it," said Lila in an effort to ease Brant's anxiety.

Unable to think of a better idea, Brant grabbed his cell and connected to Rajulk. "Can you get over here right away?"

"What's up?" asked Rajulk.

"I'll fill you in when you get here."

"So what's the big emergency?" asked Rajulk when he showed up at the ITR lab. "We have a hook on the connection to the other timeline. All the hints and innuendo in the press about activity here have calmed down, and Bromfsted has been neutralized."

"You are right on all counts except the last. There has been a complication. At Bromfsted's request, I arranged a courtesy visit to the lab. Lila here took it upon herself to whisk him off to 2010 when he meandered into the transfer perimeter with that aide of his," said Brant, turning to his lab and soul mate perched on a lab table and wearing her perennially sardonic face. "You know our mandate about not harming anyone in the process of our investigations. That not only pertains to those of the target eras but those we ourselves send whether accidently or on purpose."

When Rajulk stopped laughing, he choked out a comment. "Well, I guess I should at least troubleshoot it. Perhaps I can insert just before they turn up the rural Kansas of pre-Obamapolis and then follow them for a bit."

Rajulk looked at the black, star-studded sky and sighed. *I guess Brant can't thread a needle with this machine of his. I will have to wait a few hours … Better hunker down, that thicket of scrub brush over there should provide some cover. First, I must mark this spot in order to return to it.* He sighted an array of landmarks and took azimuth readings.

Retiring to the cluster of growth for cover, he checked out his shoulder pack. *Now, what did Lila put in this kit that's edible?*

He was jarred from a quiet slumber as the muted sound of voices cut through the morning air. *Must have dozed off … Dawn came sooner than I thought.* Two figures appeared as a splintered mosaic through the intervening brush. The faint sound of Bromfsted's voice came through followed by a response from Defoe.

"Where in hell are we?"

"It looks like Conjular and the ITR crew did a number on us," said Defoe.

Rajulk watched as the pair shuffled off to a nearby road and followed as they trudged along it. He stopped as the couple flagged down a passing truck.

I must not let them get too far ahead. I would never catch up, thought Rajulk, as another vehicle rattled in the distance. *My luck, here comes another heap even more decrepit.* The vehicle settled to a stop.

"Can I give you a lift mister?"

"Sure thing," said Rajulk as he sidled in beside the driver.

"How come you're stuck out here?" asked the driver.

"Car gave out on me," improvised Rajulk.

"I'm going as far as Cawker city. You can catch a bus there going in most any direction."

"Jeez," voiced Rajulk silently. He instinctively turned away as the heap he had flagged, gained on, and passed the pickup containing Bromfsted and Defoe. *I didn't really need to do that. I wore a mask at our only encounter, that faux celebration over the great time travel 'breakthrough.'* [25]

Deposited in Cawker City, Rajulk waited only a few minutes before Bromfsted and Defoe arrived. He watched as the pair negotiated another ride south.

They must be heading for the interstate, thought Rajulk. *I'll see if I can rent a car here. These hitches are too unpredictable. Some local should cue me in. Without funds or valid credit cards, they obviously can't rent for themselves.*

"There's a Hertz, down the street," said a local when queried by Rajulk.

He settled in the car and hurried back to the town center, cruising the outskirts for some sign of Bromfsted and Defoe.

There they are. They are headed south—as good choice as any I guess. Maybe they have something specific in mind.

Rajulk followed as they eventually caught a succession of lifts going south and then east on interstate I-70. A roadside sign read, "Fort Riley 6 miles." *That must be where they are headed. They seem to be innovative enough. It will be amusing to see how long they can fake it. I can't commit to this era indefinitely. I will give it a couple more days, and that's it.*

After negotiating a visitor's pass to Fort Riley and observing the couple for a few days, Rajulk backtracked and went through the circuitous process of returning uptime.

"I last saw them as they disappeared into Fort Riley, presumably to fake their way into the culture there," said Rajulk to an amused Brant. "The bottom line is that they didn't seem traumatized by the radical change of venue and have apparently bonded through shared adversity."

"Okay, we have too much on our plate to obsess over their plight, but we should check on them periodically," said Brant.

"I was wondering if there would be any trace of them in records of the period," said Rajulk.

"It's scary to consider it," said Brant hesitantly. "The question arises and extends to our own ventures in time: Were the records of our presence, historic, newspaper or otherwise, there all along, or did they mysteriously appear there when our change of locale was a fact? Sooner or later, we will have to pause in our willy-nilly time travel escapades and address such questions," added Brant with a sigh. "It is my fear that the mere act of checking could initiate a new timeline, which vaguely echoes one of the dilemmas of quantum theory."

———————————

A few days later Brant called together all those involved in the linkage of the timelines.

"After considerable fussing we have achieved a stable link between our timelines, which is an important development toward linking with others of our kind in particular, and fathoming the mystery of the human presence in general. Any of you wishing to return to your original timeline, please let it be known."

Francois LeBrust, Dolf, and Kara were silent.

"Okay," said Brant after a pause. "It will be productive to have reps from the only other known timeline here on a more permanent basis."

He turned to Dolf and Kara. "Francois still has his position at the Vatican. I hope you can all find a place here, including some activity to sustain you. We will help you as much as we can. At the very least, I will get Frondner to arrange some supportive activity at the GSI that will tide you over till you find your way."

XIX

Bromfsted and Defoe are Retrieved from the Nineteenth Century

Frondner glimpsed the morning headlines on his phone, winced, and dialed Brant.

"Have you seen the latest news?"

"Haven't picked up the paper yet," said Brant.

"Oh, I forgot you are still in the nineteenth century when it comes to the news," said Frondner. "In any case, I have been in a state of shock since you told me what happened with Bromfsted. Here, I'll read you the latest."

> 'US General, Chief of Intelligence disappears along with aide The State Department has confirmed that General Carlin Bromfsted, Chief of Intelligence, and his aide, Lieutenant Jebbia Defoe, have disappeared. It has been speculated that they may have defected to some foreign power, but those closely associated with them discount that theory, citing Bromfsted as intensely patriotic. More likely, other sources theorize, is that they may have fallen victim to one of several radical antiwar cults which beset our nation.'

"Maybe it will just go away," said Brant. "In any case, I can't see any solution to their plight other than bringing them back, which would not only blow the whole thing wide open, but subject us to Bromfsted's vengeance."

"The one thought I had was to research the period to see if they turn up somewhere. We can ask Rajulk if he will monitor the situation for us. We are lucky to have him with such a unique combination of talents. In addition to being our muscle man on missions, he is from that academic clan at the Consolidated Middle Eastern University and can help us because he has had indefinite leave from his obligations there."

Brant picked up his retro-paper, reread the story in more detail, and called Rajulk.

"Did you catch the item about Bromfsted?"

"How could I miss it? It was all over the net. Where do we go from here?"

"One approach would be to research the period and see if they turn up some place. I thought that you would be the best one to do it."

"I'll get on it," said Rajulk. "Many old newspaper archives are digitized now, but some are still in storage or molding in basements."

"Just a hunch, but check Washington, DC, around the date of his dispatch," said Brant. "With questionable credentials, they may have decided to migrate there and fold into the chaotic bureaucracy."

"Will do," said Rajulk. "Give me a few days."

Rajulk pored over the digitized records of newspapers. *Here, It's him, mentioned anecdotally and dated 2011—scary. Has it been here all along, or, reaching for the spooky explanation, did it come into existence only when I investigated it?*

"… was provided by Mr. Carlin Bromfsted, private consultant to the Pentagon, and reluctantly verified by the Army. How he came to possess such classified knowledge is a matter of concern and speculation. Bromfsted has been questioned and his movements restricted, pending completion of the Justice Department's investigation."

Quite naturally, they don't say what the information was, but it must have required a high level of clearance that a civilian Bromfsted wouldn't have … I Must dig further, thought Rajulk.

Here it is on a back page—I almost missed it.

"Suspect disappears
Carlin Bromfsted, a suspect in the disclosure case involving classified information has disappeared. Foul play is suspected,

although defection to a foreign government has not been ruled out" ...

Rajulk probed further. *There seem to be several items reiterating the disappearance, but it just cuts off, stops abruptly, and so far no mention of Defoe. I have a creepy feeling that the absence of further news suggests the intrusion by someone, like just what we plan to do ... Must talk to Brant about this.*

"I agree," said Brant. "It implies some intervention, not necessarily by us. But if you will pardon a lame joke, I suspect us."

"But what if we don't interfere?" asked Rajulk.

"Then it will in some way happen," said Brant with a pause to consider the implications. "Some other entity, even Bromfsted and Defoe themselves, will engineer it if we purposely choose not to pursue it. The fact is, we most of all, are motivated to get involved. These questions drift into that neverland which lies beyond the technical process of actually traveling in time. Up to now, we have been lucky. By keeping to a minimum our ventures into the past, we have avoided trapping one of ours in a time stream that was inadvertently generated by some action from which they cannot be extracted. However, the few unexpected diversions, like Adrian's quest for romance, Onsley's stumble into the transfer field, and now Lila's dispatch of Bromfsted and Defoe, are tickling the great beast of uncertainty. To avoid tickling it further, I suggest we try to extract our two wayward citizens from the trouble they have gotten themselves into, even if we have to plant them in a yet another era to keep them quiet."

"Yeah, but where?" asked Rajulk. "Any time-place we put them in, they will face the same struggle to survive."

"We can put them under the care of the Trust, if we can get them there," said Brant after some thought. "We will first send you to bring them back through the Kansas City portal. The facility there is dormant, so Seth will need to go and start it up. What we don't know is just what is there in 2010 before the house itself, but at that date you can pinpoint it with a compass if you end up in a field. Do what you need to persuade, cajole, or bribe them into cooperating, then somehow, we will smuggle them to the Fortaleza transfer point and bounce them into the Trust's timeline. Lila and I will meet you at the Kansas City house to both reinforce the mission by accenting its importance, and to provide them with some fake IDs for travel purposes. Fortunately, there is air travel in 2011, so you won't have to endure those endless treks by horse and rail to get to Washington. But you may still have to improvise once you make contact with Bromfsted and Defoe. You will doubtless recognize them from the celebration party, but as I recall, your costume included a mask, so they won't have the slightest idea who you are until you identify yourself."

"Right, I already had that faux scare during my mini-surveillance trek," said Rajulk.

Here goes, thought Rajulk as he gave the nod to Seth.

The interior of the Kansas City house was replaced by a sparsely settled suburban neighborhood. A cat, wide-eyed and tense, scampered away along with the frantic flutter of birds it had been stalking.

He heaved a sigh of relief. *It reminds me of how lucky we have been to avoid landing in the middle of some clambake. I must take some positional readings and get on with it.*

Rajulk gazed out the window of the plane as they approached Washington's National Airport. *That's the old Capitol building over there ... Not too different from the new one in Obamapolis, but it could use a bath.*

He rented a car and made directly for Arlington Bromfsted's address, which he had gleaned from a search of the local directories. It was midafternoon when he crossed the bridge and entered the working-class neighborhood. Parking on the next street, he circled the block and rang the doorbell at 332 N Emerson Street.

No answer, not home from work yet, thought Rajulk. *I'll cool my heels at that coffee shop on the corner and check later.*

After an hour or so waiting, he ambled back toward the Bromfsted residence.

That was her, he realized as he passed several locals moving in the same direction.

He continued several paces, turned, and waited as Defoe approached.

"Ms. Defoe," said Rajulk as she neared.

Defoe seemed drawn out of a fog as she sized up Rajulk.

"Do I know you?" she asked tentatively

"Perhaps not," said Rajulk. "My name is Parzan Rajulk Petrov. Just call me Rajulk. We did once attend the same function, but due to the randomness of the get-together, a formal meeting did not happen."

"What ... what occasion are you referring to?" asked Defoe suddenly sensing something out of sync with her current reality.

"The celebration at the Government Science Institute commemorating the breakthrough at the Institute of Temporal Research," said Rajulk.

Defoe was quiet. Rajulk let her simmer in silence and waited for what came next.

"I don't understand," said Defoe finally. "You must be from that other time-place, our home, before we were sent here against our will."

"That is correct," said Rajulk. "I have come to offer you a choice in return for your silence concerning the time travel issue. We will first try to extract the general from his current situation, and depending also on his agreement to silence, plant you in some setting more hospitable."

"Having engaged in what may be considered kidnaping, a criminal act, why would you and your conspirators consider such a remedy?"

"If we were criminals, we would leave you both to languish in your dreary situation. We have a sense of ethics, which is why I am here to offer you relief from your current predicament."

"We would prefer to return to that which is more familiar and in which we had an established presence," said Defoe after a pause. "Also, it will be difficult to convince the general to remain silent. He has a strong sense of what is in the interest of the country. On the other hand, what is going on back in our ... our time? There must be a big hullabaloo over our disappearance. How could we possibly explain it? The scandal sheets even now must be having a field day over it. The general's career would tank. He could even be court marshaled and lose his retirement."

"You have guessed right. All sort of speculation has surfaced about the general who disappeared with his attractive aide. It is perfectly possible he could ride it out, if all the details of his abduction were known; however, the community that has developed time travel wishes to protect the process and promote it in a controlled systematic release. This means that your return should be delayed. We need to get together with the general and sort it out. When is he due back here?"

"Any time now, but he may be tailed by the Secret Service. We started noticing it a few days ago."

"This brings even more immediacy to the situation. I will wait, and we will have it out," said Rajulk.

Defoe had relaxed somewhat as they sat silently over some coffee she had fixed in the wait. Some thirty minutes, later a scuffle and click of the door signaled that Bromfsted had arrived. Rajulk rose as he entered the living room. Bromfsted stopped short, looked at Rajulk, and then at Defoe.

"This is Rajulk from our original timeline," said Defoe. "He is here with an offer."

Rajulk picked up on Defoe's intro before the volatile Bromfsted could interfere.

I represent the forces that brought you here to protect the secrets of time travel, which we think would be a destabilizing element if suddenly let loose in the greater world," said Rajulk. "The knowledge that it can be done will eventually come to light. Any breathing time that permits both a national consensus and some kind of international agreement on its use, can help prevent chaos and unexpected consequences."

"Shouldn't that be left to the democratically elected government to decide?" asked Bromfsted.

"Ideally yes, in practice no," said Rajulk. "The fact is, knowledge of it will be revealed in due course. I am not from the technical branch of those who developed the technology. But it is a process in its infancy, with multiple unknowns and dangerous consequences, such as stranding those prone to careless adventurism in time streams from which they cannot be retrieved, or worse, including attempts at exploitation by rogue nations seeking advantage."

"What you point out is certainly to be considered, but we remain in fundamental disagreement. However, you and your cohorts seem to have the upper hand," said Bromfsted evenly. "What did you have in mind for us?"

"First of all, to rescue you from eminent arrest for what appears to be the miscalculation of using the foreknowledge of events to some advantage," said Rajulk. "It is irrelevant what that was. The task before us is to extract you from this situation, which, in spite of your own actions to expose us, is our responsibility for putting you here in the first place. Related to your immediate situation is this: An unexpected aspect of time travel is our encounter with an alternate time stream. It is a discrete reality with its own history and which, due to some pivotal event our timeline, broke off at a point and created its own time stream. In this, the one case we know of, the pivotal event was the insertion of the personage of Jesus Christ as an adult into the culture of ancient Judea.

Setting aside the question of how this occurred, we have now established a permanent link with this, the original timeline. Its worldly makeup is somewhat different from ours, being composed of nations living in fragile alliances sprinkled with autonomous, progressive enclaves. It is to one of these that we propose to send you until the practical and political issues of time travel are resolved and the process is revealed—at which time your disappearance can be more easily explained, and hopefully, your reputations restored."

The silence that ensued reflected a realization by Bromfsted and Defoe of the complexity of matters related to time travel.

"We agree that return to our familiar world has its problems," said Defoe. "How would we escape the scrutiny of the Secret Service in order to proceed with your plan?"

"With difficulty," said Rajulk. "If you agree and we manage to elude them, we will temporarily return to our own timeline and start from there."

"How will we do that?" asked Defoe again taking the lead. "We started in your lab in Obamapolis."

"There is a standby transfer point in Kansas City which will deposit us in the uptime front of this timeline, the present as you would have experienced it had you not been, shall we say, hijacked. With luck, we can avoid running into anyone who might recognize you and perhaps eliminate any temptation you may have to make a run for it," said Rajulk with a witty twinkle.

The increasingly stoic Bromfsted remained noncommittal.

Rajulk commented casually, "I hope you will see the wisdom and reason for this path forward. Once in Kansas City, we can make connections through Miami to Fortaleza on Brazil's north coast."

"Fortaleza?" asked Defoe.

"Yes, it is the location of the settlement where we wish to send you. They call it Blairton in the other timeline. The complex issues of its naming and location there will be explained later. For now, we must concentrate on getting you there. Have you noticed whether your trackers keep a twenty-four-hour vigilance?"

"Yes, for the last couple of days," said Defoe.

"Is there a back way out of here?"

"We can probably sneak out between the houses in the block behind once the neighbors go to bed," said Defoe.

"Good, my car is parked there," said Rajulk.

They waited amid small talk broken by extended periods of silence.

"The neighbors' lights have dwindled to a minimum," said Rajulk, looking out the window. "It is 2:30. Let's give it a try."

They slipped out the back and scanned the rear of the houses opposite in the block.

A few are probably still watching TV, but it won't get much calmer than this, thought Rajulk.

"That one seems quieter than most," said Rajulk indicating a dark structure silhouetted against the sky filled with the wash of the city lights beyond.

Rajulk climbed up and over a low fence and assisted Bromfsted and Defoe as they negotiated the barrier with some difficulty. Feeling their way forward, Rajulk gestured toward a dark opening between the houses that would lead out into the street beyond. An explosive bark shattered the silence. Its low, gravelly timbre signaled that a canine of considerable size had been disturbed by their presence. Two glowing orbs of ominous character closed on the three as they hustled toward the black egress. With Defoe and Bromfsted in the lead and Rajulk coming up behind, Rajulk turned in the coal black darkness of the corridor.

Can't see him, thought Rajulk? A painful yelp broke the silence of the night as he sprayed the darkness with his stunner. *I hope he is out ... had to beam him on wide angle.*

Bromfsted and Defoe had reached the end of the corridor and negotiated the exit. Flipping the latch the two emerged from the passageway followed by Rajulk. A light flickered on in the darkened house followed by the muffled sound of a door opening in the rear.

"Quick, this way," said Rajulk, as he led them to his car.

They piled in. With Rajulk at the wheel, they zoomed out of Arlington heading north.

"We will stick with this car. Air travel could expose us once they get the idea that you have flown the coop. We will head north to pick up the turnpike, and follow Route 70 to Kansas City. We will need some rest stops on the way. I figure if we keep moving we can get there in about twelve to fourteen hours."

Rajulk and his charges approached Kansas City from the east.

"We will stay on Route 70 until we pass through the city. Our destination is on the other side," said Rajulk as he appraised the situation.

"Here," said Rajulk as he took an exit leading to where the A.D. 2287 rented house would stand. Once there, he led Bromfsted and Defoe to the transfer perimeter. *I don't even need GPS thought Rajulk. There are enough landmarks to zero in on this spot?* He activated his TR. Brant and Lila greeted the trio in the interior of the rented house.

Bromfsted and Defoe stood silently as Brant greeted Rajulk and then turned to the couple.

"General, you doubtless recall your unexpected temporal displacement when you and Lieutenant Defoe visited the lab. We will call it an accident that the transfer field was activated when you slipped into it, but we will not go into that now. We must deal with the present. Rajulk has doubtless told you of the hubbub in Obamapolis concerning your disappearance together, which would likely persist even if you went back and tried to expose our activities at the ITR. After all, the lab is just a place with a pile of apparatus. Outside experts unfamiliar with it cannot fathom what it can do. Beyond that, you know how the press is. They gravitate toward the juiciest version of anything."

"We propose, then, to place you temporarily in a place of relative safety either to buy time for some kind of international agreement to develop or other events surface that suggest a controlled way forward. At which time, you can return and resume your life after plausible explanations of your disappearance are revealed."

"This agreement—you are not likely to get it. Each nation will want to exploit time travel for its own ends. Beyond that, there wouldn't even be any hullabaloo, if you hadn't captured us in the first place. But I can't see we have much of a choice," groused the general while he reluctantly considered Brant's logic.

"You may have a point about the technology," said Brant after a pause. "What would you suggest?"

"I would have to think about it, but first off, we could use it for strategic advantage. But like the atomic bomb, if it is discovered that we can do it, others will find a way," said Bromfsted.

"Then we must press forward," said Brant tentatively, somewhat shaken by Bromfsted's view. "I have some fake passports and IDs for your air travel. You can take commercial air transport to Fortaleza and make the transfer to the alternate timeline from there. Rajulk will accompany you and introduce you to the Trust leaders."

Bromfsted gave a grunt, indicating that he understood the plan but was still baffled by both the existence and the unexpected complications of time travel.

They tread through the busy terminal toward the Transform Airways boarding gate encountering numerous travelers from arriving flights. A passenger in uniform slowed to a stop and initiated a tentative salute as they approached.

"General Bromfsted Sir, is it really you? It's me, Captain Carley."

"Carley, uh … it's nice to see you. I have not heard from you since your transfer," said Bromfsted, picking up the rhythm of the exchange. "As a matter of fact, I have gone through a couple of aides since you left. This is Lieutenant Defoe, my aide now."

Things are about to get out of hand, thought Rajulk.

"Sir, it is a pleasure to see you again, too, but General, it is all over the media that you have disappeared with … with Lieutenant Defoe," said Carley with a glance at Defoe.

"That … is just a front story. You will notice that I am in civilian clothes," said Bromfsted, lowering his voice. "It is to prevent being compromised while on a covert mission. I would not be telling you this if we had not had this chance meeting. You are to forget we ever met. All will eventually be revealed."

Carley surveyed the trio, lingering for a moment on Rajulk, wondering what he had to do with the General's mission.

"Yes sir," he said finally with a salute. "Good luck on the mission, whatever it is."

"That won't hold him for long," said Bromfsted as they scurried through the terminal. "If we don't surface sometime, he will conclude that there was more to my disappearance than meets the eye and start blabbing."

"Hopefully you will be safely ensconced in the Trust enclave by that time," said Rajulk, wondering why Bromfsted hadn't seized the moment to blow the whole thing.

Using the fake IDs provided by Frondner, they traveled to the standby facility in Fortaleza and transferred to the common downtime transfer point. The carved-out wedge-shaped configuration of the Trust's counterpart location appeared after the six-hundred meter trek. With the Trust's TR, Rajulk initiated the transfer uptime. The bright, palm studded landscape of the new Trust enclave at Blairton lay spread out before them.

It's damn pleasant here, thought Rajulk as he panned the bucolic scene against the background lap of not too distant surf. *If I live long enough, I might just gather up Meriam and the kids and retire here.*

"Okay, we're here at last. I'll introduce you to the Trust leaders and explain your situation," said Rajulk. "If our previous experience is any indication, they will receive you with open arms. In the face of ever-present threats, they may be able to use your military knowledge to enhance security."

"It is great to see you again," said Binzing sizing up Rajulk's companions, "but we now have a problem. The balance of the enclave scheduled to arrive by ships has been intercepted by—I guess you would call them pirates—and are being held for ransom. They have been taken south to some unknown destination."

"I am anxious to hear about that. First, I would like you to meet General Bromfsted of the Intelligence Service of the US Army and his aide, Lieutenant Defoe. We need to sequester them in this timeline and have their permission to do so. He can provide you with the details of this, if he so wishes. In any event I would appreciate the Trust's indulgence and cooperation in accommodating them, hopefully on a temporary basis."

"After the services of you and your colleagues in resettling us, we can certainly do that," said Binzing.

Now transformed by the revelation, experience, and complexities of time travel, Bromfsted focused on his new venue. "This problem of your missing personnel—perhaps I can help."

"Well, perhaps you can," said Binzing after a pause to size up Bromfsted.

"Do you have any maps of the area south of here?" asked Bromfsted.

"Only rough ones from the previous owner of the estate," said Binzing

"Let's have a look."

"All Right," said Bromfsted, consulting the map spread out before him. "Of course, all the places familiar to us in our uh … timeline, as they have explained it, have different names."

"Yes, you will notice this timeline reflects a different colonial history of the South American continent," said Rajulk.

"So I see. It seems the fickle winds of history squeezed the Spanish and Portuguese out. But to the issue of your missing personnel, I need to be filled in on the main mode of travel here. Do you have access to such information?"

"Yes," said Binzing. "Our probe of the neighboring areas has revealed a surprisingly diverse array of commercial activity, not as advanced as many of the isolated enclaves of our home continent, which you call Europe, but adequate in a make-do situation."

"Well, first we should make a good guess or consult the locals as to where your colleagues may have been taken, and hire someone to transport us there," said Bromfsted. "Once there, we can either to pay the ransom or retrieve your cohorts by force, threats, or stealth."

"I will delay returning to my timeline and stick around to see what you come up with," said Rajulk. "All of us may be needed to address the problem of your missing citizens."

"Should I go too?" asked Defoe, breaking in to the concentrated exchange between Bromfsted and the Binzing.

Bromfsted turned and viewed his aide, who, through shared adversity had morphed from an impersonal assistant to something more. "No, it may be dangerous," said the general, his eyes lingering on Defoe.

A day or so later, Binzing again briefed the Trust leaders and Bromfsted.

"According to the locals, the pirate activity is several hundred miles to the south in a natural harbor called Portsmouth. They gave no details."

"That's likely to be what we call Salvador in our timeline," said Bromfsted recalling what he knew of the Brazilian coast. "What sort of transportation for hire is available here?"

"The usual balloon mode but that destination is off limits for commercial flights," said Binzing. "We need to find a rogue transporter for hire, but before we embark on such a mission, we need a plan."

"If we can get transport, I think I can help with the plan," said Bromfsted. "What kind of weapons do you have?"

"We have the usual projectile ones, and stunners and lasers that we are hesitant to use," said Binzing

"It is my understanding that you neglected to use them when your enclave was routed from your home in what we call Judea," said Rajulk. "You need to compromise your ethics and unleash your more potent weapons now that your very existence is threatened. It is possible to use them in a nonfatal way. On one occasion, I used a laser to disable a Roman *bireme* without harming anybody."

"All Right," said Binzing after a pause. "I will impress upon the council the gravity of the situation."

Two days later, they met with Binzing. "It's done. The council has given its go ahead, and a man of questionable reputation and a somewhat tattered balloon, has agreed to take us most of the way to the pirates' hideaway."

"What's 'most of the way'?" inquired Bromfsted.

"For a considerable sum, he has agreed to approach by night and deposit us somewhere to be determined after we get an idea of the situation there," said Binzing. "An airship such as his is vulnerable, so he will retire up the coast, wait for a signal from this small *wavant* device he gave me, and take it from there. If we again need to travel north by balloon, he will be there. We hope. He will get only half the fee upfront. I have painted a rosy picture of the rescue of the armada. I hope it works out for the better. In any case, if we are successful, the bulk of the captives will have to be transported to our new home by ships—their own if intact, otherwise we will have to improvise."

Even with half the fee, he's liable to run if the going gets tough," said Bromfsted. "He's scared since pirates, even if clad in monk robes, can deal harshly with anyone caught on their territory."

"The fate of the enclave is at stake. We will have to take that chance," said Binzing. The only other uncertainty is the somewhat bizarre picture the balloon captain gave of the pirates."

"What did he say?" asked Bromfsted.

"He described them as a bunch of disgruntled monks."

"What the hell could he mean by that?"

"I have no idea, but we can ask him on the way."

"Let's concentrate on getting the Trust people free," said Rajulk. "Portsmouth— so that's what they call it in this timeline. The captives are probably in some sort of temporary confinement pending some payment of ransom. Let us hope their ships are still intact."

Darkness closed on the balloon as it traveled south.

The ship's captain spoke over the drone of the engines in a gruff but articulate rendition of English. "By direct route overland, it's about seven hundred miles. If I have judged the winds right, we should get there just about this time tomorrow night. If it is as you suspect, the armada carrying your comrades is corralled in the bay, which extends west of the city. Lacking a containment center for masses of people, they most likely have left the passengers and crew on the ships and given them a small amount of provisions to survive. After all, they are more valuable alive and for ransom, than they are dead."

"Let us hope you are right," said Bromfsted. "By the way, what did you mean by calling the pirates a bunch of disgruntled monks?"

"Just that, from all reports it's a monastery gone rogue."

No one responded to the captain's comment.

Hours later, the balloon's captain appraised the situation. "The winds are blowing toward the west, so we will approach from the east with the motors off," said the captain. "The drift should take us over the northern part of the peninsula out over the bay where the armada of ships is likely moored."

The dark outline of land finally appeared as they drifted westward. Dots of light from random settlers peppered the fields below. Suddenly the wide expanse of the bay spread out before them, and another forest of flickers appeared to the south.

"It's them," said Bromfsted, pointing. "It has to be, and just as we suspected, they are still sequestered on the ships. Even in darkness, I judge from the number of discrete sources of illumination that here are some twenty-five of them. The pirates doubtless have the entrance to the bay blocked and guarded. That's where we should stage a little 'demonstration' and maybe torch one of their control centers, if we can spot one."

"That's up to you," said the captain. "I am vulnerable up here in this ship. A few well-placed shots can bring me down."

"Okay," said Bromfsted. "Put us down … there," he said, pointing to a dark patch of the beach. The Captain deftly released the gas in spurts, decreasing the balloon's lift and maneuvered the ship to the chosen spot.

"I will retire up the coast a few miles," said the captain. "When and if your mission has concluded, go there and light a smoky fire. I will find you. I am still due half my fee for your transport."

With a grunt, Bromfsted said to the others, "This way."

The three of them alighted from the balloon, careful to avoid any random wanderer who might question their presence. Proceeding southward along the beach, they began to encounter an increasingly populated area of small boats, neatly groomed ships, and well-kept landings illuminated by the wash of starlight.

"That's the armada they conger up when they need to transfuse their roguish existence with wealth. Looks like they're still using sails, probably with some primitive motorized assist," said Rajulk speaking softly and gesturing toward the small armada of ships. "How about we stage a little demonstration and sink or damage one of the larger ones? That should bring the unholy fathers out of seclusion."

"If we do that we may not have to," said Bromfsted. "They may cut their losses and let the Trust personnel go, but more likely they will ask for a parlay."

"Don't bet on it," said Rajulk.

"Whatever course you take, I hope the Trust personnel will be safe," said Binzing who had remained sullen during the tense exchange between Rajulk and Bromfsted.

"We will do our best," said Rajulk. "Now, that large one there, I will put a couple of nice holes right at the waterline. We are a little far to do it from shore even with the laser in tight beam. I could swim out, but it might disable the laser. On the other hand, there is a small dinghy over there that should do the trick. Wait here."

"Be careful. Even with little fear that the unexpected could happen. There is probably a watchman or even a token crew aboard," said Bromfsted. "The minute you torch the bow, they will come running."

Rajulk quietly rowed to the first ship. *The crew is probably below in a perverse meditation or some bizarre version of prayer.*

Only the squeak and groan of the boat's members punctuated the otherwise soundless night as he drew near the ship's bow.

About ... here, thought Rajulk as he took out his laser and let loose a blast, sending the smell of burnt wood into the night.

He quickly backed away and returned to the shore and was greeted by Bromfsted and Binzing.

"We could see the flash from here," said Bromfsted. "So far, I can't see activity on the—wait, I can see some movement now. You also must have attracted some attention on shore. Here come a couple of the rogues up the beach. Get a load of those robes. Whatever take they have on material things in the outer world, they have retained the image of the ascetic."

"Let's fade into the shadows and see what the reaction is," said Rajulk.

"*Quod est damnum? Qui vides eam!*" shouted one of the monks from shore.

"*A contritionem in alveus. Non ignoramus quid est,*" was the response from on board.

"Latin," whispered Rajulk, somewhat impressed. "They are trying to figure out who did the damage. We have superior arms. We could just tell them it was us and that there's more where that came from."

"We don't know what reserves they have," said Bromfsted. "And even with inferior weapons, they could battle us to a standstill."

"Okay," said Rajulk tentatively. "But we may have to put on a more potent demonstration before they are impressed enough to rally the whole cloistered community. If things get sticky, we can always retreat up the beach. For now, perhaps a more spectacular display may be in order. I think I can torch the sails of the ship from here."

Rajulk put his laser on tight beam and aimed at the mainsail of the already damaged ship. For a moment, nothing happened, and then the sail burst into flame.

As the monks stood appraising the initial damage from shore, shouts came from the ship as all witnessed in dismay the sailcloth was consumed by fire. Several others emerged from the bowels of the ship to fight the fire and keep it from spreading.

"Here goes," said Rajulk as they emerged from the shadows. The monks turned to confront them as they approached.

Both parties stood mute, each pondering how to move forward.

Binzing broke the ice. "You have our countrymen captive, and we have come to liberate them."

One of the monks stepped forward.

"I take it you are referring to the several ships we recently appropriated in the open seas to the north. We have learned from Mr. Lenyon, after the confusion of the intercept subsided, that they are part of a larger contingent destined for some new place to settle. You seem to have superior weapons and means. Our following uses weapons only when necessary to assure our survival on sorties and to sustain the logistics of our enclave."

"Lenyon, he was in charge of the balance of our fellow citizens arriving from the east. Where is he now?" asked Binzing.

"He is sequestered on his ship, as are the others, awaiting response to our request for an equitable remuneration for their release."

Bromfsted cut in. "No price is, as you say, 'equitable' when piracy is in play. You have seen the power of our weaponry. We can torch the balance of your ships and maybe your facilities on land if necessary. Who with authority can speak for you?"

"I can. We have a hierarchy to deal with matters of faith, but any of us can speak to the secular affairs of the community. We are committed to martyrdom if such is our fate," said the Monk.

Standoff, thought Rajulk. *We need to try something else before this thing gets messy.* "Wasn't there sufficient wealth aboard the ships to satisfy your greed?"

"We didn't board the ships for plunder. We used threats, harassment, and an overwhelming cortege of ships to corral them into captivity. We avoid violence beyond the necessary minimum to intimidate, although, sadly, there have been occasional casualties by accident. In this case, there were no soldiers aboard, only simple sailors and their cargo of passengers. They stand sequestered, and we supply them with the necessities of life until their allies come for them, with appropriate compensation, of course."

"With our arrival here, things have changed. Release our countrymen, and we will call it even," said Rajulk who drew his laser and turned toward the ships scattered at anchor. "Perhaps I should stage another demonstration to convince you."

"Wait!" said the monk as he observed the crew of the already inflamed ship still trying to contain the blaze. "I will consult the abbot. Perhaps some arrangement can be made."

The monk left, and several minutes later a group appeared moving slowly and clustered around a bent figure walking carefully with the aid of a cane. Pausing to observe the burnt ship with the fire now all but contained, the abbot appraised the trio of strangers and spoke in a clear voice belying his apparent frailness.

"I see you come with potent weapons. Perhaps we should talk."

Dismissing his entourage with a wave, the abbot gestured to Bromfsted and the others to follow.

"There is no need to press this matter further," said the abbot as they settled in his quarters in a nearby cloister. "Your ships were the booty of opportunity, and it hasn't worked out. I will instruct the guards to release them."

"We will wait until that seems to be the case," said Bromfsted ever suspicious of an accommodating enemy.

They turned to go but Binzing cut in. "I am interested to know what series of events brought you and your following to go rogue."

The abbot paused and looked at the trio of strangers who had just disrupted his group's orderly scheme of mischief making and sighed. "We are originally of Spanish origin, lured here by the expectation that our culture would prevail in the struggle for dominance in this hemisphere due to the strength of our host countries. It did not turn out that way. Barred from returning to our homeland because of our alleged desertion of it, we became increasingly isolated and estranged due to the domination of our neighbors. We assimilated the language, but little else, and gradually turned to activity outside the law to survive."

"Those I represent have no particular ties to the Anglo culture that seems to dominate here," said Binzing. "We would welcome allies of any persuasion, short of those engaged in the roguery your following is locked into. Have you considered another path?"

"As the abbot here, I have often pondered it."

"When we return to our newly settled enclave, I will send some of our specialists here to plumb the possibilities. Perhaps some natural advantage or local product can be exploited to your benefit.

"Your generosity is unexpected considering our contentious encounter," said the abbot. "We will await your contact."

"It will take some days to transport and settle the balance of our citizens at our new home near Fortaleza," said Binzing. "When that is done, we will send our experts to plumb the possibilities here. At first glance; however, the natural harbor is an asset; it is a convenient stopping place for travelers going to the south. I suggest you exploit that advantage, since any friendly port of call draws profit from visitors. The transition will be difficult, but surely, the foundations of your order would not sanction the activity you engage in. Your immediate problem is to control your following and shed your reputation for plunder and ransom.

By daylight, the armada assembled and sailed from the confines of Portsmouth. Rajulk, Bromfsted, and Binzing retired up the coast and lit a smoky fire. After an interval, the swollen blob of the balloon appeared in the distance.

"I feared things might not have gone according to plan, and I would lose the remaining half of my fee," said the relieved captain over the clatter of the ships engines.

"It was certainly not quite what we would have expected, but the situation has been satisfactorily resolved," said Rajulk. "The commandeered ships are on their way to the newly established colony."

A week later, the armada of Trust ships entered the bay at Fortaleza and were greeted by their already established colleagues. Bromfsted stood watching on the wharf with Defoe.

XX

Barry

Satisfied that the balance of the Trust's populace was safe and united with the rest of the enclave, and that Bromfsted and Defoe were safely integrated there, Rajulk made the circuitous trip back to his timeline by way of the new Fortaleza link. Flying directly back to Obamapolis, he arrived somewhat burned-out from the continuous trouble-shooting of missions to preserve the secrets of the time transfer technology.

It was late as he slogged through the terminal. Even though a few flights had still not departed, most of the gates were closed. Maintenance personnel were already at work clearing away the day's discards and droppings of the hundreds of passengers. He dodged an attendant pushing a large cart and almost collided with another worker. The latter stood back to let Rajulk pass, but his eyes widened as he locked onto Rajulk. Rajulk gave the attendant a cursory glance, walked a few steps, and paused. Some subliminal persuasion lifted him out of the sullen hangover from the complexity of his latest activity. He turned and saw that the man had stopped work and stood staring at him. For a moment, both stood frozen in indecision before the worker spoke in highly accented, but understandable English.

"Is your name Rajulk?"

"It is. Do I ... know you?" replied Rajulk hesitantly.

"You probably remember me from another ... another place," he said, struggling, for the right word to express himself. We were last together in the square of the city Jerusalem. I had just taken you there to search for Thaddeaus."[26]

Another period of silence passed as Rajulk stood in openmouthed appraisal of the man standing there before finally voicing a choked, "Ba—Barabbas! [27] Besides the fact that I hardly recognized you without your beard, it defies reason that you are even here."

"Yes, it is I Barabbas, but I am known here as Barry, Barry Bass. I changed it to avoid trouble since the name Barabbas seems archaic. It even draws sneers from some more devout citizens, and it has some negative association here, since the name itself coincides with a treasonous character in the bible. Had I been more aware of the history of this place, I would have discarded it sooner. As you noticed, I have discarded the beard of my homeland. I am surprised you recognized me at all."

"Yes, your mention of the incident in Jerusalem struck a chord. I can certainly understand the reaction to the name Barabbas," said Rajulk.

The unintended humor of Barry's remark broke through the aftermath of his stupor and intruded into the otherwise serious exchange.

"But now providence has asserted itself in a most unusual way," continued Rajulk. "How could you possibly even be here? In our brief association, I withheld many things from you because they were not only alien to your earthly experience but also irrelevant to the events taking place. Most important were where I was actually from, how I got there, and why I was there in the first place."

"Whatever you didn't tell me, it now falls into place," said Barry. "I can infer much of it now and fill in the blanks, having gone through the process of getting here myself, combined with the reality of your presence. The first hint I had that there was a connection to you and your colleagues was a picture of Ms. McEntire in the newspaper. As to how I came to be here, I can only tell you what happened," said Barabbas revealing to Rajulk an unexpected level of expression.

"You must remember," continued Barabbas, "we had gone to the market in Jerusalem to look for Thaddeaus, that disciple of Jesus. You left me suddenly, citing the need for privacy."

"Yes, I remember," said Rajulk. "While there, I received a communication, by one of the devices you must now have experienced in this era that Thaddeaus had been spotted in the cemetery where Jesus disappeared. I dropped everything and headed there."

"That explains it," said Barabbas. "At the time; however, since you didn't return to the market, I was consumed by an overwhelming curiosity, so I took a chance and guessed you may be going back there.

Sure enough, I got to the cemetery just as you, Thaddeaus, and that woman who freed you from the garrison prison were leaving. The woman and Thaddeaus separated and headed toward the Jerusalem bypass road while you continued back down into the bowels of the city. I followed as you disappeared into a blind alley bordering the wall of the Roman base and terminating at the city wall. I could not fathom what you might be doing there, but I waited, increasingly consumed by the mystery of your activities. I was just about to leave when you emerged with what looked like a Roman soldier, minus his weapons and part of his uniform.

"I retreated from the mouth of the alley and watched as you and the soldier again moved into the inner part of the city. Not wanting to interfere in some unknown situation involving the Roman authority, I held back, as you and he seemed to be in a hurry to be somewhere. The day was passing, but having committed so much time already to watching your strange behavior, I was determined to see it to some sort of conclusion. I continued to follow you until you disappeared into one of the service entrances of the water tunnels. I waited for a period, and when you and the soldier did not emerge, I decided to take a chance and go to the north of the city where the water feeds into the system and wait to see if you would emerge.

"When I got there, all hell was breaking loose, as you sometimes say here. You and the soldier had just come out of the tunnel. A woman, the same one who liberated you from the garrison prison and whom I have now recognized pictured in the local newspaper, held base commander Belator captive. He and some troops had apparently been waiting for you. His men milled about, making frequent charges, but were repulsed by the frequent flashes of fire thrown at them from some weapon she held. The three of you, with Belator still captive, commandeered some horses from the cowed soldiers and left for some place or other. Anxious to know the outlandish ending of it all, I followed on foot as fast as I could. In the meantime, Belator's men had rallied and galloped past me in pursuit. As I approached a certain spot, I saw that Belator had been released for some reason and was being un-trussed by his soldiers. I passed by unobtrusively as an innocent itinerant. They all stood watching the cloud of dust churned up by your horses as you mounted a hill not far away. I heard Belator mumble something. Curiously, he and the contingent of soldiers mounted and left the scene."

Rajulk interrupted Barabbas saying, "That is exactly what happened. What did you do then?"

"Against my better judgment but still consumed by the mounting mystery of it all, I was drawn to the direction of the hill. When I reached the summit, the three of you had disappeared. I wandered about for a moment, sadly let down, since the uncanny events stemming from my association with you had given new life to my dreary day-to-day existence. As I prepared to leave, I was suddenly enveloped in a dizzy sickness like one gets from bad food."

"It's possible that in the euphoria of escape from that dangerous situation that we delayed in deactivating the transfer field," mused Rajulk. "But go on, what happened next?"

"When the surrounds stopped whirling, I looked around and prepared to descend the hill, but nothing seemed the same. It was almost dark. Lights were sprinkled about the valley below and glowed from the windows of a domed structure nearby. Sounds of laughter came from there, which frightened me."

"That would have been us celebrating our safe return from an arduous jaunt into the past including the things you have just described," said Rajulk.

"Perhaps so," said Barabbas. "In any case, in my anxiety of experiencing such a jarring change of venue, the thought never entered my mind. I hastened to quit the place, since I thought it was haunted. I soon encountered several natives who stared relentlessly at the way my clothing, since it was nothing like what everybody else was wearing. I was sighted by the authorities traveling in one of the now familiar vehicles moving about through no means of propulsion observable, and was taken to a place of confinement. Since I did not know the language they were speaking, I was mute and unable to answer their questions. They thought I was daft, but they eventually released me and gave me some clothes suitable to the new world in which I had found myself. I achieved a modest degree of communication with some men they had brought in with special language skills, but they were as perplexed as I was at my presence there and my situation in general. The authorities finally gave up and set me free. I managed to get some menial employment to survive and figured that the key to it would be to learn as much of the language as I could. One of the languages commonly spoken was the vaguely familiar Hebrew, but English was more universally spoken. I worked hard in my off time to master it."

"You certainly seem to have done that," said Rajulk, fascinated as he listened to Barabbas' tale unwind. "But how did you end up here, so far from your homeland?"

"If that was the homeland I knew, it was unrecognizable. The change was so radical that and until recently, I never made the connection between my previous association with you and this place until, by accident, I came across a picture of that woman who came to your aid in the dungeon of the Romans. I concentrated on efforts to improve my lot and discovered that the United States was the dominant power in this world. After some difficulty, I made my way here to its capital. Unfortunately, in spite of my mastery of the language, my ability to advance and improve my lot in this world was still hampered by my background. One of the things I discovered; however, is that the Jesus we all knew is still alive through his teachings as interpreted by several branches of the Christian Church. I attend one of these faithfully to lift up my spirits."

I hesitate to squash his belief with the truth about Jesus in all its detail. It is what sustains him, thought Rajulk.

"The thing which only recently came to light was a picture in one of the newspapers. It was the woman who rescued you from the Belator's prison. The newspaper identified her as a Miss McEntire. It began to come together. The new place I had been transported to was somehow connected to you and your colleagues. Looking back, I am surprised I didn't realize it before."

"I have nothing specific in mind, but we could possibly use your services sometime," said Rajulk on a whim. "Can you give me some way to contact you?"

"Yes, I will write it down," said Barry

Rajulk took the paper, and giving Barabbas a final look to assure himself that he had not imagined it all, turned and left.

Momentarily revived by the bizarre encounter with Barabbas and still in a state of incredulity, the fatigue of his recent travels again set in.

I will bring Brant up to date in the morning, thought Rajulk. *He will certainly have something to say.*

"He what?" said Brant.

"He showed up at the airport terminal as a worker. He has taken the name Barry Bass."

"Figures," said Brant laughing. "Beyond its archaic sound, the name Barabbas wouldn't go over so well even in this secular age. The Christian cults would be eager to do something symbolic, like make an example of him. But how—that is, what happened? How could he possibly be here?"

"To make a long story short, he followed me after I left him and headed for the cemetery. He witnessed all my subsequent encounters, ending at the transfer point on the hill. Then, he accidently slipped into the transfer perimeter in that brief interval when Seth had failed to deactivate it. You remember, there was a great sense of euphoria when we all emerged from that complicated mission unscathed. We put celebration before all else."

"I'll be damned," said Brant. "Well, he saved your skin at least once and was of help to us at other times. Maybe, since he is already in the exclusive time travel club, we could use his muscle on some future mission and avoid running the risk of bringing in others. You say that he's completely fluent in English?"

"Remarkably so, highly accented of course," said Rajulk. "If you are interested, we could rescue him from the menial jobs he has been reduced to taking. There is no issue of secrecy. He is already in the time travel club. Since we are awash with uncertainties in our dealings with the other timeline, his brawn and perspective could be of help."

"Okay, you contact him," said Brant. "We can put him on the staff here more or less in a job similar to that he has now. It will enable him to survive. Since he is in our exclusive club, and if needed we can also use him on missions."

"I'll do that," said Rajulk, but I warn you, he is still captive of the idea of Christianity and the genuineness of Jesus Christ. With exposure to the details of our thrust into the past, early on, it will dawn on him that something is amiss."

XXI

Pans to Discredit Mormon Origins Are Disrupted

LeBrust resumed his role as Vatican press secretary after a long absence and a dressing down by Senior Cardinal Alofi at the Sacred Congregation for the Doctrine of the Faith. Evoking his divinely inspired urge to take extended absences for spiritual contemplation, he managed to escape demotion and relegation to a menial job pushing paper at the Vatican press office.

He grumbled in silence as he plowed through the heap in his inbox. *He could have saved his breath. This office runs itself, and my worthy assistant, Father O'Malley, has got my back,* adding in afterthought, when wafted by the image of the somewhat fay O'Malley, *so to speak. Days to day operations of the Press are on automatic, but I guess I need to bring myself up to date on things. First, Adrian and I must get this Mormon thing out of the way. An anonymous posting on the net should do it, and we still need to convert those azimuth readings to GPS.*

That's done, thought LeBrust as he finished the pile, and turned to the forest of e-mails to be addressed or deleted. Stepping away from the computer, he uttered a sigh as he stared at yet another stack of papers on his desk.

What is this? He paused over a paper with a note attached. The letterhead read, Congregation for the Evangelization of Peoples. *It's from Cardinal Alohi himself.* "Please examine the attached and respond with appropriate action," the note read.

LeBrust scanned the letter.

Memo to the Vatican Press:
Priority: Secret

Preliminary discussions are underway to embrace the Mormon religion and welcome it into the fold of the True Church. The conflicting underpinnings of our belief systems are the chief obstacle to any merger. We are working to resolve such differences by giving sanction to the Mormon idea that our savior Jesus Christ, through the all-powerful grace and divine presence of god, did indeed appear in the western nations to continue his good works. The question of the pope's supremacy over the totality of the faith seems to be less of a problem as long as the melding of the fundamentals goes smoothly and the Mormon elders are given appropriate recognition and respect. It is expected that the Vatican press with its resources will support this effort.

To this end, his Holiness Pope Wang has instructed me to orchestrate a measured revelation of this idea. I call upon you to float a vague editorial suggesting the virtues of such an ecumenical thrust without mentioning the Mormons specifically. Then, in calculated installments, we will reveal our goal.

Yours sincerely,
Cardinal Alohi

"Damn," murmured LeBrust under his breath. *I just posted the junk about the Mormons on the net. Some idiot will go looking for the gold plates and find them. The Mormons—all that fussing Adrian and I went through to discredit them. Now this, a fine time for him to be off in pursuit of some liaison. I need him here with me to deal with this. I must get a message to him some way.*

LeBrust grabbed his cell phone.

"Get me the GSI in Obamapolis, USA."

"Government Science Institute.' How can I connect you?"

"Dr. Conjular, please."

"Brant," said LeBrust as he connected and before Brant had a chance to say anything.

"I need to get a message to Adrian. I must either go back temporarily to 1860 and post a letter to him, or have someone do it."

"You are in luck. He is in Obamapolis with his wife because of some medical emergency. You can speak to him directly. He is at the embassy guesthouse. You can get the number from directory services."

"Thanks."

He actually married her, thought LeBrust as he got the number and dialed.

"Adrian, Congratulations on your marriage. Is everything all right?" asked LeBrust.

"It is now. Eugenia has more or less recovered from her illness. What's up?"

"I just got word that the True Church is planning to embrace the Mormons and incorporate them into the True Church family," said LeBrust.

"They what?" responded a flabbergasted Adrian. "That would be a giant step for such a conservative branch of the faith. What sort of ideological contortions will they go through to justify it?"

"It doesn't matter. It is to be a merger," continued LeBrust. 'Embrace' is the term Cardinal Alohi used. The point is: I have been ordered to prepare the way with a media blitz suggesting what a good idea it is. Whatever its refinements, it changes everything. I just published a hint on the net that the gold plates containing the sacred words of Moroni are to be found on the Hill Cumorah. It's out there. Somebody will pick up on it, likely the Mormons themselves. Of course the whole site of Mormon origins is now fixed up as a museum, and the hill itself is squeaky clean, but if the hint I floated takes hold, they will be digging up the side of the hill until they find it."

"Then we went to that effort for nothing," said Adrian. "Maybe the church fathers won't translate the plates before they blab to the media about it. In that case, when they find out what is on them, they will either suppress it or try to dub it a hoax. The trouble they would have with that is that all the characteristics of the find, including the disintegrated suitcase we carried the things in, will show age."

"We can't chance that someone else will find them," said LeBrust. "We had better do damage control, get up there right away, and see if we can dig the damn things up. Can you get away from Eugenia for a few days?"

"I think so."

"Good. My own situation here at the Vatican is tenuous. I have too many unexplained absences. Cardinal Alohi has been making threats about sacking me. Maybe that's okay. This job is getting boring anyway."

"It's up to you. I suppose I could try doing it alone," said Adrian.

"Wouldn't think of it," said LeBrust. "How could you manage those heavy plates by yourself? Beyond that, there is the question: Should we do it now or go back in the past to do it?"

"We may be stuck with the now," said Adrian. "Brant is unlikely to sanction another jaunt into the past. He thinks the whole thing is frivolous to start with. I will book some accommodations and tell Eugenia that we will be gone a few days. We will need some digging implements to do the job. I will get a couple of those folding shovels we had when we put the plates there. They are primitive but will fit in our luggage."

It was dark when the taxi pulled up in front of the Palmyra Inn.

"I assume you are here for the pageant," said the clerk. Do you have reservations?"

"No—" began Adrian, but was interrupted by the clerk.

"That's strange, all the participants should have made reservations," said the clerk consulting his ledger.

"Participants?" asked Adrian, whose query was again cut off.

"You are in luck," again interrupted the clerk. "We have a cancellation."

"What's he talking about?" asked LeBrust.

"Haven't the slightest," said Adrian in a subdued hush-speak. "I'm bushed. Let's get some sleep and do some snooping around tomorrow. We can blend in with the tourists and try to zero in on the exact spot where we buried the plates."

Morning sun illuminated the periphery of the blackout curtains.

"Guess the trip tired us out," said a sleepy LeBrust. "We'd better get to it, but first, a bit of breakfast."

Adrian sipped coffee and looked around. "It looks as if the inn is full. The faithful will be all over the place. I took a quick look outside. The place we put the plates is completely wooded over, but the slope leading to the high point on the Cumorah ridge, while usually clear, is temporarily filled with a theatrical setup for some kind of pageant, complete with stage and seating for the audience. That's what the clerk was talking about when we got here."

They finished breakfast and wandered back to the room.

"The rehearsal begins at 9:00 a.m.," said the clerk as they passed the desk.

"It's the pageant again," said LeBrust. "He seems to think we are here to participate."

"Let him think that. It will take any suspicion away from what we are actually here for," said Adrian.

Back in the room, Adrian eyed the two folding shovels. "We can't go out with these things exposed, just asking for questions. Grab those pillow cases to cover them."

Carrying the covered implements under their arms, they strolled out to the well-manicured lawn and blended in with the tourists.

"This way," said Adrian. "We can circle around this theater setup and mosey up the slope. About half way up, we can melt into the forested area. We can't see our reference points, so the azimuth readings we took will be useless with all that cover, but we know in general where we buried the plates—that level spot. It was the only one on the slope upward."

A green canopy closed in over the pair as they left the hubbub of the improvised theater and sidled into the overgrowth.

"Let's go in further," said Adrian. "As I recall, the path we took upward was this way and ran parallel to the cleared-out area we just came from. If there is anything left of it, we can use it to zero in on the location."

"Here," said LeBrust after they had poked around another fifteen minutes. "The path is grown over, but there are still traces of it. If we follow it we should be able to find the spot."

They made their way upward for a few more minutes before Adrian said, "There, it's the only level place on the slope. Unfortunately there's a good-sized tree right in the middle of it."

"We can dig to the side," said Adrian. "It is just our luck that the plates will be directly under it."

They busied themselves, hacking away at the loose soil.

"Damn, there's a big root in the way," said Adrian. "Stand back. I'll give it an overhand whack."

Adrian swung the shovel a couple of times. "Just about through."

Clunk. The shovel severed the root and struck a hard surface.

"That may be it," said LeBrust now excited. "I'll scrape away some of the top-soil."

They cleared away the scraps of decomposed leather. The remnants of the decomposed suitcase mingled with the glistening reflections of gold.

"We can hide the shovels and use the pillow cases to cover the plates as we take them out of here," said Adrian. "We had the wheelbarrow when we carted them here in the first place, but we now can only retrieve a few at a time."

"Okay, let's get to it. Drag a couple of the plates over here and cover the rest for now."

A shout shattered the tranquility of the setting.

"Who is there? You are trespassing on Mormon property!" shouted a uniformed officer as he approached the pair. "I was suspicious when I saw you two disap— "

He stopped short and stared at the sparkle of the gold plates, now partially uncovered.

"Holy Moroni! Wait until the Elders hear about this. For now, you two come with me. You are under arrest for trespassing."

Adrian looked at Francois, and with a sigh, they followed the guard back to the security office appended to the inn.

While Adrian and Francois waited in a secure holding area, the guard spoke quietly to the security chief, whose eyes widened as the guard went on. The chief scratched his head and finally reached for the phone. In a muffled voice, they heard: "Sir, there has been a discovery on the church's property which I thought it important enough to call about." After a few more seconds, the chief said, "a cache of gold." After another pause the chief said, "Yes, gold, it appears to be in the form of plates ... Yes sir. I'll wait."

"Now what?" whispered Francois.

The chief waited for some response, which eventually came evoking only a curt "okay."

"We will just have to play it by ear," said Adrian. "They are shaken up by the appearance of the gold, and even if there are secret doubters in the bunch, they are now reassessing their views of the fundamentals of the faith. We will have to wait and see if they try to translate the things before revealing their existence. Trouble is, there are at least two other people who know about it now, the deputy who captured us and the chief himself. We will have to wait and see if they can keep a lid on it."

It was another half hour before a solemn group of Elders entered the security office. Subdued exchanges followed with frequent gestures toward the captives. Finally, the assembly approached them.

"Here they come," whispered Francois.

"Sir, by what right did you invade and defile the sacred grounds of the Church?" asked one of the Elders who had separated himself from the pack.

"Through inspiration impressed upon me by the great god who rules us," said Adrian without missing a beat.

In an effort to circumvent the concept implied, the sullen Elder responded hesitantly. "The gold you have found verifies one of the precepts of our faith, but being unknown to us and with uncertainty as to whether you even accept our beliefs, your involvement in this has still to be explained," said the Elder.

"It was only after entering the sacred grounds of the Mormons on a modest tourist sojourn did I receive the inspiration," said Adrian.

After a moment of silence, the elders retired to a corner and engaged in deep discussion. Eventually, the chief Elder again approached, this time with as close to an ingratiating countenance his austere nature would allow.

"You have done us a great service and uncovered items, which support the founding precepts of our movement. Whatever divine inspiration motivated you to do so is between you and the Creator. We are sorry to have detained you. You are free to enjoy the rewards of our founder's setting, or to go."

Francois and Adrian hurried to the car and away from the Mormon enclave.

"We will see how it works out," said Adrian. "They will either blab the whole shebang to the press to neutralize all the perennial naysayers, or take the conservative route and examine the plates first. We need to watch the media for clues."

Back in Obamopolis Adrian paced the floor.

"Nothing, it's been a month, and the Mormons have not said a word and appear to have quashed any leaks," said Francois.

"Yes, unfortunately they figured out what was on the plates and have suppressed it," said Adrian.

"Well, not quite. In addition to the closed bunch at the Mormon compound who know about it, we know about it. It is no surprise that within their ranks, an admonishment to secrecy was requested, but what if we blab it to the press and all over the net?"

"Who would believe us?" asked Adrian. "No doubt, the Mormons already have a rough translation of the plates. It's fortunate we didn't put that image of Winnie-the-Pooh on them. At the very least, they will be in a dither trying to explain how and why such an anomaly was found in the site of Mormon origins. In any case, I have been absent long enough and must get back to Eugenia."

XXII

Adrian Attempts to Establish a Trust Related Church in New York

Adrian sat mulling over the sermon he had prepared for the following Sunday. He squinted at the shadowed copy and looked up as Eugenia appeared in the doorway. Warmed by her presence in spite of the gray of overcast and shortened days, he was filled with a fleeting awareness that in periods of bliss, time passes quickly.

"I didn't want to disturb you when you were preparing tomorrow's sermon, but I thought you may want to know that the doctor has suggested that I come in for some tests."

"By all means," said Adrian with a pause. "I wasn't aware that anything was bothering you."

"Yes, I haven't been feeling well too well lately, but I didn't want to disturb you. I know you work hard to refine your Sunday message and must deal with problems of the congregation during the week."

"Well … we will have to pay close attention to it," said Adrian his voice trailing off as he stared at his beloved.

"What do you have for this Sunday?" asked Eugenia, changing the subject.

"A … a new tack," said Adrian tentatively, a nascent worry for the moment hindering his thoughts from moving forward. "I am trying to subtly move away from the commonplace subject of Christian morality in the direction of a universal ethic."

"That should please my father, who is full of cynicism when it comes to religion," said Eugenia with a laugh.

Sunday's sermon was going well until unexpectedly, a shout came from the congregation.

"Where is our savior Jesus Christ in your Church?"

"What kind of church is this where there is no mention of our blessed redeemer," shouted another standing beside him."

"Gentlemen," said Adrian, taken aback by the sudden interruption. "I had no intention of bringing insult by omission of that which you may hold sacred."

The congregation had turned to discover the source of the interruption. Two staid looking men stood in the rear of the auditorium gesticulating with an expression of outrage. Tentatively, Adrian started again to speak, and was again interrupted by the two visitors, who seemed intent on preventing the meeting. A few in the congregation quietly rose and left. Adrian managed to finish the sermon in spite of the repeated chides and interruptions. As everyone filed out of the meeting place, a small boy remained sitting in the rear of the seating area.

Adrian approached, stared at the child, and asked, "Are your parents here?"

"No," said the child. "I am by myself."

"Are you lost? Can I help you get home?"

"No, I know how to get to my house. I came to listen to you talk about things. I was here last week."

Funny, I don't remember seeing him then, thought Adrian. "Did you understand what I was talking about?"

"Yes, about everybody being good to each other."

I guess that is as fitting an explanation as any, thought Adrian.

"Those men were not here then," said the boy.

"You mean the two who interrupted the service?"

"Yes."

"Let's hope they don't come back. What is your name?" asked Adrian changing the subject.

"What is your name?"

"Felix."

"Felix. Felix—?"

"Adler, Felix Adler."

Probably Jewish, if my crash course on this timeline has taught me anything, thought Adrian.

"Felix, you are welcome here, but I worry that your parents might be concerned about where you are and what you are doing. They may not like my message as well as you do."

For the first time, the boy did not respond.

"Well," said Adrian, after a pause in an effort to revive some momentum in the exchange. "I would hope next time you will have their permission to come here and if they would themselves care to attend, they would be welcome."

Once again, Felix was silent.

"All Right, I must close the meeting hall now, and if you need someone to see you home, I will gladly do it."

"I can get to my house. It isn't far," said Felix who then left.

An odd kid if I ever saw one, thought Adrian. *He should be out playing instead of contemplating the mysteries of life.*

In the weeks following, Felix was always there. Then, suddenly, he was not.

I didn't see the kid today or last week, thought Adrian. *Parents probably caught on to his delinquency and put a stop to it.*

The two troublemakers periodically attended the meetings and began to bring others with similar complaints about the secular nature of Adrian's message to the exclusion of Christian references.

The weeks passed and Eugenia's condition worsened. She ate little and slept late. Disturbances in vision, balance, and coordination intruded on her daily life.

She is getting worse, thought Adrian. *My medical background doesn't extend to the realm of esoteric diseases, and this age doesn't have the extensive diagnostic tools that are available uptime.*[28] *But taking her there will mean revealing everything ... I may have no choice. The Kansas City portal is still open. I must get her there and make the transfer for her sake.*

"I have made a decision," said Adrian as the family assembled. "I must take Eugenia and go to seek out a specialist to diagnose and treat her condition."

"I realize we have given her over to you in marriage, but I would advise against subjecting her to any strenuous activity," said Edgar. "You have told me of your experience in medicine, but common sense would seem to go against your plans. It would be even dangerous to subject her to the stress of travel."

"Your caution is well intended, but I know enough to judge her condition as serious. For her sake, we must go … go south to Philadelphia where there is a specialist in brain disorders," improvised Adrian."

"It will also mean suspending your activity at the church," prodded Edgar. "You will lose some parishioners if you are gone for long."

"Yes, I expect so, but it can't be helped, unless you would like to take over temporarily."

"I will consider it," said Edgar after a pause. "I am pleased with your secular approach to the spiritual, but we seem to have collected a group of complaining misfits bent on creating disturbances. This is unfortunate, because after some skepticism, I have become increasingly interested in your efforts and surprised at the dormant dissatisfaction in the populace with organized religion. It will challenge my time allotment for business, but I may be able to manage it—until you return, that is."

After a contrived explanation interrupted by prolonged embraces, Adrian persuaded Eugenia of the gravity of the situation. They packed a minimum of provisions and departed the Winthrop household. It was some time before she awoke from frequent dozing to realize they were traveling westward.

"We aren't going to Philadelphia?" said Eugenia, sensing that Adrian had something else in mind.

"No my dearest," said Adrian. "I had to use a bit of deception to take you to the place where you are sure to get the best care. All will be explained when we reach our destination."

"I trust you to do what is best for me," said Eugenia in a fog of fatigue.

She was weak and exhausted as they finally pulled into Kansas City in the evening.

"We will rest the night in a hotel and will continue with the plan I have for you," said Adrian.

The next day he took Eugenia and headed for the suburbs.

It's beginning to look familiar, thought Adrian as he surveyed the dreary fog shrouded landscape. He focused on the surroundings. *I will back azimuth from those reference points there to be sure.*

"Adrian, what are we doing in this depressing place?" asked Eugenia, for the first time fearful of Adrian's unpredictable actions.

"Be patient for just a little longer," said Adrian as he took out his TR and activated it.

The bleak environs were immediately replaced by the interior of the Kansas City house.

"Brant Conjular, please, Mr. Beike calling," said Adrian as he connected to the ITR. After a moment's pause, Brant answered.

"Adrian, is that you?" asked a surprised Brant.

"Yes, it's me and I must consult with you. Eugenia has suffered a health reversal. That which ails her is outside the realm of my medical experience and the scope of intervention procedures of the nineteenth century. I made this decision to return her uptime to diagnose and hopefully cure her condition."

"Okay, hold tight. I will see if I can get the GSI chopper to pick you up. It will take at least two or three hours to get there."

A confused Eugenia spoke. "Dearest Adrian, who were you talking to and where is this strange place? How did we get here? I gaze through the window and see houses of unusual shape and an occasional carriage passing by at enormous speeds, propelled by nothing visible."

Adrian took a breath. "First of all, it was only with reluctance that I brought you here, but it is the only place I could hope to restore you to good health. It is also something of which I have not thought necessary to tell you. I have felt guilty about not being truthful. The vehicles passing by are called automobiles and are only one of the strange and unfamiliar things you will experience here. The hardest thing for you to grasp; however, is how we got here. The 'here' I am talking about does not mean place, but refers to time. We have moved through time to the future where new discoveries have been made and developed."

"How is this possible unless ... unless you yourself are from this place, that is, this time?"

"You have guessed right," said Adrian. "I am not from the time period in which we met. I was there for a specific purpose which I won't go into now, but I was blessed to have met you there and decided at the time to remain there with you."

"When is this time in relation to my time?"

"It is some four centuries forward, 2287 A.D., to be exact."

The hours passed, and the faint clatter of the chopper intruded on the cascade of questions about the novel venue in which Eugenia found herself.

"It's here," said Adrian. "We need to get to Obamapolis and see to your diagnosis and treatment."

"Will I again meet those two incredible women who rescued me from

Quantrill's rabble?" asked Eugenia, with a dawning that there might be some connection between their somewhat mysterious appearance and her new situation.

"Yes, and others you have encountered since we first met," said Adrian, surprised that Lila and Vanora had made such an impression. "If your treatment is successful, you can decide whether to stay here or return to your time. In any case, some communication with your parents will be necessary. We need first to get settled and arrange for you to see a specialist."

The flight back flight back to Obamapolis filled Eugenia with wonder and added to the numerous questions about the strange venue she in which she now found herself.

With some apprehension, Adrian and Eugenia faced the doctor, a neurologist who had taken the case.

"I have reviewed your history, considered the symptoms, and consulted with my colleagues," the doctor began. "We have concluded that you are suffering from a pituitary adenoma. Your symptoms—problems of vision, hearing, and balance, along with trouble with coordination and reflexes—confirm it. It can be relieved with endoscopic surgery. We can schedule it for next week."

"I don't know if I can bear the discomforts of surgery," said Eugenia after they had left the office. "Is not the cure more stressful than the disease?"

"The surgery you know is primitive compared with the painless procedures possible now," said Adrian. "Due to dramatic changes in anesthetics, you will not experience pain during the operation although in the recovery period you could experience some minor discomfort. In any case, I will be at your side."

"I have trust in you," said Eugenia.

"So, we meet again," said Lila as she and Vanora entered Eugenia's hospital room.

"Yes ..." said Eugenia as she struggled against the remnants of anesthesia. "It is so nice to see you both again. I cherish memories of our time together, but hunger for the truths behind it all."

"Adrian will have to explain to you from the beginning just what he was doing in your time period in the first place," said Lila. "For us, the important thing is that you regain your health."

Several days later, Eugenia was well enough to leave the hospital.

As they sat in the smart quarters of the GSI visitor's residence, she once again appeared alert.

"Adrian," she said suddenly, "please tell me more about this strange world I find myself in and what you have to do with it."

Adrian stared at her for a prolonged moment and then began.

"First of all, to add to your confusion, I must tell you that not only am I not from your time period—I am not even from this timeline. The idea of different timelines, each with its own history, will be new and bordering on the fantastic to you, but now, at least two timelines are known to each other and in contact. How many others may exist in parallel with us has yet to be determined, but this timeline was created by a specific action in my original timeline. It happens through some unpredictable and mysterious interaction between the stark physical realities of the universe and pivotal human events. In the case of this timeline, the triggering event was the introduction by my original timeline, of an agent, the adult figure of Jesus Christ"... *No use further confusing her with the details of that,* thought Adrian.

"As for myself, my presence and purpose here was to instill a new ethic into the course of humanity in the name of our sponsor, the Trust for the Fusion of Science and the Spirit. It was not what resulted. With all our good intentions, the action created a Christian religion centered on the persona of Jesus rather than the ethical ideals we promote. Myself and Francois LeBrust, whom you met in Dodge, are here to correct as much as possible, the drift of this religious movement, and to do it without once again disturbing the flow of time. Such was my mission until I met you. Now, after a considerable number of close calls, I am emotionally exhausted and want to settle down and pass on the mission of the Trust to whomever the leadership chooses."

Adrian stopped talking. His convoluted narrative hung suspended in silence until finally Eugenia was moved to speak.

"The fantasy you have woven ties the mind in knots, but the reality of my affection for you is what sustains me now. I hope it lasts forever."

"It will," said Adrian, embracing her in the sheer joy of the moment. "We must somehow get word to your parents concerning your recovery since they will be anxious," said Adrian as they came back to earth. "We can either go back together, or I can return briefly to your period and post a letter from Kansas City."

"We should know after a few weeks if my recovery will last," said Eugenia. "Then, perhaps we should return to ... to my time. In the near term I am most happy there, even though the marvels of this place have captured my imagination."

"We can have the best of two worlds," said Adrian with the thought, *maybe of several.*

Weeks past, and Eugenia rallied to her old vibrant self and mingled freely with those both new and those whom she had met previously.

"We have decided for now to return to Eugenia's home period," said Adrian as they met the others for dinner one night. "Eugenia's parents need to be informed of her improved condition. Also, I must contend with the riffraff that keep intruding on my services."

"What's that?" asked Brant. "You didn't mention it before."

"A rogue element that started coming to my services and causing disruption," said Adrian. "I have tried appeasing them, but they are a bunch of fundamentalists who are convinced that I am preaching heresy because I make no references to Jesus. I thought they would get tired of harassing me and go away."

Lila perked up. "Oh, I really should make a little visit to your church and take Vanora. I thought that period had its quaint charms."

Brant rolled his eyes knowing what she had in mind. *She cannot leave things alone. She gets a high if there is a remote possibility she can crack some villainous heads.*

"I would be happy to welcome you to my congregation if only temporarily," said Adrian, naively oblivious as to what she had in mind.

"That's great," said Lila with hyperbolic enthusiasm.

Brant stood with a sour expression on his face. *She's going to get herself shot by some nineteenth century lunatic ... And in the never-land of time travel, we still don't know what happens in the time stream when someone from a future period dies in the past.*

Do what you have to do and get back here. We need to consolidate the contact with Adrian's timeline. And take some weapons," barked Brant, stirred by a subliminal impatience.

Preparations were made, and the van left for the transfer point.

"It shouldn't take long," were Lila's jaunty parting words.

They arrived at the Kansas City house and transferred. The ever-gloomy landscape didn't seem so depressing now, with Eugenia's recovery and Lila's stream of sardonic remarks. They once again made for the city center and the railroad. Arriving in New York and the Winthrop homestead, they were joyously greeted by Edgar and Sally.

"We were worried since we had heard nothing from you," said Edgar. "The war to the south has delayed communications, and we feared you had been caught up in the conflict."

"We are both all right. Eugenia's condition has been relieved, and she seems to have recovered," said Adrian with the mordant thought; *sometimes a war can be convenient.* "We have brought the two friends I told you about who rescued me from Quantrill's rabble. We happened upon them in … Philadelphia," said Eugenia with a glance at Adrian. "Could they stay in the guest house?"

"Certainly, it would be my pleasure," said Edgar. "I'll have the servants prepare it immediately."

"How did things go at the church?" asked Adrian as they sat at the dinner table.

"Not so good," said Edgar. "The trouble makers were there every Sunday, each time bringing more of their friends. Much of the congregation has drifted away, with the exception of a few hardy souls."

"With your permission, we would like to persuade your … visitors to behave themselves," said Lila.

"I don't know," said Edgar, stroking his beard. Eugenia has told me in general terms that you used physical violence to rescue her. The church is no place for such activity."

"Then what, if such were necessary, it were done outside the church?" asked Lila.

"Well … if it can salvage the movement Adrian has worked so hard for, perhaps it can be permitted," said Edgar.

"Perhaps you can stand outside the church and tell me who the trouble makers are, and then we can prevent them from entering in the first place."

The now sparse collection of parishioners filled into the Church for the Sunday service.

"That's them," said Edgar, as two men of medium stature approached.

Lila stepped forward with Vanora slightly behind and to the side fondling a stick of considerable proportions. "I'm sorry, sir, but due to your disruptive behavior on previous visits, you will not be permitted to enjoy the benefits of the service."

Somewhat amused, the men looked at one another and started to circle the pair.

Lila did a quick sweep with her leg, upending the man in the lead. His companion helped him up, and the two retired to a safe distance in heated discussion.

"That does it for now," said Lila as they waited for the men to leave for good before reentering the church. I have a feeling we have not heard the last of them. I think we will stay around for a few weeks and let Brant cool his heels. This may get nasty."

The next week, the two showed up again with three beefy cohorts.

"There they are again, this time with reinforcements," said Lila. "This is getting interesting."

The troublemakers remained at a distance as their advance guard started to enter. Lila was there with her gentle warning as the group pushed her aside and swept past her.

Vanora was not so easily pushed aside, and when the first of the rabble brushed against her, she dealt a fist into the side of his head.

Surprised at the fury of the assault, the remaining two hesitated for an instant then attacked Vanora in a body while the first of the riffraff struggled to unscramble his brains from Vanora's blow. As the still intact duo turned and focused on Vanora, Lila dealt a well-placed foot between the spread legs of the trailing one. The remaining assailant oblivious to the fate of his moaning colleague, grabbed at Vanora, but was simultaneously upended by Lila from behind and creased with a blow from Vanora's stick, which she wielded like the gladiatorial weapon of her origin.

As the trio limped, crawled, and slithered away. The trouble making two who had stayed behind, retired back down the street affronting the church.

It's okay for now, thought Lila, *but those two have an endless capacity to make mischief, and we w on't be here to prevent it.*

Later, after dinner, Lila cornered Adrian and expressed her concerns.

"We can't stay here permanently to troubleshoot the problems of your movement. My judgment is that you have not heard the last of these riffraff. You might consider alternate plans should things go out of control. We will stay a few more days and hopefully, things will die down."

"I know this," said Adrian. "I am sorry to get Edgar and his family involved in it. Should things degenerate, I will consider returning uptime with Eugenia."

Two nights later a frantic knocking on the Winthrop's residence door signaled trouble.

"They have set the mission house on fire," exclaimed the breathless messenger.

All rushed to the scene, as locals worked to extinguish the blaze. An hour later, Adrian gazed woefully at the remnants of the building.

"I guess it was inevitable," said Adrian with a sigh.

"I somehow feel that it may have survived, had we not so heavy-handedly interfered," said Lila remorsefully.

"Don't blame yourself," said Adrian. "It was destined to happen. Rogue elements have had it in for us from the start. We all relished their temporary comeuppance. The question is, where do we go from here?"

"You are always welcome back in our timeline," said Lila. "You can even concentrate on reconnecting with your own timeline and finding a place for your skills."

"I will have to consult with Eugenia about returning uptime," said Adrian.

Later, in the privacy of the Winthrop house, Adrian sounded her out on the move.

"I feel guilty in withholding our future plans from my dear parents, but if you wish to do it in secret, I can always use the excuse of the property bequeathed to me in California. You remember, I was returning from there when we first met. We can suggest we are going there for a new start. It is far enough away to expect infrequent communication. I will have to arrange a caretaker for the estate, but I can do that from here along with any confidentiality needed."

"For now, at least, I believe it is the best course," said Adrian on consideration. "In the future, perhaps, we can reveal all including your miraculous recovery from illness."

Bidding a tearful goodbye to Edgar and Sally, the couple along with Lila and Vanora, once again journeyed to the Kansas City portal. An anxious Brant met them as they appeared in the transfer perimeter.

"It didn't work out," said Lila. "It would have required continual policing of the meetings. Adrian and Eugenia have decided to cast their lots with this era."

"That's good," said Brant. "Given the paucity of knowledge of the Trust's timeline, it will be helpful to have Adrian around as we develop our contact."

Adrian in a Moment of Déjà vu

"Well Adrian, as long as you are committed to this timeline, maybe you can attach yourself to some activity similar to what you tried to start in Eugenia's nineteenth century setting," suggested Brant. "Other than the odd directions the Christian movement has taken away from the aims of the Trust, there should be some spinoffs of it that are closer to what the Trust originally intended. Once committed, your ingenuity should enable you to derive some income from it."

"A helpful suggestion," said Adrian. "In fact, I came across a notice in the newspaper about a movement called Ethical Culture. I thought I would look into it even though I was suspicious that it was there, amidst the Christian, Jewish, and other manifestations of the correct answer to it all."

"Yes, the Ethical Culture movement has been around for several centuries, always there but has never seemed to take off like some of the conventional denominations," said Brant. "When Obamapolis was founded, a branch was established here. I'm sure Rajulk could give you a more thorough rundown."

With little else to do, I think I will look into it myself," said Adrian. "A little visit to the internet should fill in the blanks."

Adrian sat staring at the screen. The man in the period photo, the founder of the Ethical Culture movement, stared back. The name in the caption read "Felix Adler." He recalled the child who had frequented his services in a vain attempt to equate the image he summoned up to the mature countenance that inhabited the screen.

It is too much of a coincidence. It must be him, thought Adrian.

XXIII

Time Travel Exposed

Bryce Carter spent a day following anemic leads in hope of nailing a story to pitch to Ninor Conroy, senior editor at the *Tribune*. He picked up a copy of the paper at the corner stand and headed to his favorite bar. Settling in a corner booth with a double scotch, he mulled over his prospects as a free-lance reporter. He unfolded the paper and took a sip of scotch. A minor headline on the front page caught his eye, beginning on the front page and continuing inside.

INTELLIGENCE HEAD DISAPPEARS

"GENERAL CARLEN BROMFSTED, ARMY CHIEF OF INTELLIGENCE
HAS DISAPPEARED ALONG WITH AN AIDE ..."

"Bromfsted," muttered Carter as he shuffled through to the continuing page, which showed photos of both. *That's the brass that corralled and grilled me the other day. Now they are both missing. What's going on here? What the hell was it they wanted to know? ... Oh yes, about some time travel malarkey Lenny Barre floated ... Maybe Barre wasn't so crazy after all and was just being cagy. Now the general himself and his aide are missing. If there is a connection, it could be because Bromfsted was getting too close to the truth, which brings me back to that bunch at the GSI and the time travel stuff. I must run this by Conroy.*

Ninor Conroy sat listening to Carter. "I thought that time travel thing was dead."

"I thought so too, but now even the team that questioned me about it is missing," said Carter. "Maybe we should call those magicians over at the GSI on it. We could float some connection to the disappearance of the general, put the whole thing out there, and let them squirm. We can beef up the story by relating the retention of both me and Barre."

The next day a banner headline leapt off the page of the *Tribune.*

Time Travel a Fact?

Brant was on the phone to a drowsy Frondner. "Did you see the *Tribune?*

"No. What's in it?"

"They apparently felt confident enough to blow the whole time travel thing up in our faces. They got the jump on us. Our idea of a controlled release is now gone. They put two and two together and figured they had enough to expose it. We all know that when it all comes out, it is the story of the century. Bromfsted, or shall we say the lack of him, is mentioned along with his aide. They may be able to pinpoint Bromfsted's disappearance with his visit to the lab. If anything can be proven, we could be charged with kidnaping. We might weather it, if Bromfsted was willing to go along with the idea of a voluntary absence. A simple 'no comment' will blank the press but may not work with the authorities. Some bigwig will see it as a chance to make a name for himself. We need to get together for a response. I will be at the ITR. You can join me there. The GSI has been targeted, and they will be down our throats at any time. Gird yourself for an onslaught. The press, as usual, will get there first, but the authorities will follow up quickly."

"Got it," said Frondner. "I'll see you at the GSI."

When Frondner arrived at the GSI, it was already ringed with reporters. A cursory "no comment" put them off as he plowed his way through the herd. *We'll need something else for when the senators and the FBI get here.*

Brant met him along with Lila and Rajulk in the ITR lounge.

"Okay, how shall we handle this?" asked Frondner.

"I say we keep stonewalling," said Lila. "They can't prove a thing. Any forensic probe of the wall of junk here will reveal nothing definitive."

"Okay, the lingering aspect of this chatter is that we will be under the constant eye of both the press and the authorities," said Frondner.

Brant spoke up. "What happens when we finally bring back Bromfsted and Defoe? We can't leave them in Fortaleza forever."

His query was met with silence until Frondner himself finally said: "We can deal with that later. Meanwhile, I will go and speak to the Press." He stepped outside to confront them.

"Now, just what do you want to know," said Frondner.

"What's all this about time travel, and what do you know about the disappearance of General Bromfsted?" asked several of the reporters in a series of overlapping queries."

"As far as the General is concerned, he did make a courtesy visit to us, but left." *He did leave, so to speak,* thought Frondner.

The reporter persisted. "But he hasn't been seen since."

"We are as concerned about the general's disappearance as you are and hope he and his aide are safe, wherever they are," said Frondner.

"What about your employee's statement concerning items retrieved from ancient times?"

"I questioned him about that, and he said he was inebriated and just trying to impress his uh … companion. Aside from that, you have our previous announcement of the minute breakthroughs at the Institute of Temporal Research, which continues to pursue penetration of the barriers to the past.

"He's wearing them down," said Brant who had been listening to the exchange from the inside.

The phone rang.

"Get that," Brant said to Lila as he continued to monitor the standoff between Frondner and the press.

"It's senator Levendorf." said Lila with her hand over the phone.

"Here comes Frondner. Let him deal him deal with it", said Brant.

"That will do it by now. Most of them are drifting away," said Frondner.

"Good," said Lila handing over the phone. "You take this. It's Senator Levendorf"

Frondner took the phone with a grimace and intoned a pleasant, "Senator Levendorf."

"Sir, I am chairman of the senate Committee on Intelligence. We, as you know, deal with current and projected security threats to the nation. Recent items on the media concerning activities at the GSI have sparked our attention anew, in particular the experiments in time travel and the results, along with a bundle of anecdotal evidence suggesting that the GSI has achieved the capability and is sitting on it. This may be an attempt by the press to lift some modest scientific advance to the levels of science fiction. But if there are discoveries beyond the event you celebrated some months ago, we as an instrument of the government need to know about it." [29]

I didn't even know he was at the event, thought Frondner. *We should have realized that they have a finger in everything, real and imagined.*

"The press seems to promote the most spectacular extrapolation of any occurrence in the human sphere," said Frondner. "Our specialists at the ITR are constantly working to further the modest advance we celebrated. They have just initiated new strategies to enhance temporal penetration. I am waiting to hear if there has been a breakthrough. *That's benign enough to hold him until we can engage in a more confidential setting.*

"I would like to hear more about your progress," said Levendorf

"You are invited to the lab at any time. Dr. Conjular will show you around."

"How did it go?" asked Brant.

"I put him off since we were on an unsecured line, but I have invited him to the lab for a look-see. In any case, we are getting in deeper and deeper. We have to come out soon. Once we do, we should probably give the press something more to chew on. We can get some government rep of the astronaut type to go back and witness the worst incidents of history."

"If we have a choice in it, that gives me an idea," said Brant. "We could claim that, at this time, we can't control where the transfer takes us. We could, by mistake, whisk some sucker off to the era of the black plague."

"Good idea. That should turn the good senator and the civilian population off to the process for now. But it might not phase the military if they're looking for some application of time travel. In any case, if we had to stage such a demonstration, we would have to immunize the subject to death. It would still leave the Bromfsted and Defoe situation in limbo, but, with their permission, we could doctor their disappearance later."

Brant and Frondner greeted Levendorf when he showed up at the lab the next day.

"Senator, it is a pleasure to see you," said Frondner. "With me here is Dr. Conjular, head of the ITR, the Institute of Temporal Research. I must tell you first hand that I could not disclose the true state of things over an unsecured phone line."

"What … what is it that was not disclosed before?"

"The details concerning the fate of General Bromfsted and his aide, Lieutenant Defoe," said Frondner.

"What do you mean? What happened to them?" asked Levendorf, now confused.

"It involves technical aspects of the transfer process. I will let Dr. Conjular explain it."

"Even with the state of temporal transfer still in its experimental stage, the penetration into the past is more than we have previously disclosed," said Brant. "This was our choice, in the interest of national security. Regarding the general and his aide, they inadvertently stumbled into to an active transfer field when they visited the lab. We have not yet determined where or when they went. We hope they are safe, and we still hope to retrieve them, but that will require a much more precise analysis and control of the transfer process. We are near to solving it."

"As a representative of the people, I feel I must disclose this," said Levendorf uncertainly.

"It would lead to the great embarrassment of us all, including congress in general and your committee in particular, and the end result may be the dissolution of the GSI whose contributions to the national prestige are well known?" said Frondner.

"Then … what would you suggest?" asked Levendorf after a moment of silence.

"Give us some time to solve the dilemma, and we can all emerge from the quandary unscathed. In the worst scenario, you can deny any knowledge of the whole thing."

"We are under time constraints," said Levendorf. "A rational explanation of it all will have to surface soon. The press will not let up when they smell something fishy, and we will be under increased pressure." He turned to go adding, "Keep me continually informed."

"That buys us some time," said Frondner after Levendorf was gone. "We need to connect with Bromfsted to see if he will cooperate. Fortunately, we have the new link in place in this hemisphere."

"I'll go," said Brant. "I will explain the situation and see if he will go for it. Hopefully, his experience of time travel has given him a new perspective."

Brant made the now familiar trip to Fortaleza. Taking advantage of the new western hemisphere link, he transferred to the alternate timeline. A short walk brought him to the vicinity of the Trust's new home, but the busy scene at the nearby docks gave pause to his purpose for being there. An armada of ships stood anchored off shore, and the hubbub of noise accompanied a euphoria of greetings. He spotted Rajulk in the onlookers and waved for his attention.

"I don't know what developments have brought you here, but you are just in time," said Rajulk. "We have liberated the remainder of the Trust personnel who were kidnapped by pirates. They are just now returning. Bromfsted took part in the rescue and seems to have adapted to his new situation."

"That's great to hear, especially that Bromfsted is cooperating with us. It is timely because it is exactly the reason the reason I am here," said Brant. "The whole story of our discovery and use of time travel is about to break. Someone we have previously butted heads with has put two and two together and thrown it out there. The burden of time travel has subtly shifted. We have to either insist that it isn't so, or to come out with the truth."

"Since Bromfsted is the key to a smooth release of the whole thing, we need to consult with him and explain the situation," said Rajulk, wincing at the thought.

"So, now the shoe is on the other foot," said Bromfsted as a humbled Brant and Rajulk stood before him, figurative hats in hand.

Bromfsted let a moment of silence fill the anxious void.

"I understand your dilemma and have come to appreciate your concern about making the whole thing public. Having stumbled on the capability of time travel, your first instinct as scientists was to plumb its potential for clarifying history without disturbing it, which can result in alternate realities. Since I am of the military, I would look to the possibility of using it for defense in the greater interest of the country. Now that things seem to be out of our hands, we must make the best of it. I will make an appearance before chief of staff General Morehouse and explain everything."

"We are glad you see it that way," said Brant. "There may be unforeseen results from rogue forces ending up in timelines from which they cannot return or be extracted. We can emphasize that. My take is that once the consequences are known, mischief-makers will tread carefully. The technical process is complex, but an occasional kook will engineer it and end up in never-land. It can't be helped. Therefore, we seem to be in some kind of agreement. When we return, I will have

Frondner prepare a statement. We will explain your absence in any way you suggest.

"Yes, how about this as a start: 'I as Chief of Army Intelligence, having become aware of the phenomenon, chose to investigate its potential in the interests of security. Just as you laid it out to Senator Levendorf, Lieutenant Defoe and I visited your lab and accidently slipped into a transfer field. You were in a tizzy and worked frantically to solve the problem. Finally, having done so, the scientists have managed to return us to the uptime present to explain what happened and reveal the startling fact of time travel to the world. We will, for now, leave out the little detail of a parallel timeline.

"That may work," said Brant with a relieved nod from Rajulk.

Bromfsted, Defoe, Rajulk, and Brant bounced back to the Christian timeline and made the journey from the Fortaleza site to the States, and Obamapolis.

Strolling anonymously into the Obamapolis office of the Chief of Staff dressed in civilian clothes, Bromfsted pronounced, "Please tell General Morehouse that General Bromfsted wishes to see him."

The young lieutenant in reception looked at the person dressed in civilian clothes standing before him and suddenly realized who he was.

Bromfsted heard the muted voice of the excited aide as he spoke to Morehouse.

Morehouse rushed from the office and stood mute, staring at Bromfsted. Amused, Bromfsted did a cursory salute and walked past him into his office. The open-mouthed Chief followed him in. Bromfsted closed the door.

"Where on earth have you been?" asked the confounded Chief. "Rumors have been flying that you were abducted, deserted, or went off you rocker along with that aide of yours, and where the hell is she?"

"All will be revealed when I tell you what happened."

"Go on," Morehouse blurted out in exasperation.

"First of all, Lieutenant Defoe is well and will appear in due course."

"Here's how it went. When we, from curiosity, visited the facility at the GSI to investigate the absurd rumors relating to time travel, we didn't expect anything beyond a pile of unfathomable gizmos and claims of some minute highly theoretical advance in the field. It turned out that the GSI's esoteric division with the pompous name ITR, standing for Institute for Temporal Research, had made extraordinary advances. Lieutenant Defoe and I accidently blundered into one of the transfer perimeters and ended up in another timeframe.

"You mean you were actually somewhere or some—some time else?"

"Yes," said Bromfsted, "In a previous period—the twentieth century, to be exact."

Morehouse sat down, stared at Bromfsted, and then off in space.

Bromfsted was the first to speak. "The capacity to travel in time is a monumental advance in both science and humankind. I think if we release the information selectively, emphasizing the danger and unpredictability of the process, rogue forces will shy away from it."

"I'll accept your judgment on that," said Morehouse after a moment's thought. "Of course, the press will want details of your adventure, if you know what I mean, and we will have to make up a plausible story for Levendorf and his damned committee."

Epilogue

A muted cacophony filled the room as the club of exclusive time travelers sat, stood, and lounged in the GSI rec room.[30]

Frondner tapped his glass and all faded to a quiet.

"The secret is out, or at least some of it. The technical process enabling time travel has been revealed, but not the stories of your individual experiences within it. We hope to keep those in the confines of our exclusive club.

"I would like to pitch a suggestion. I have been considering those of you in the exclusive trans-temporal club we have brought back from other periods. Even if the exchange between timelines goes dormant, as Brant has suggested, you will be the artifacts of our efforts. For this reason, I have brought you all together to honor your uniqueness under the name of some sort of society or organization. Of course, our young friends, Aspira and Aran, won't yet understand what I am talking about. No matter, in time it will be explained to them. As to the club name, let's see if we can come up with something."

"We could give it a duplicitous name," said Lila after a pause, like ... ATFV for Action Task Force for Virtue, but with the real meaning of ... Alternate Timeline Family Vagabonds."

Frondner broke through the explosion of laughter that ensued. "Shouldn't we keep it serious? What if the press decided to cover it?"

"Whatever we call it, if anyone chose to zero in on it and start digging, we might well have problems," said Brant only partially recovered. "In the meantime, we might as well have some fun with it and have our reunions under the blanket of the—what was it?"

"A-T-F-V," intoned Lila reverently.

"Yes, the ATFV"

"We would put a public face on the advocacy of virtue," said Lila with a straight face, to a resurgence of laughter.

"In this permissive age, wouldn't we come under the reticule of the press?" pressed Brant.

"The joke will be on them," said Rajulk.

"We need a logo," said Lila. "How about that babe who is pictured on those old Columbia Picture intros?"

"There may be copyright problems with that," said Frondner, now somewhat weary of the frivolous drift of the discussion.

"We can get permissions for some generic virgin to fill the need. I will engage the quest," said Lila grandly.

"And I commission you to the task," said Brant, matching her feigned pomposity.

A week later, Lila called the club together for the unveiling.

"I'm with her most of the time, but she's been up to something," said Brant.

"We will soon find out," said Rajulk, already sensing the unexpected from the unpredictable Lila.

Lila leaned against the drink dispenser talking to Barry as Brant and Rajulk entered the rec room of the ITR.

"There you are." She gestured to the draped easel. "I was getting ready to unveil the surprise without you."

She strode over to the easel and stripped away the covering.

"Behold our new logo."

"You've got to be kidding," said Brant against a background of uncontrolled laughter.

Notes

1 - A chronicle of the first mission, entitled *The Gospel Probe*, was placed in the Restricted Archives of the Government Science Institute (GSI), parent organization of the Institute of Temporal Research, the ITR.

2 - An account of the second mission, entitled *The Romp of LeBrust,* was rendered in duplicate by Lark Zakraven, a participant of the mission. One copy is in the restricted archives of the Government Science Institute (GSI), and the other in the archives of the Ecumenical Council.

3- Garuletzsky: An agrarian cult in the Trust's timeline in a symbiotic relationship with the Trust.

4- Xerjinko: A roving band that warred with the Trust and encroached on Garuletzsky lands, as detailed in *The Romp of LeBrust,* the second novel of the Gospel Probe series.

5 - Flood of Deutchia: A metaphor for the dissolution of the federated sovereignties of Deutchia, the geographic equivalent of Europe in the Trust timeline.

6 - Temporal Reciprocators (TRs): Handheld devices connected to the instrumentation devised to enable time travel.

7 - The Great Inland Sea and the River of Majesty: Names given to the Mediterranean and the Nile River in the Trust timeline.

8 – *Wavant:* Communication by superimposing information on

disturbances in the electromagnetic spectrum, the Trust's scientific equivalent of radio.

9 - Lieutenant Carl Onsley: Bromfsted's assistant who was sent on a mission to shadow Francois LeBrust, only to be ensnared in a time transfer. The incident and subsequent events are recorded in *The Romp of LeBrust*, pp. 242 - 283.

10- *Mumurastation:* A Gallogermanian word in use by Trust operatives meaning a deception that exploits superstition; equivalent to the English expression "mumbo jumbo."

11 - Anglo: The English language equivalent in alternate use with Gallogermanian in the timeline of the Trust.

12 - The period during which Adrian assumed the role of Jesus to further the Trust's aims is detailed in *The Gospel Probe*.

13 - William Clarke Quantrill was a Confederate guerrilla leader during the American Civil War who led a Confederate bushwhacker unit along the Missouri-Kansas border in the early 1860s, which included the infamous raid and sacking of Lawrence, Kansas in 1863.

14 - Hogback Ridge: Now known as Mount Oread; is a lift in the landscape of Lawrence, Kansas, which has become the seat of the University of Kansas.

15 - A chronicle of Adrian's venture into biblical Judea may be found in *The Gospel Probe*, previously cited.

16 - An account of Adrian's ordeal on the cross as the Jesus figure may be found in *The Gospel Probe*, pp. 145 and 182.

17 - As detailed in The Gospel Probe, Rajulk was commandeered by Roman soldiers and forced to join a road-building contingent east of Jerusalem.

18 - Saul of Tarsus (Saint Paul) met unexpected resistance to his message in *Iconium*. The meeting descended into chaos and had to be quelled by

Francois LeBrust's use of a lachrymatory agent. The incident is recorded in *The Romp of LeBrust,* p. 45.

19 - Carlen Bromfsted: US Army Intelligence chief and recurring nemesis of the ITR.

20 - Van Croizen: Francois LeBrust's pseudonym in the post of Vatican press secretary as presented in *The Romp of LeBrust.*

21 - The staged "celebration" of a scientific breakthrough regarding time travel brought together a menagerie of period costumes. Bromfsted's unfortunate choice, a Teutonic Knight encountered Brant bedecked as the conquering Alexander Nevsky.

22 - Wild hair - A twentieth-century expression for the abrupt appearance of dubious inspiration. The expression springs from the idea that there is a deviation in the normal course of rational thought when confronted with the unexpected presence of a wayward follicle in the rectal area.

23- Flood: The Flood of Deutchia was not a flood in the usual sense, but the metaphor of uncontrolled water fit the course of events in the Europe of the Trust's timeline—the disruption of the European Council of Nations due to irreconcilable differences and the dissolution of areas of defined authority.

24 - Mark Vanor Petrov takes his given names from two brought back from the Roman period: Marcus Petrilius Petrov, a Roman centurion, and Vanora (Vanorissiama-por Vibia Vivius), a Roman female gladiator. Both were rescued from the Roman period as detailed in *The Gospel Probe* and *The Romp of LeBrust.*

25- As a diversion, the time travel team staged an event to commemorate a modest advance in penetrating the time barrier, inviting all participants and potential nemeses. See *The Romp of LeBrust,* p. 201.

26 - As detailed in *The Gospel Probe,* Thaddeaus was the assumed name of Francois LeBrust in the role of Trust agent during the biblical period. The name itself has come down to us through the lore of the period.

27 - The story of Barabbas's detention and trial before Pontius Pilate and his subsequent interaction with Rajulk is related in *The Gospel Probe*.

28 - Adrian acquired and used medical knowledge in preparation for his role as agent of the Trust. See *The Romp of LeBrust*, pp. 160 and 162.

29 - In order to divert attention from the real progress, the Institute of Temporal Research, (ITR) staged a faux celebration celebrating a minute breakthrough in penetrating the time barrier. See *The Romp of LeBrust.* pp. 266-276.

30 - Those who were brought back to the uptime present of the Christian timeline in this series, which includes *The Gospel Probe, the Romp of LeBrust,* and this title, are Marcus Atrius Petilius, Belator, Elisheva, Vanora, and the children Aspira and Aran.

Characters Listed In Order Of Appearance

Barry Bass – Assumed name of Barabbas in the uptime present.

Lila McEntire – Scientist in the ITR, martial arts expert, and confidant of Brant Conjular.

Danner Binzing - Leader of the scientific wing of the Trust for The Fusion of Science and the Spirit.

Danbro - Security Chief of the Trust.

Adrian Beike - Agent from the Christian timeline inserted into native cultures in various guises to instill the values of the Trust.

Brant Conjular - Chief scientist of the Institute of Temporal Research (ITR).

Marzin Jut - Primary Rector of the Alcon Enclave.

Kara Satin – Trust agent chosen along with Dolf Barret to reestablish contact with the Christian timeline after the demise of the Trust enclave.

Lors Roux - Technician of the Trust overseeing the process of time travel.

Dolf Barret - Lieutenant of the Trust Security Force chosen with Kara Satin to probe for a renewed contact with the envoys of the Christian timeline.

Francois LeBrust - Prime agent along with Adrian Beike in the quest to promote the values of the Trust.

Gerald Frondner - Head of Government Science Institute (GSI).

General Carlin Bromfsted – Chief of Security of the US Army and recurrent nemesis of the ITR.

Rajulk - Parzan Rajulk Petrov - Scholar and prime field operator of the ITR.

Joseph Smith - Founder of the Mormons.

Seth Richards - Operations tech of ITR.

Eugenia Winthrop - Wife to be of Adrian Beike.

William Clarke Quantrill - Confederate guerrilla leader who sacked Lawrence Kansas in 1863.

Calvert Bliss - Undertaker in Manchester N.Y.

Booster Claven – New York resident who befriended Adrian in his journey to reunite with Eugenia.

Edgar and Sally Winthrop - Parents of Eugenia Winthrop.

Vanora –(Vanorissiama-por Vibia Vivius) - a Roman female gladiator brought back from Roman Era and confidant of Lila McEntire.

Larson - Sheriff of Lawrence Kansas.

Anderson - Supply envoy for Quantrill.

Thoth - Rajulk's ally when he was captive aboard the *Roman bireme.*

Aspira - Child discovered during Rajulk's journey from Alexandria back to his transfer point near Pelusium.

Lt. Jebbia Defoe - Assistant to General Bromfsted.

Bryce Carter - Freelance reporter.

Ninor Conroy - Senior editor at the *Tribune.*

Lenny Barre - Secretary to Gerald Frondner.

General Sneed - Chief of Intelligence Ft. Riley.

General Norman - Base Commander at Ft. Riley.

Longton - Owner of property in Blairton purchased by the Trust.

Fenart - Leader of first Trust migration to Blairton.

Lenyon - Leader of second wave of Trust citizens migrating to Blairton.

Onsley - See footnote 9.

Captain Carley - Previous aide to Bromfsted.

Cardinal Alofi - Senior Cardinal at The Sacred Congregation for the Doctrine of the Faith.

Cardinal Alohi - Press attaché at the Vatican.

Felix Adler - Founder of the Ethical Culture movement who as a child frequented Adrian's Church.

Senator Levendorf - Chairman of the senate Committee on Intelligence.

General Morehouse - Chief of Staff US Army.